MIRROR OF THE
BLESSING

M C Warner

Book Cover Design by M C Warner
Edited by Quick Fox Editors

ISBN: 979-8-9995186-0-6

First edition 2025.

To my teenage self, desperate to be an author. It took longer than we planned, but we did it.

CHAPTER 1

Saturday night for Levi Beckett wasn't that different from any other night of the week. The television droned away in the background, while a glass of cheap beer slowly added another set of condensation rings to his side table. The cheap bulb in the kitchen overhead light cast an unnatural blue hue, turning his tawny skin gray. The glare it cast on the television screen was right over the news anchor's face. With the volume turned down, Levi was left with only the visuals to dictate one news story from the next.

Emergency lights were swapped out for an image of a building under construction. The captions changed from an attempted robbery of healing spells, to the feel-good story of the week: the new low-income housing complex under development from Mr. Townsend.

Levi didn't have to read the subtitles to know that the anchors were praising Joseph Townsend for investing in the community, and fighting back against the rising cost of housing in Ashton. He'd seen it enough times to know their monologue word for word. No one had bothered double-checking the real estate magnate's other developments, or noticed the whistleblowers vanishing in broad daylight. Worst was the woeful ignorance of the blatant, preferred treatment of families that had a magical member, over those without. No one questioned the historic homes being bulldozed, or how the former residents were left with a pittance and without a roof. Levi didn't have to imagine that scenario; he had lived it.

When the image of Mr. Townsend flashed across the screen, Levi flipped his middle finger. A tired act of protest that he followed by turning his attention back to his beer.

1

The drink was getting warm, but it was better than the continuous praise for a man who'd earned the moniker, the Devil. Uttered in hushed tones far, far away from the bright lights and security cameras of Ashton's upper-class levels. Down where Levi lived, citizens vandalized the few surveillance devices that graced the city blocks, and no one bothered to replace them.

It was nights like these that Levi thought about getting a hobby, as the hours slipped by. But hobbies cost money, and every cent was already going to his funeral. When he'd made his deal, Levi had been thinking small: a roof over his and his best friend Sammy's heads, food in their stomachs. He had no idea how it would take its toll on his body. How the lies would become chasms between him and any relationships he hoped to gain. If he had known, he would have asked for a lot more. Then he could have afforded Sammy's own place with ease. Maybe at least get some better beer.

Still, waiting for a death that would arrive without warning was a waste of his time. Taking a sip of his drink, Levi pulled himself out of the recliner and headed into the kitchen for a snack. It was the little wins in life that made a difference, like the fact that the recliner hadn't yet molded its shape to his body from sitting in it too long. Other than his bed, it was the only piece of furniture that comfortably fit his tall, lanky frame.

The recliner wasn't the only piece of furniture in the room. An old couch that had been saved from the dumpster also took up space. The patterned flower design, narrow cushions, and wood trim had been in fashion at one point, long before Levi had been born. But it was better than sitting on the floor. Between the television, his chair and the couch, the living room barely had room to move. Add in the low ceilings and yellow stained walls from tenants past, and the place wasn't aging any better than Levi himself. But Townsend's name was nowhere on the building, and that mattered so much more than floor to ceiling windows.

The kitchen was sparsely stocked. A collection of dust on the top of the refrigerator marked where cereal boxes had once stood. Running a hand down his face, his fingers brushed over the week-old beard; Levi needed a shave too. He'd have to go shopping in the morning, if he didn't want to run completely out of the basics.

But he still had some coffee; the empties were creating a precarious tower of large metal canisters in the corner. Did he need to keep all of those? Not really. But there was something about seeing how long he'd survived that made the pile of recycling look like art.

The fridge was mostly condiments: a carton of eggs that would have to work for tomorrow's breakfast, a splash of milk left in the gallon, a jar of salsa that had dried bits around the lid. Salsa... Levi hummed as he investigated to see if that bag of chips was still there, or if Sammy had finished it off the other night. Their late weekend shifts meant Levi didn't expect a call from them until Monday.

He was reaching for the cabinet door when it hit. First, the warm life blood pooling up against his shirt. The sensation was odd enough that he looked down. Crimson liquid was already blossoming around his left shoulder.

The pain hit second; it always did. It was as if his body was still reacting. It didn't know its skin and muscles had already been torn apart. There wasn't time to think, to press something against the wound, to get to some place safer to bleed, before his body screamed out in agony.

His knees were already trembling, begging to collapse. But Levi had survived before, and he could survive again. He just needed to get to the first aid kit.

With one hand pressed to his clavicle to stop the bleeding, Levi stumbled to the bathroom, nudging the switch with his good shoulder until the tired light flickered on.

He had to cut off his shirt to assess the damage. Sammy would yell at him later about taking the hair cutting scissors to fabric, but they were the one who'd left the shears on the bathroom counter. He had to cut down the front of the shirt and the sleeve to get out of it.

All it was good for now was to wipe the blood away, and press against the still-bleeding wound. In the light of the bathroom, the patchwork of scars cast strange shadows and highlights across his skin. Burns along his neck from a curling iron in a clumsy hand had faded with age. A scattering of injuries that had left no scars caused his joints to ache in the cold, or seize in times of stress.

The ache in his wrist as he pressed the remnants of the shirt against the wound should be the last thing on his mind, but his brain didn't get the memo.

When Levi pulled back the balled up fabric, a round hole was looking back at him in the mirror. Round was new.

He turned in place; it was somehow even worse. Bright red blood was draining down his back from a reflection of the wound from the front. Was this an exit wound? From a *gunshot?* He couldn't imagine rebar, a sword, or another non-projectile was the culprit; he'd have even more injuries if that was the case. There wasn't much time to speculate. He had to fix the damage to his body, before he bled out.

The first aid kit was the only luxury item in his apartment. He had given up keeping it in the quaint plastic container it had come in over the years; the toolbox was far more suited to heavy trauma treatment. The giant plastic clasps were easy to flip open with one hand, and the packs of gauze were on top, right where he always needed them. The only item that he'd purposely left out was a pair of forceps. The Blessing only passed on the injuries, not the cause. No bullet would be transferred with the wound. As long as he kept it clean and let it heal, he didn't have to worry about infection.

The process would be easier with another set of hands, but it wasn't like he could go to the hospital. If another wound transferred while Levi was still on the table, people might suspect, and then he'd have an even worse problem on his hands.

Bloody fingers grabbed a few of the sterile packs and set them on the counter, one at a time. With his teeth, he ripped open and layered the sterile material on top of the wound at his front. Fingers fumbled to tape the layers of gauze to his skin. His mind was screaming in pain, begging for an end that wasn't coming, if Levi could help it.

The wound on his back was just barely within his reach, pushing his joints past the point of comfort. Years of using kitchen tools to smooth medical tape that was just out of reach, or bracing injured limbs with paint stir sticks to reinforce a makeshift cast, had made the tedious process a practiced art. He'd kill to have one of those healing scrolls, but the only way he could afford one was to steal it.

There was only a single spell in the toolbox. It wasn't anything like a healing scroll, but it would buy him time. There was so much more blood than he was used to, and he couldn't imagine how he was going to deal with the wound on his back without passing out.

The cardstock spell was small enough to fit into a wallet. It had cost him the bulk of his funeral fund a few years ago; had its potency faded since? His eyes scanned over the corners for the blue expiration square that appeared whenever a charm had faded. Flipping the card over, Levi bit back a curse. Bloody fingerprints covered anything that would be of use. With nothing left to lose, Levi slapped the spell to the front of the wound and broke the seal. Skittering starbursts of energy tickled along his shoulder and back.

Days like today made Levi wish he could go back in time and stop that conversation from ever happening. He'd been too young back then to make the right choice, and the man that offered had known it.

Frozen, starved, and days from losing the house, teenage Levi had never felt more trapped. If he hadn't had Sammy back home doing their best to keep the pair of them alive, Levi wouldn't have seen that winter. Any chance at earning money back then was an easy yes.

A benefactor in a fancy car, a nice suit, and the offer of a future had seemed too good to be true: a simple magical compatibility test for cash. A job, if Levi could best it. No one had warned him that it would set his nerves on fire. Or that the moment that he'd passed, he would gain the worst side effect of all—hope.

But when the man had offered the money, and a life where he would no longer be hungry or cold, Levi's empty stomach reconsidered. When he'd been told that his choice could save someone's life, Levi had folded.

A decade later, Levi wished he had trusted that instinct. That pain had been a warning. And yet, every injury after (save for the day that Levi felt like he had been tossed through a windshield), hadn't come close. Bumps, bruises, cuts, concussions, and more wrist and ankle injuries than he could count. Tonight's gunshot wound was like nothing he had ever felt. He didn't even have the luxury of passing out.

Packing the wound on his back, Levi bit back curses as his knees gave out. Bloody fingers smacked into the floor, and his head dropped back against the wall. Black spots danced in his vision. This wasn't the worst pain he'd ever had. That honor still went to the broken leg. Intermixed with bruised ribs and cuts and scrapes, it had him hobbling around the apartment while he'd choked down his own screams. This, this was nothing, he lied to himself. Forced himself to believe it the same way the reporters believed theirs.

With each moment that passed without another injury, Levi could only guess that she was done getting hurt for the night. The tightness in his chest loosened, and it felt like he could breathe for a few moments longer. One day, the wound would be fatal, and there wouldn't even be any warning before the curse traded his life for hers.

God, he hated her. What was she doing to get a bullet to her shoulder, and how come this was the only shot that had hit?

At least Sammy was working late. There was no way to explain any of this mess without putting them in danger. If his benefactor ever found out Sammy was a Healer, they would be Chained themself. Forced to heal the wealthy elite time and time again, until they were drained of power and their life force along with it. Levi could never decide what was worse: he and Sammy surviving under someone else's total control, or death itself.

Levi's hands were still shaking as he pulled himself off the bathroom floor. His fingers left red smears in his struggle to hold onto the countertop, to turn the handle to the faucet. It would be easier to clean off in the shower, but he had to keep his shoulder dry. The gauze that he had fought so hard for was already staining through.

He'd been on autopilot as he'd worked, but now Levi was left with the mess and the pain of Vicki's choices for tonight. Tossing back a small handful of pills, Levi chased them with his now-warm beer. Everything tasted bitter as he forced the last of it down his throat.

Scrubbing the blood off the floor with his good arm, Levi wished he could afford a cleaning scroll. Every movement sent pain radiating down to his fingers. The pills needed time to take the edge off; there was another hour to go before he would get any relief. If he was lucky, sleep would kick in soon after, though luck was never on his side.

A shrill *ring* interrupted his work. He threw the rag to the ground; it landed with a worrying *thwap*. How much blood had he already lost? "Levi speaking," he answered.

"I'm really sorry to ask you, but can you come get me?" Sammy asked, their voice hurried and anxious. "My car kicked the bucket again, and everyone else has gone home."

Levi really shouldn't. Between the pain medications and his arm, it would be a disaster. But Sammy was the only person who kept him sane; he'd be damned if he'd let them get hurt walking home alone because he'd said no.

"Lock up, but stay inside if it's safe. I'll be there in ten," Levi replied. He pulled himself off the floor with a wince and a grunt, and went to wrap more gauze around his wound. If he packed it with enough bandages and tape, wore a dark shirt, Sammy wouldn't be able to see it in the dim street lamps. The club was only a couple of blocks away on foot; he could manage it.

The rest of the mess would have to wait until morning. He could handle it on his own, as long as Sammy didn't decide to follow him home. If they did, hopefully Sammy wouldn't comment on it. So far, they hadn't pushed when he'd said that his injuries came from work.

Levi filled his pockets with the necessities: wallet, keys, and cell phone. He grabbed a baton and some pepper spray. Even reaching with his uninjured arm caused pain to flash through him. But the danger of walking through their neighborhood at night, without a defense, outweighed the agony. Keeping the baton where it was visible should deter opportunistic thieves. His hands hovered over the lockbox with his pistol; a good idea on any other night, Levi left it where it was. It was too dangerous, and the pain was already making his mind fuzzy.

Flicking through his closet instead, he grabbed a stretched out sweatshirt. Biting back screams, Levi maneuvered his damaged arm through the sleeve and over his head. There were spots in front of his eyes as he dropped to his bed. Forcing himself to breathe, he pulled himself back to standing. He still wasn't done.

Between the winter cold, and Sammy's immediate suspicions, Levi couldn't justify leaving the apartment without a coat of some kind. So, with an already aggravated wound, he pulled on the jacket, doing his best not to move his arm too much. The strain from the added layers was enough that he'd be sleeping in both tonight. Tucking his left hand into the pocket of the coat as the world's worst sling, he was out the door.

The wind on the streets was biting cold. On any other night he might have turned back for a better coat, but there was no getting out of this now. Levi could have gotten there faster if he didn't have a limp. The broken leg from a few years ago had healed as well as it could without a cast, though he would hate to see what it looked like under an X-ray.

The strip club was a bold building, easily spotted even at a distance. The cement block exterior had been painted a bright pink over a decade ago, but it had since faded under the harsh sun. Neon lights between the metal security grates over every window made it look like a trashy jail cell. The interior was only a little better. There was a reason the lights were always kept down low and focused solely on the stage and the performers. Levi had met most of the dancers here, though the only one he knew by their real name was Sammy.

Sammy must have been watching his approach; they opened the door before Levi could knock. The Connection helped with that. A magical construct, it could give two people an extra boost from the rest. They were so rare that most didn't believe Connections existed at all, despite those like Levi and Sammy who had lived with it ever since they'd met. Though among Levi's neighborhood, those that claimed to be so lucky were either grifters or cheats, just trying to get into someone's wallet or bed, or both.

His and Sammy's Connection wasn't like the ones in the movies. There was no undying romance between them. They were family that no one else understood. Levi would do everything in his power to make Sammy's life better, and Sammy would do the same for him. They already claimed to get an uneasy feeling in their stomach when he was hurt; Levi didn't want Sammy panicking every time they felt nauseous. If they ever found out about his work, they would burn themselves out trying to fix a problem that had no solution.

Sammy was shorter than him, but that was only noticeable when Sammy wasn't wearing thick-soled shoes. The light brown skin of their face had recently been scrubbed free of makeup; their cheeks were still red from their efforts. Baggy jeans, a loose sweater, and a patch-covered trench coat hid the rest of their form. The knit cap on Sammy's head didn't entirely cover the newly bleached short hair though; it had seen better days. That cap was almost as old as either of them, and neither knew who the first owner was. They had swapped ownership too many times over the years. For now, it was part of Sammy's look, patches and all.

Somewhere under all of their layers, Sammy had a wad of cash tucked away. Despite the recent push for digital currency, patrons of the strip clubs preferred the untraceable paper. Once the weekend was over, Sammy would go to the local exchange to get some of it back to digital. Landlords only accepted digital currency anymore, and the exchange places always took a cut in the process. Levi didn't know exactly what Sammy did with the rest. Most people around here had cash tucked into cupboards and under mattresses. Any place that delivered food to their neighborhood took cash payment, so did the small markets and shops. Cash kept in a way that digital currency didn't. Areas like Levi's neighborhood were a holdout in the old ways.

With that much cash hidden on their person, even the brief walk home was a risk that Sammy didn't like to take alone. It was only with their junk of a car that they'd offered to take closing, so that the other dancers and staff could get back safely. It was a risk that Levi hadn't been fond of.

"So are you going to admit that always taking close is a bad idea?" Levi asked, as Sammy stepped out into the street.

"I had it handled," Sammy pointed out. An unfamiliar ring of keys jingled together as they found the door key and locked up. "I could have stayed the night if I needed. But I knew you would answer the phone."

Levi bit the inside of his cheek, keeping his tongue squarely in his mouth. The pain was nothing compared to the pulsing throb in his shoulder. If the shooter had aimed just a little to the left, he wouldn't be here at all. Tomorrow wasn't certain either. If he didn't keep on top of it, he could still bleed out.

"Careful, people might think that you like me," Levi teased, holding up his right hand to placate Sammy from playfully punching him in the shoulder.

It only made his best friend suspicious.

"Levi, did you get hurt at work again?" Sammy asked, their voice pitched with concern. Eyes scanning over his body, their gaze narrowed on Levi's left arm as if they could spot the injury through his clothes.

"Yeah, nothing a little sleep shouldn't patch up," Levi said, stepping between Sammy and the street beside them.

That was the one lie between them. He kept it close to the truth: Sammy thought Levi did security work. A hired detail for someone rich enough to pay the kinds of money that helped Levi afford the life that he had, but shady enough that Levi kept away from hospitals. Some low-level mob or gang. Levi didn't even have to lie about a name; Sammy didn't want to know.

"So, if we go to your place, I won't find your first aid kit covered in blood?" Sammy asked, arching an eyebrow. With a turn on their heel, they started back towards Levi's with a motion for him to follow.

Levi frowned, glancing in the other direction towards Sammy's place. It would be a shorter walk; only a few blocks and with better street lights. But when he turned back to his friend, Levi knew that there was no chance of keeping them out of his mess. Sammy had paused, arm held out for Levi to take so that he didn't slip on the icy patch he'd barely dodged on the way in.

Together, they picked their way along the sidewalk. There was a thin patch along the center where businesses had shoveled the gray, black, and yellow snow out of the way. Piles from the plows narrowed the sidewalks by half until spring. What remained had compacted the slush into ice. Levi still preferred the winter over hot summer months; the freezing temperatures covered up the odor of the meat processing plant at the edge of town. In the summer, when nothing was comfortable and being inside was almost worse than being out, no one could open their windows without breathing in the stench.

"Maybe a little," Levi grumbled, tucking his hands into his pockets. This was exactly why Levi had found a new place to live; he could bleed all over without issue.

"Where did you get hurt?" Sammy asked, looking him over. It was dark, and both of them were bundled up. Unless Levi's limp was worse tonight, Levi didn't think that they would find it.

"My shoulder, but it's fine," Levi replied, waving away their concern. "Like I said, it's already healing. But, you're right. It bled a bit, and I'm not done cleaning up."

Sammy frowned, squinting at him. "Why don't you want me to help? You know I've been practicing."

"Because my employer already knows about this one, and I don't want it to heal too quickly and make them suspicious," Levi lied.

A Healer, even one as untrained as Sammy, was worth a lot. As long as both of them kept those powers under wraps, it gave Sammy a get-out-of-jail-free card. It had been more than luck that Sammy had missed the ability tests at school. Newly Chained to the Townsend family and aching with the aftereffects of the Blessing, Levi had fallen ill. Sammy had stayed home to take care of him and missed the state inspection. There wasn't enough funding to follow up. It meant that Sammy had fewer job prospects. No one would hire them without testing papers proving they lacked any magical ability. It also meant that Sammy was free.

"Which shoulder?" Sammy asked.

"It's healing on its own," Levi started.

"I'm going to punch one of your shoulders. Tell me which one is injured so that I can avoid it," Sammy replied, shooting him a glare.

Levi stopped in his tracks and bit back a groan of annoyance. He had hoped to avoid this conversation until they were warm and inside. The shops on his block all closed at sundown; even most of the late owls in the apartments above them had all gone to bed. None of the windows he could see had any light coming through. It left the few streetlights to see by, and those were few and far between.

It was hard to get a read on Sammy in the dark.

Levi pointed with his good arm, trying to ignore the burning pain. "Please don't punch that spot."

Sammy took Levi's good hand and interlaced their fingers as much as they could with a pair of mittens in the way. Leaning their head against Levi's good shoulder, they let out a breath. "I won't heal your wounds, but I can check the bandages and clean your apartment," they offered. "Let me help where it's safe, okay?"

Levi relented with a nod and kept moving, pulling Sammy along with them. It wasn't safe, not a hundred percent. But there were only so many ways that Levi could push his only anchor away, before it would be too much for both of them.

Levi's brick apartment building was shorter than the others around it. A remnant of a time when landlords still had a chance of going up against Townsend for properties. The other buildings hadn't fared the test of time any better than his own, but they were several stories taller, with a facade of concrete instead.

There were only a few badly worn concrete steps into the building, and the door to the lobby was always unlocked. It was warmer once they got inside, though Levi wouldn't call the lobby comfortable. Tile floors echoed under foot falls, and three sets of doors made up the space. No welcoming plants, fake or alive, had graced it during his residency. There had been a bench here for a time, but that luxury was gone too. An office that was locked and magically sealed when no one was inside, the unlocked doors into the first floor apartments, and the doors to the stairwell were all that greeted any resident or guest.

He bypassed the rows of locked mail boxes. The only mail he ever got was of the junk or bill variety, so Levi only checked it on the first and last day of the month.

There were no elevators by design; he never loathed it more than tonight. He and Sammy climbed the stairs up to his floor without conversation, pausing only at every landing for Levi to gather his breath.

The warmth of the apartment washed over them as soon as Levi opened the door. There were still drops of blood on the floor of the bathroom, and a spot on the kitchen floor where he'd been standing when the bullet wound had transferred.

Sammy's mittens went into the pocket of the coat, the coat on a hook by the door, and the heavy shoes were kicked into the pile underneath it. Already in a plastic bag, the stack of cash went into the lockbox where Levi kept his pistol. Levi didn't even remember giving out the code.

In that time, Levi had only managed to take off his coat and put it on the rack next to Sammy's. The pain in his arm had numbed with the cold and the meds; only movement set it off now. Sliding the coat off had been a series of sharp shocks. He felt the shirt over the bandage and was pleased to find that it wasn't damp. A check on the gauze underneath said that he was still in the clear.

"I swear you make the biggest messes," Sammy remarked, stealing a pair of house slippers. Rolling up the sleeves of their long-sleeved shirt, Levi could just make out the tattoo sleeve. It wasn't done yet. It had started with lots of disconnected designs that were finally getting incorporated into something cohesive. Some of them were getting corrected or covered up, and others were incorporated into the final piece. The line art around their wrist had been completed about a year ago, and a few other sections had been started and stopped in the last few months. It was going to take a lot of time and money to get everything done, but Sammy always said that there was no reason to rush.

Every time he saw the ink, Levi felt a rush of fulfillment. Thanks to him, Sammy had gone from starving, to splurging on little luxuries while thinking about the future.

"It'll get done or it won't," Sammy said, catching his eye as they looked for something more than the wad of paper towels that Levi had been using before. "Where do you keep the disinfectant?"

"It's where you put it," Levi replied, which meant it was under one of the sinks.

"Ah ha!" Sammy exclaimed, finding the stash of cleaning supplies under the kitchen sink. There were a lot of things that

Levi didn't remember being there. For one, there was a little cleaning basket with a handle. Disposable gloves. Rags. More spray bottles than he'd ever owned.

"When did that get in my apartment?" Levi asked.

"A couple of months ago," Sammy replied. "Remember that mess on your leg? I thought it would be nice to have a few more things in the kit, especially if I'm going to be cleaning up after your sorry ass."

Levi had no idea what pocket dimension Sammy had pulled that from, because he had never seen any of that in his life. How could Sammy have slipped all of that in without his notice?

Either way, it was a gift now as he collapsed into a chair. The guilt, which was always there when he had to ask for help, ate into his stomach. Somehow, Sammy had never missed calling on one of his bad nights. The moments where Levi was tempted to down a whole pill bottle, instead of just enough to cut through the pain. When the bleeding would not stop, or the ache that filled his ribs made it hard to breathe. The time that he had to lie about being a car crash victim, without having left his apartment. Sammy had taken every excuse and did their best to patch and fix what they could.

"One of these days, your job is going to get you killed," Sammy grumbled in the other room. "And I will track you down and tell you I told you so."

"Even in the underworld?" Levi teased from the couch.

"Especially if you're in the underworld," Sammy replied, looking up from where they were scrubbing. "You know how easy it is to convince Hades to let a begrudged loved one through for a lecture? He doesn't even ask for anything in return."

Levi was confident that if there was an afterlife, it wasn't a place that Sammy could visit. No known powers on earth could interact with the dead. Still, it was a running joke between them. Sammy had once promised they were going to find the people that had abandoned Levi to the streets and give them over to Cerberus to use as a chew toy. The next time that Levi had met up with Sammy, they had a new tattoo of a cartoon Cerberus on their shoulder blade. It was chewing on a stick figure form of Levi's parents.

"Well, I promise that if my job kills me, I will stick around for the lecture," Levi replied.

Sammy didn't like promises that Levi was going to live forever, regardless of when they were talking about it. They said it was too fake to be real. A promise that could not be kept.

When they were this worked up, agreeing to wait for the lecture seemed to be enough. When they weren't, promising that they would want to wait on the lecture until both of them got to pet Cerberus got a grin.

"Good boy," Sammy replied, with a curl to their lip.

Levi pulled a pillow off the couch and threw it at them. Sammy cracked a smile before getting back to work. Tomorrow, Levi promised himself, he was going to get Sammy something nice. Maybe another plant, or something good to eat. Sammy hadn't needed to stay in this messed up life with Levi. Sammy could travel someplace warmer, like a tropical island outside Townsend's reach, where the cold wind didn't rattle the windows in the winter, and the possibilities were endless.

Levi thought of his funeral savings in the lockbox, and wondered if he was going to live long enough that Sammy could go somewhere warm when he was gone.

CHAPTER 2

On the main floor of the nightclub, there was hardly any room to move; people were clustered around the bar and every seating option, crowding the space. Owen, protector of drinks, stood off to the side of the table as he watched his friends dance. More than once, another patron had tried to steal a chair, or outright sit to give themselves a reprieve. Between Owen telling them to shoo, and the bouncer-sized guard at his back reinforcing his statement, no one stayed for very long.

Glancing back, Owen caught sight of one of the guards, standing with his hands crossed over his chest. A scowl was on the older man's face.

"Careful, your face might get stuck like that," Owen said with a grin. The table he'd picked tonight wasn't the usual one that he and his friends camped at when they were downstairs. With the winter break ending, and the new college semester starting, the crowds had doubled. Owen had to pick through what remained before scoring this space. The guard had settled into position a few feet back to shoo away anyone that tried to get too familiar with Owen and his friends. Vicki's friends, really, since it was her dad that owned the club; every extra perk that Owen and the others enjoyed came from her.

The security detail huffed, but Owen saw the quirk of a smile before it was quickly hidden.

The table shifted, and his attention was pulled away to address it. Friends this time, rather than chair stealers.

"Owen, stop flirting with the bouncer," Janie teased, settling into the chair to his right.

Owen ducked his head, trying to hide the heat on his cheeks. He wasn't flirting. But he couldn't help trying to get a smile out of the person who insured that the table didn't get stolen, and the drinks didn't end up on the floor.

Janie was the tallest woman in the group, stretching an inch or two above him in the right heels. Her dark hair was cropped into a pixie cut, and a trail of earrings went up both of her ears. The sleeveless black corset top she was wearing tonight showed off the tattoo that went across her collarbone and down to her chest. A twisting vine, it draped almost like a necklace. Janie was the most sensibly dressed tonight, even if that was a stretch. Tight black pants that could have been painted on completed her look. Owen had been stuck in too many conversations about how much those pants didn't breathe to appreciate the effort Janie was going for. But she looked the least tired among them, perched with one leg on the stool as she leaned against the table.

Brooke on the other hand was struggling just to sit down. Her legs wobbled across from him, before Janie reached out to catch her. Out of all of them, Owen wasn't sure if Brooke, or Alicia, had had the most to drink tonight. The pink blush across Brooke's cheeks and nose wasn't all make up. The silver sequin strapless dress she was wearing kept slipping, catching in her long dark brown hair; the fashion tape had failed from being covered in body glitter. Owen couldn't tell if Brooke had brushed against someone else, or if that was all from Brooke's own supply. A heart locket draped across her chest, nearly identical to the one Alicia wore. Alicia's necklace had been a gift from Vicki, whereas Brooke had purchased hers to match.

Alicia looked the most distracted out of all of them. She had fully settled into the chair to his left, but her green eyes kept casting around the room like she was looking for someone. She almost looked hopeful. Like the person she was waiting to see was somewhere in that crowd, she just had to find them. Her blonde hair was pulled back into a ponytail; it bounced as she turned her head back and forth.

Out of all the people here, Owen and Alicia were the closest. After Alicia's older brother had died when she was in middle school, she'd come to live with Owen and his dad for a year. Her necklace had been given to her by Vicki soon after the funeral, and Owen had never seen her take it off. Not even to go swimming.

The dress that Alicia was wearing at least had sleeves, so she wasn't pulling it up every few seconds like Brooke was. Instead, she was struggling to keep it pulled down over everything she wanted covered. It took her a few tries to get it how she wanted as she fidgeted in her seat.

Janie snagged his attention as she made to grab one of the drinks that Owen guarded.

Owen only offered her a small bottle of water, keeping the alcoholic beverages close. Janie had a tall glass of dark red tomato juice and liquor, topped with several green olives and not a single stalk of celery. Brooke's contained a pink slush with an umbrella and glitter dust along the outer edge. Alicia's vodka soda was plain, but he knew it would pack a punch. Each of the beverages were still sealed with a tamper proof enchantment. His task was to keep them here, and not let them be thrown away by a stranger.

He had passed out two more of the small water bottles, when Alicia snapped back to attention. "Owen, give me my drink," Alicia bit out, making a grabbing motion at him in the universal sign of "give me" used only by toddlers, and the intoxicated.

"You made me promise you would have at least one of these tonight," Owen replied, motioning to the water. Brooke had at least opened hers, though some of the water was splashed on her face and down her front. Seriously? Again? What was with these three overheating on the dance floor? Brooke had nearly passed out during the summer; Owen and the bar had needed to put ice and cool dishcloths on her just to keep Brooke out of the hospital. After that, Brooke, Alicia, and Janie had each asked him to prevent that from happening twice. A few months later, they were already back to complaining about him being a stick in the mud.

Janie smiled as she downed hers, the small bottle crunching as she drank without stopping. Owen was glad that it wasn't his car that he was going to be driving them home in. If someone puked in Vicki's, it would get professionally cleaned that night. His car didn't get the same treatment.

Janie replaced the lid and slid it across the small tabletop to him. "Drink?"

Looking down, Owen grabbed the Bloody Mary. He double-checked that the name in the enchantment over the top was Janie's and passed it over. He didn't dare slide it. Janie's reflexes at this time of night would cause her to backhand it onto the floor.

"I'm going to check on Vicki," Owen said, as he passed out the other drinks. "See if she and Edwin are ready to leave."

Alicia had at least opened her water and taken a sip. What was left of Brooke's water would end up on the floor if he pushed it.

"Already?" Brooke exclaimed, her eyes wide. "It's not even that late!"

Owen shrugged, not bothering to point out that it was already after their agreed upon ending time, and yes, it was that late. He was long ready for bed; the caffeine in his system was the only thing that was keeping him going for the drive home.

"If Owen says it's time to leave, it's time to leave," Janie said, grinning over the rim of her cup. "We wouldn't want the guard coming after us."

Owen rolled his eyes.

"Can you wait a little longer before asking Vicki?" Alicia asked. Her eyes were looking anywhere but at their group. "I'm not done dancing yet."

"Not done?" Owen asked. His friends looked dead on their feet, ready to kick their high heels into the nearest corner to never be seen again. Alicia was chewing her lip as her attention was pulled back to the dance floor. Perhaps she was hoping to go home with someone, instead of sleeping off tonight's decisions alone. Owen sighed.

"Please?" Alicia asked, making her eyes big and wide. It was a tactic she'd used since they were children.

Owen wilted. The time for them to leave wasn't even up to him: it was up to Vicki and her whims for the night. It was his responsibility to keep everyone safe and not lose one of them, as their permanent designated driver and as their friend. "A few more minutes, but I'm going upstairs instead of waiting down here."

Alicia beamed and gave him a kiss to his cheek. It was wet; he could still smell the stink of alcohol on her breath. Great. He watched her stumble back to the dance floor, before using a napkin to wipe the sticky lip gloss off his face. He couldn't wait to find out what kind of mess she was going to get into, while he tracked down the other two. Owen only hoped that they were still fully dressed when he got there.

Vicki's booth was up a flight of stairs and past a pair of security guards. More of the bouncer types, but instead of being dressed in a T-shirt with the club's name on it and jeans, these two were dressed in suits. Owen knew they were armed with more than muscles and hard looks.

"Vicki upstairs yet?" Owen asked as he stopped at the edge of the stairs. He only recognized one; the younger was a mystery. It was the only reason Owen had stopped to ask at all.

The new guard looked at him and glanced over at Bill, a veteran to the Vicki's antics who Owen knew well. It was Bill that replied, "Not yet," He looked at the new guard and added, "Robbie, this is Owen Mills. He gets free run of the place, same as Miss Vicki."

Owen made note of it; he tried to make a point to know all guards here at the club. It made his life easier if he didn't have to prove who he was when he needed extra help to get Vicki home.

"I thought no one was allowed upstairs unless Miss Vicki personally invites them," Robbie replied.

"First day?" Owen mouthed to Bill, who smiled.

"Something like that," Bill replied, before grabbing the velvet safety barrier and unclasping one side. He motioned Owen through; Owen didn't have a problem stepping past them to head upstairs. Even over the sound of the club, he caught snippets of the conversation.

"Miss Vicki is allowed everywhere because she owns the place. Owen is allowed everywhere because he's our extra eyes and ears," Bill explained. "Can't tell you how many times he's given us a heads up that we're in for a busy night, before we're in the thick of it."

Owen should have felt a swell of pride, but honestly, he felt tired. It had been a long night already, and he hadn't even planned to be out. It was the first week of classes, the start of his senior year in college. Dual degrees in risk management and magical security would help him follow his father into private security, but the syllabi alone had Owen exhausted. He was ready to sleep through the weekend, not party it up. Unfortunately for him, Owen was the only one with any interest in staying sober to drive the rest of the drunkards home.

**

As fun as her father's club had been, Vicki was ready to start the next part of her night. The lights still danced in her vision, even after she was off the dance floor and swaying back to the private booth. The only person allowed close enough to her when she was like this, was her off and on again sex friend, Edwin. The two of them had been back together for about a month; it was nowhere close to their longest relationship to date, but it was getting there. Edwin's arm was wrapped around her waist as he swayed with her.

They continued on past a set of guards, who did not even blink as they let her through, and up a dangerous flight of stairs. An elevator would have been nice, but the only one in the building was a freight elevator for equipment and food. Vicki would not get caught dead in that dirty machine.

The private booth had been redesigned just for her. The dark green plush seats were easy to collapse into, and the dim lights kept her headache at bay. If there was one upgrade to the Blessing that she could ask for, it would be for the headaches and hangovers to go away too.

Vicki's feet ached as she threw them up onto the wooden table. The window overlooking the dance floor let the occasional laser lights in from below. A set of green velvet curtains was pulled to either side of it. At any moment, they could be closed with a remote, in case Vicki wanted more privacy. The same one controlled the lights, but Vicki was the kind to set and forget them. The glass was bulletproof, but there was nothing to protect against aside from the remains of someone's drink being smashed against the glass. The alcohol had long evaporated, but the mix-ins had left their mark.

Drinks had been delivered while they'd been out, their names and protective seals over the tops. She grabbed the one with her name and pulled off the paper. The enchantment insured only Vicki could remove it, and there was no way to fix it once it was broken. Something, something, drugged drinks and all that. Her father's security measures were ridiculous sometimes.

Beside her, Edwin was sprawled out with his new drink in hand. His dark, curly hair was only barely contained by the earlier heavy applications of mousse, and his attempt at a five o'clock shadow needed another trim. The buttons of his teal satin shirt had started coming undone in the last few minutes. The stupid necklace that her friend Alicia had got him over Christmas was reflecting the lights off his bared chest as he took in deep breaths. If Alicia wasn't her best friend in the whole wide world, Vicki would have snatched the necklace off the man's neck and thrown it into the crowd the second she'd spotted it earlier tonight.

Speaking of men, the door to her private room opened to reveal Owen. Dressed in his normal club wear—a dark red button-up shirt with the sleeves rolled up, gray slacks, a necklace and ring—Owen looked more like a poser than someone that should be her friend. He was standing there completely sober, and hadn't even been to the dance floor once tonight. If he wasn't so efficient at being a servant free of charge, Vicki wasn't sure she would ever bother with him at all. It wouldn't matter who his father was, he would have been kicked from the group a long time ago. Whatever she wanted, he got her. The trade-off was that she had to put up with him being *responsible*.

"Are you ready to leave?" Owen asked, hovering near the door. "I can track down the others for you."

Vicki waved him off, annoyed that he already knew what she wanted before she'd gotten a chance to tell him. She would have contemplated sneaking out to drive herself and Edwin back for a private party, just for two. But Mr. Owen "designated driver" Mills had taken the keys early in the night to keep her from doing just that. Spoil sport.

"Do you think he's going to get a drink dumped on him again?" Edwin asked as Owen left the room.

"That'd be funny. It's been a while since the last one," Vicki grinned as she took another sip of her drink. The room empty again. The guards outside wouldn't dare check in on her, unless she signaled for help, and Owen was going to track down three other women who were trying to have fun. She had plenty of free time.

Throwing a leg over Edwin's lap, Vicki drew him into a kiss. She made sure to be extra vocal as she grabbed and twisted the necklace that he was wearing. The grin on her face spread as she felt some it snap between her fingers. All it took was running a hand along Edwin's neck to distract him as the necklace fell from her fingers, into the booth and out of sight. He might get it back. The cleaning staff were rather good about not taking what wasn't theirs, but she wouldn't have to see a gift from another woman on him for the rest of the night.

The door opening stopped her hands from straying further; she and Edwin turned towards it and the loud noises from the other side. The door must have been bumped by accident, because no one was there. Still, there were a lot of sounds from the bottom of the stairs. What was happening at her club now? And was it worth knowing about?

Poking her head out of the door, Vicki surveyed the scene below. At the bottom of the stairs, the two security guards were blocking the way from anyone trying to get past. A number of people had gathered around, while the guards wrestled to contain a fight.

"Hey, go down there and ask what's happening," Vicki poked at Edwin.

"Me? Why me?" Edwin asked.

"Because you're big and strong and won't get accidentally elbowed by the guards, and the guard won't lose his job, house, and hope," Vicki replied, giving Edwin a sweet smile.

Edwin grumbled as he buttoned his shirt and started down the stairs. She might have caught a few words about her dad being an overprotective jerk, which was as true as it came.

Leaning against the doorway, Vicki crossed her arms as she watched the scene below. People were being thrown out, and others still being threatened. Father's rules for the club were strict. No rushing her, or rushing the stairs. No pushing the guards. No violence. If the guards deemed anything a threat to her safety, every guest involved became trespassed. Those that argued could find themselves banned from the club. Among the crowd, she saw Owen had found Alicia, Brooke, and Janie.

Brooke kept adjusting the top of her sleeveless dress, as the material kept trying to slip off her body. Vicki didn't bother hiding her laugh. Brooke should have learned how awful that dress was when Vicki had worn the same style last week. Instead, copycat Brooke had to try it for herself. Even the fashion tape had given up after a night of dancing.

Janie and Alicia were leaning against each other. Vicki could see their mouths moving as they talked. The group had to stay away from the stairs where the guards were working. Edwin wasn't with them; instead, Vicki found him sitting only a few stairs down from her perch. "What are you still doing there?"

"They told me to get out of their way, let them do their jobs," Edwin replied. "I think that someone tried to sneak up and use your bathroom. Then that mess broke out."

Vicki watched as more people were booted from the club with a put upon sigh. It meant that she was going to have to go out the side entrance tonight. That sucked!

***

Owen had just gotten down through the security barrier, when a runner tried to bolt up the stairs to Vicki's private booth. The crowds were surging close to the door, while he pulled back just to keep out of the way of security. This wasn't the first time; around the holidays, there had been a paparazzo who had slipped into the club with little more than a cell phone camera. He'd tried to slip upstairs to catch Vicki and her friends unaware. A few months before that, a private detective who'd been interested in Edwin had tried to make it up. Each time, security would get beefed up, and the detail for Vicki would change.

While Owen was at the nightclub to have fun as much as the rest of his friends, the moment those new security plans were drawn up, he would get involved. He would point out flaws, namely pointing out how Vicki would actively sabotage their plans to enjoy her night out. As someone that had to live with those security plans, it made sense to keep his dad up to date with how it actually looked from the ground.

So Owen's first thought when the stairs got rushed wasn't curiosity, it was annoyance. The intended intruder didn't even make it three steps past the velvet ropes, before they were tackled and restrained. Exactly how the plan was supposed to go. Except Vicki's father would see that as three steps too many, and want the plan changed, again. Owen was going to live with Vicki griping and trying slip away from the guard. Again.

"That's going to take a while to clean up," Janie commented, when Owen finally found them again. Like many others, his friends had stepped off the dance floor to get a better look.

Owen shrugged, trying not to let his frustration get to him. It would be a few more minutes before he would get the all clear for Vicki to come downstairs. The bigger issue would be if Vicki saw this delay as an opportunity.

"Maybe," Owen relented. "It'll just take a little longer to get upstairs to grab Vicki and Edwin."

Alicia made a face, but Owen ignored it. Whatever weird thing was going on between Alicia, Vicki, and Edwin, he did not want to hear about it. He knew too much about the three of them and their relationships already.

***

The music from the club bounced around the concrete buildings surrounding the parking lot. Vicki could still feel the bass under her feet as she swayed and danced back to her car. She'd at least managed to make it back upstairs for another drink before heading out. She still wanted to party, and a little disturbance would not stop her. Besides, the annoyed look on Owen's face was more than worth it.

"Hurry up!" Vicki called without looking back. She knew her friends were behind her, trailing along like the little ducklings that they were. Owen would be at the back of the line with keys in hand. That man always tried to say goodnight to every single guard that Vicki's dad had on staff that night. *Suck up.*

The pain in her feet would not go away, another annoyance that the Blessing didn't take. Only injuries were taken, not the aches of living well. She was dying to take these heels off, but she had crossed this parking lot barefoot before, and the paparazzi had helpfully splattered that all over the newspapers by morning. As soon as she was in the car, though, all bets were off; she could throw the shoes out the window for all she cared. They went with this dress, and the dress was going to be burned before she ever had to wear something like this again. It chafed like nobody's business *where* it was nobody's business.

She couldn't wait to see Brooke dealing the same issues next week.

"Vicki! Wait! Something's wrong," Owen called, sounding like he was right behind her, and out of breath. Either he was walking faster tonight, or he had jogged to catch up.

Vicki rolled her eyes as she and Edwin continued to walk. What a loser. Always looking at the dark side of life. It had been his idea to be the designated driver, but without the thrill of someone driving with reckless abandon. Boring Owen bringing up his "concerns" again.

The thing was, this club *was* safe. Only a few paparazzi showed up from time to time. Nothing here could hurt them. All kinds of precautions were being taken even out here, including the half dozen security guards that patrolled this parking lot.

As expensive as this was place was to maintain, with all the guards' salaries and precautions, crowds were still wrapped around the block every night. The cover fee to get in could be raised on a whim, and nothing changed. Everyone was willing to pay it to be among them, to talk about Vicki's designer clothes for the night, and partake in the drink special that she sipped in public, before going back to her drink of choice.

"Owen," Vicki snapped as he tried to grab her arm to pull her back.

She was met with worried eyes.

"Stop that!" She yanked her arm back and turned away from him. "You're such a worry—"

The words died in her throat as her eyes landed on the shadows. There was something moving. It wasn't a guard; they all had flashlights and reflective gear. *Where were the guards?*

The shadows took shape into the form of a man. A man dressed in black, body still melting back with the night. A shiver run through her. The yelp from those around her only made the fear grow.

"What's this? Security? Guards?" Vicki called, her voice getting louder and higher pitched with each request.

"Quiet," the voice replied, muffled and unfamiliar. The figure was moving towards them. A glisten of something reflective was where the man's hand should be. "Or I'll shoot."

Shoot? What was happening? A kidnapping for ransom? An attack? Where were her guards? Her eyes left the man as they darted around the space. Where were the reflective lights of the men that were paid handsomely to protect her?

"Give me your wallets."

Where was the security? Vicki had never been outside without seeing at least one other person watching the lot. She stumbled back, hoping to at least flag something in the cameras. *Where were the guards?*

Around her, she could hear her friends scrambling to put their hands on their wallets. In the center of it all, Vicki was frozen in place. She didn't have a wallet; there was nothing she needed to carry to the club. No one even tried to ID her.

"Hand over your purse," the man with the gun stated, pointing it at her.

Purse? She didn't have a purse. The clutch in her hands was empty, except for a flask and some condoms. There was no way she was handing any of that to this creep.

"This is mine," Vicki replied.

"Your money, or your life."

This was ridiculous. Why was she afraid? Her mind had seen the weapon as a threat and forgotten the truth. She was Vicki Townsend, the daughter of the most powerful man in the country. This mugger would be dead before he could hurt her.

Standing up taller, Vicki stared the man in eyes. "Do you know who my father is?" she asked. Horror melted off her as boredom took its place. Around her, she could still feel the terror from her friends, but they had something to lose. She didn't. "This is your last chance to walk away. Touch me, threaten me again, and your whole family dies."

The shadowed face seemed to think she was bluffing. "No."

A crack of the muzzle split through the air and a red-hot pain burst through her shoulder. Her knees buckled, and she dropped. Shock and pain burst through her as a familiar power enveloped the wound. It screamed red hot, then melted away like it had never been there at all.

The air was filled with screams. Voices commanded Vicki and her friends stay down. There was the reflective gear of the guards, with their lights and firearms drawn at the ready. Vicki pursed her lips as she watched them rush in. They were too late.

She only vaguely heard that the shadow man said anything else. It was cut off by a second shot ringing through the night.

"Miss Vicki?" A guard rushed to help her off the ground, gently brushing away the gravel that had collected in her palms. "There you are, Miss Vicki."

The guard was moving to step in front of her, but she still saw it. The man from the shadows was no longer among the living. The body on the ground was in a rapidly growing pool of his own blood.

Looking down, she could see the bloodstain on her dress and a hole in her sleeve. The wound, however, had already healed into nothing. There wasn't even a scar.

"Miss Vicki? Your father wants you home right now," the guard in front of her instructed.

"What happened?" Vicki asked. The mixture of alcohol and adrenaline was making her stomach curl. She needed to get out of here, before she puked where the flashing cameras could catch her. Stilling her stomach, she looked away from the mess and focused on the guard at her side.

"We intend to find out," another guard said, crossing over to look at what remained of the shadow man.

The guard that had helped her up guided her to one of her father's vehicles. The windows were dark and tinted; no one was going to see her inside. Getting into the back seat, she looked around for the others. They were getting loaded up too, but no one was sharing a ride. Edwin was holding his arm; there was a dark patch near his crotch.

This was not how her night was supposed to end, collapsed alone in the back seat, without Edwin's touch or her friends' laughter. The healthy, comfortable buzz beneath her skin had quelled, replaced with the weight of sobriety and the beginnings of a hangover. Tension thrumming through the air, Vicki knew that her guards would take her straight home. But she wanted another drink!

A small piece of satisfaction flashed through her as she looked back at the parking lot. While the rest of her friends were taken away, the only one that was still standing was Owen. Sober Owen, holding the keys to her car, was stuck waiting with the guards. If he hadn't corralled them out to the parking lot, she'd still be dancing right now. He could wait for all she cared.

***

The screams still rang through Owen's mind as the security forces surged forwards and took control. Beside him, Brooke was retching out the contents of her stomach, not even avoiding the splashes of vomit against the pavement. Owen cursed his own sobriety as the world moved around him in a blur.

The keys were still in his hand. The metal biting into his palm was the only thing keeping Owen grounded.

"What the fuck, what the fuck," Janie was saying to his right. He turned to look at her to give him something to look at, instead of the body of the man on the ground. She was pacing back and forth, wringing her hands, looking everywhere and nowhere all at once.

To his left, Alicia's eyes were filled with tears. Her shaking hands were trying to press against Edwin's arm. There was blood between her fingers, dripping down Edwin's shirt.

"You're going to be okay, you're okay, it's going to be okay," Alicia whispered.

"I'm shot, I'm not supposed to be *shot!*" Edwin's eyes were wide as he went into shock.

A guard with a first aid kit took over, wrapping Edwin's arm and giving Alicia wipes to clean her hands. Owen heard the promises to go to the hospital; he turned to look elsewhere instead.

Vicki was being led away by a guard, someone else taking her home tonight. The keys biting into Owen's flesh were no longer of any use.

After Vicki was loaded into a car, so was Edwin, then Alicia, Janie, then Brooke. Each given a guard, and each being driven away. Out of the parking lot, away from the crime scene that smelled of blood, death, and vomit. But Owen was left alone. Just him and the single guard standing next to the body. The guard was the new guy, the one that he'd met earlier at the bottom of the stairs.

Robbie's posture was tense, and he still held the gun in his hand like he was going to use it. Tension radiated down the man's arms, and his eyes glanced between the surrounding area and the now cooling body. The shadows of the night seemed to stretch further than usual. Owen kept seeing movement, where all was still.

There were supposed to be more guards out here. Thinking that surely he'd missed one, Owen counted on his fingers. One here with him, then one each with Vicki, Edwin, Alicia, Brooke, and Janie. Six. Six guards, but two of them were from inside.

"Were you fully staffed tonight?" Owen asked, his stomach dropping as the question left his lips.

"We were," Robbie replied, narrowing his eyes at the dark. The gun in his hand didn't tremble, but the hold was still anxious. It was pointed down at the body that Owen was desperately trying to pretend wasn't on the ground. "I can't protect both of you. Wait until your father gets here."

Owen nodded as he took a step back. His heart pounded as he tried to find some place safe to look. In all the years that he'd been part of Vicki's friend group, it had never been this dangerous. Owen stayed sober, so that his friends could get home safe. This parking area was assigned its own pair of guards at all hours, even when it was just an empty lot.

The guard pressed a finger to his earpiece and replied to someone on the other side. A minute later, two police cars and an ambulance pulled up.

A K-9 unit leaped from the car and got to work. It seemed excessive, until the police found more bodies. Blood drained from Owen's face as he learned what had happened: the bodies of the missing guards were stuffed under and behind Vicki's vehicle. Whoever had put them there, hadn't planned for Vicki to make it that far.

Owen had had enough. He'd wanted to spend tomorrow getting ready for a full week of classes, and doing some last minute reading. Now, he didn't think he would get to leave before last call.

"I'm waiting inside," Owen stated to anyone that wanted to listen. He needed a drink. Something strong enough that he could pass out for the rest of the night. Something that could make him forget. He had enough to take a cab home—he doubted his father was going to take him home before morning. Head of security would be needed until dawn, if they even let him go that early.

Owen was no longer needed, which meant that was it was a damn good time to drink.

***

Something small and metal poked at his side as Owen laid on the long bench in Vicki's private party suite. Everyone else had gone home, except for security. Most of the patrons didn't know what had happened. The lights and sirens were in the private lot; anyone that could have gone outside to see them had already gone home, or continued their nights elsewhere. Owen had had no problems weaving through the previously packed crowds to order his drinks.

Downstairs, the regular lights were on, unfortunately illuminating the room that Owen had deemed his place to rest. The remote wasn't where it was supposed to be, so Owen couldn't close the curtains. But even if he wanted to, he knew he shouldn't. He needed to go home and sleep in a real bed. At least it was still the weekend, and he could sleep in.

Someone turned up the lights as they walked in. The normally dim overheads seared Owen's eyes; he threw a hand over to cover them.

"It's time to get you home," Dad said.

"Are you done for tonight?" Owen asked, dropping his feet to the ground, and trying to use that leverage to pull himself to a sitting position. His head ached, and he knew his words were slurred.

"I'm going to let the investigators work," Dad replied. "They'll give me their reports as they find our more. Did someone take your statement?"

Owen nodded, wincing as even that small motion jostled his brain. "I did. There wasn't much to it. I saw a shadow that looked odd next to Vicki's car, turned out to be a man with a gun. Guy tried to mug us, which doesn't make sense, shoots Vicki, then gets taken out before he can get another shot." Owen rubbed his head. "It doesn't make sense, right?"

"No, it doesn't," Dad agreed. "But I believe you. We've got the best of the best looking into this, so don't be poking your nose where it doesn't belong."

"That was one time," Owen muttered as he pulled on his coat.

When Owen had introduced Janie to the rest of the friend group, he'd immediately felt left behind. Janie had latched onto Vicki, and Owen had felt used. His invitations to hang out had been turned out with always the same excuse. So, he'd went digging. Had their spontaneous friendship of two wandering souls at a gay bar turned out to be a planned meeting? Was that friendship a ruse for Janie to get to Vicki? The idea that his first queer friend had been using him felt like a slap in the face.

He didn't find out until later that Vicki and Janie had started sleeping together. It had taken time for him to repair his relationship with Janie after that, but they had gotten there in the end, even if they didn't hang out one-on-one anymore. Owen wasn't sure how much of that had been him pulling away to protect himself from getting hurt again, and how much of that was Janie not trusting him anymore. A mixture of both, and a desire not to rock the boat more than he had to, meant that Owen was no longer close to the one person who'd been a friend, without Vicki's influence.

After that, Owen always felt like he was on thin ice, so he'd started hanging back. Somehow, that pullback from being so involved had placed him into the role he had today: the sober one at parties that watched out for his friends.

Owen paused as he stood up, remembering the metal thing that had been poking his back. He reached back, feeling around until he pulled out the necklace that he had seen on Edwin earlier tonight. The broken links gave him way too many ideas about what this couch might have been already used for. He delicately placed the necklace on the table and went to go wash his hands.

"I'll follow in a moment," Owen said, wandering off to find the bathroom. It wasn't far; the lavish overdone stall always creeped him out. There was no reason that a bathroom at a nightclub should have anything velvet in it. His friends had gone back to it enough times together that he really didn't like touching anything in here that wasn't stainless steel or porcelain. If it couldn't be disinfected, then he didn't want to go near it.

"Remind me to take a shower when I get home," Owen stated, as he stumbled back to where his father was waiting. He could see the amused look on his dad's face and frowned back. He waited for the comment about watching where he was laying, but Dad didn't jump at the chance. Too many had died tonight to make a joke.

The ride home was quiet, any meaningless conversation forgotten as the soft sounds of the radio drifted through the air. Neither of them were listening to the late-night music, but at least it kept the silence from being awkward.

The condo that Owen and his father lived in was dark when Owen stumbled in. It was smaller than most of his friends' homes. No indoor movie theater like Edwin's family had, or expensive gardens like Vicki's mansion, or private the way Janie had an entire condo for herself. Owen couldn't imagine him and his father needing more space.

He didn't bother with the lights as he moved towards his side of the home. He and his father had lucked out in getting a place that had enough space for separate wings on either side of the main living area. Owen kept his bedroom and bathroom clean and orderly, and took care of his own laundry, the same as if they were roommates. But Dad helped with the groceries and paid for the place. Plus, they paid for cleaners to show up weekly.

Owen and his dad had come to that arrangement when he was in high school, and they hadn't changed it since. After all, Owen was still in college, and didn't need his own place yet. His infrequent one-night stands didn't come back with him. None of them had been "meet the family" types.

Walking into his bedroom, Owen flicked the light switch on. Wincing, he focused on getting to his dresser and finding something comfortable. He'd never had the patience to really put away his clothing, focusing instead on sorting it into categories, and then steaming or ironing as needed. It took some digging to pull out the pajama pants and old ratty shirt. It wasn't lost on him that he'd been wearing them since he'd finished his growth spurt, despite having more than enough to purchase something nicer. No one was going to see him in these, so it didn't matter. He was going to wear them until they were actual rags.

As he peeled off the layers of club attire and dumped them into the laundry basket, Owen had to keep reminding himself to take a shower before falling into bed. He was going to feel better in the morning if he did. Despite downing shot after shot of vodka, Owen could still remember the flash of the gun and the shrill of those screams.

Tonight didn't make any sense. The mugger in the secure parking lot. The shadows drifting around the cars. The shot that missed Vicki.

Owen stopped, his hand on the handle of the shower. Missed? It missed Vicki? It had to have. Vicki wouldn't have walked to the car if it had hit. There would have been screaming and crying. The response of the security would have been different, speeding out of the parking lot with promises to get to the hospital quick. Or she would have been helicoptered away. So Vicki couldn't have been shot.

But why did Owen still remember the bullet rending through flesh, and the blood dripping down Vicki's back?

Nothing about tonight made any sense.

CHAPTER 3

Night bled into morning. The early hours of sleeplessness had given way to a restless doze. The armchair Levi awoke in wasn't as comfortable as his bed. Sammy had rolled up a few towels and tucked them around his arm to keep the pressure off, and leaned the recliner back as far as it could go. It kept him from rolling onto his bad arm in the night.

Sunlight had begun its kiss through the windows as Levi blinked and looked around. Pain had awoken him. The medication that he'd downed the night before had faded, and a throbbing ache had pulled him from sleep. He had vague memories of pushing Sammy to take the single bed. They could have shared the space, but this way he wouldn't bleed on them.

There was a blanket draped over him, something that he didn't remember grabbing before sleep had taken hold. The buzz saw sounds of his friend's snores echoing through the space should have been enough to wake him, but nothing about last night was as it should have been.

The side table had a small stack of pain meds, a bottle of water, and a note. *For when you wake up.* He swallowed the pills without question and washed them away with the water. The medication was sure to get his stomach turning without food, but hopefully he'd be asleep again before the nausea hit.

The sun was up higher the next time he opened his eyes. The smell of toasted food and the sulfuric bite of cooking eggs took hold. It should have been way better than the smell of the disinfectant that had been drifting through the air as he'd fallen asleep—but eggs. What he wouldn't give for eggs not to smell so horrid right now.

Pulling the blanket up over his nose, Levi opened his eyes. Sammy had changed. Their outfit looked suspiciously like the clothes Levi had recently laundered and hung up in his closet. A dark-colored turtleneck that Levi sometimes wore going out was paired with ratty old sweatpants that sagged loose on their hips. Most of the clothes that Levi and Sammy could swap back and forth were shirts and shorts. Sammy's pants were a few sizes larger than his own.

The beanie that Sammy had been wearing was gone; they had already showered and brushed out their hair this morning. Any pretense of a bra or binder was missing, and their chest swayed as they cooked. Sammy rarely wore chest compression at home, so Levi didn't blink.

"What's the plan for your car?" Levi asked, remembering the reason that Sammy had joined his party last night.

"I'm not sure," Sammy replied, leaning against the counter. They crossed their arms and frowned. Worry flashed through the knit of their brow, the pull of their lips, and the sag of their shoulders. "I'll call around tomorrow, see if I can get it towed to a shop."

This wasn't the first time the car had refused to start at the end of Sammy's shift, and it wouldn't be the last. Levi knew that Sammy only held onto it (despite being a money pit) because it meant something to them. The vehicle had been purchased during a fight that the pair of them had had. Levi had realized how dangerous his deal had been, and tried to push Sammy away and find his own place. Sammy had threatened to move out of town, and purchased the car as a first step. When the anger and hurt had cooled, Sammy decided to stay, but kept the car. It had been patch worked and duct taped ever since.

It would make both of their lives easier if Sammy scrapped it. No more trying to find places with street parking, no more insurance and tags. One less falling apart, unreliable mess in Sammy's life. But Sammy had kept the car and Levi both.

"If you ever need anything, tell me," Levi said. If there was any good to come out of selling his life, making sure that Sammy was okay was his only request.

"Always. What do you take me for?" Sammy replied. "I called you last night, didn't I? A good thing too, since your pride seemed to think that you could handle a bullet wound."

"What? When did you—" Levi asked, drawing up to the bandage on his shoulder. It had been changed. There was a new flash of pain there, too.

"After you passed out, I cleaned the wound and stitched it up," Sammy replied, waving their hands as if to indicate magic. "I also pushed it to scab, just a little. It's not healing-"

Bullshit. Levi stared at his friend, wondering how they were trying to justify the healing magic this time.

"-just what you would have gotten if you had gone to a hospital, instead of doing it yourself again."

Panicked worry flashed through him. Levi could see the newly darkened circles from exhaustion that hadn't yet faded. Bloodshot eyes he was certain came from the strain of using their powers, though Sammy claimed it was just from crying. With a grunt of pain, he forced himself to sit up and properly look Sammy over. The worse signs of overuse were rapid aging, or intense hunger, but he didn't spot either.

Sammy narrowed their eyes at him until Levi leaned back, feeling defeated.

"You know why I can't go to the hospital," Levi pointed out.

"Yeah, but if they're going to get you shot and stabbed, it'd be nice if they had a little mob clinic you could go to as well," Sammy grumbled, handing over a plate.

The plate itself was supposed to be shatterproof; Levi had hoped it would stand up to his abrupt abuse. It was also made for toddlers. There were little divided sections on it, bearing the cartoon designs of children's shows that Levi didn't really remember. Sammy had bought them as a joke for one of Levi's birthdays, for all the nights that he was too weak or hurt to carry a nice ceramic plate.

"I'll bring it up to my bosses," Levi replied, sliding into a chair and picking at his food. He wasn't hungry; the pain medications still made the eggs smell and the toast unappetizing. He would stir the food around and take a few bites, though, and hope to settle his stomach.

***

The next morning, Vicki had done her best to avoid her father. The man had a temper, and while it had never turned to her, his idea of protecting her involved the same logic as a dragon locking a princess in a tower. Her freedoms would include whatever she wanted to do, as long as it was on the estate. From threats to her school, to the car accident that she had been in, keeping her under house arrest was his first reaction. The first attempt on her life? Yeah, she was going to be stuck inside for a while.

Her endeavors only lasted until late afternoon, when her father sent for her.

Vicki paused outside the office door. A rich oak with panels of glass to let light in, it allowed for people to see when her father was not to be disturbed. With the door open a crack, she could both see and hear him. Her father's voice was clear, but it wasn't until she heard Mr. Mills that she realized that this was a conversation with the head of security.

Last night had been the first time that the Blessing had triggered on an injury that it had been designed to protect her from. The fear of staring down the gun, even though she knew it wouldn't actually hurt her, still flashed through her mind and made her palms sweat. Wiping her hands on her skirt, she pushed those thoughts away. She was Vicki Townsend. Nothing could hurt her.

"Continue searching," Father ordered. "There's got to be a connection somewhere."

There was a stormy look on her father's face as he sat on one of the two couches in the room; he did not like the news that he was getting. Both her father and his head of security were out in the conversation area. A set of couches with a long coffee table set in between. It was more comfortable when her father was working overtime.

One the second couch, Mr. Mills tapped away on a tablet. "All we have is a cash deposit into his bank account," he said, not looking up from his screen. From where Vicki was standing, she couldn't see what was on it. "You see it too? It's the amount that we flagged as suspicious from…" His voice trailed off for a moment, and Vicki wondered why he'd paused. It was hard to see if he was trying to find it on the tablet, or spacing the answer. "The play money account."

Father looked contemplative. "Which means we agree that one of them hired him, but we don't know which one took the money."

"I'm afraid so," Mr. Mills replied, a resigned look on his face. "How do you want to handle this?"

Father leaned back, and Vicki could see how tired he looked. Had he slept at all last night? The amount of magic thrumming against the door to greet her suggested that he was using other means to stay awake.

When Father leaned forwards again, all the tiredness had slid from his face. He picked up a tablet of his own and tapped the screen a few times. The chime on the Mr. Mills's device signified the transfer of a file.

"This plan is need-to-know. The smaller the circle, the better," Father explained.

Mr. Mills opened the document, and his eyebrows raised. Vicki contemplated walking in to see what he was seeing. If it was need-to-know, shouldn't she also be informed? This was her life they were talking about!

The decision was taken from her as Mr. Mill's tablet went dark. "I'll handle this one personally," Mr. Mills replied. "Will that be all?"

"For now," Father replied. "Thank you for taking the lead on this."

Mr. Mills gave Father a polite smile before he walked out. Mr. Mills was built large. Vicki took a few steps back to pretend that she wasn't eavesdropping. The man still stopped when he spotted her in the hallway.

"Your father has been waiting for you," Mr. Mills said kindly, opening the door further to let her pass. It also kept her from slipping away.

"You wanted to see me?" Vicki asked, stepping into the room and taking the space that Mr. Mills had been in previously. The tablet had been taken, so she couldn't see what had been on it, but her dad's device was still there. She reached across the table and snagged it from his hands. The passcode was her birthday, but the document he'd sent wasn't on the screen anymore. Frowning, she raced to find it.

"Vicki, there's nothing in there that you need to get into," Father reprimanded, but his voice was soft. He only did that with her.

Vicki stared at the tablet for a long moment, hating the small bubble of shame that welled inside of her, before she glanced back up at her father. There was still that hardness around his eyes. Locking the device, she set it back down.

"As of right now, we don't know who went after you last night," Father said. "The pawn that shot you was simply that. A pawn. We found evidence of another person that took out two of the security guards, before you and your friends stepped outside."

"Someone else? How can you tell it wasn't only the mugger?" Vicki asked, her mind reeling from the new body count. The nightclub was supposed to be her home away from home.

"We found evidence of another attacker," Father pressed. "Which means you are still in danger."

Vicki swallowed under the harsh weight of his words. That meant that somehow the mugger had killed the guards and then come into the club. Or worse, someone inside her nightclub last night had been helping them. Maybe one of the staff. It sent a shiver down her spine.

Vicki shook herself. While the scream that had escaped her the night before had been unbidden, the pain had vanished with her cry. The wound was gone in moments, because Vicki was untouchable. "I survived last night," she pointed out. "Not a scar on me."

"Others were not so lucky," Father reminded her. "You are to take the next week off from school. There are too many questions and not enough answers, and I will not let you back out into danger until we have less of the first and more of the second."

"A week?" Vicki blurted out. "You want me to be locked away for a week? We barely started the semester. My friends are out there."

Father's eyes flashed, dark and angry. "Someone was after your life, and their accomplice remains at large. This is only the beginning."

"I have the Blessing, Dad," Vicki pointed out. She sat up straighter, tried to show him the daughter that he would be proud of: a young woman that could think on her feet. "We should show them we're not scared, that their little attempt did nothing. Draw them out of hiding."

"You know nothing about the Blessing," Father stated. His voice was firm. "Do not argue with me. We will gather more information before we make another move. I will not lose you like I lost your mother."

The dead wife card. While Vicki expected it, it still sucked. He used it whenever he was being *really serious* about Vicki obeying his commands. She didn't even have any memories of her mother; only that her death was the reason that he had developed the Blessing in the first place. It worked like a charm, offered her a life that she wouldn't have been able to experience without it. But she didn't mourn the woman who'd died; how could she? Outside of guilt trips, no one dared to mention her. Vicki knew nothing about her, except that she was gone.

"I understand," Vicki replied, the response almost automatic. A week stuck inside. A week before she would be allowed back into the sunlight.

Her father's cruel words crossed her mind as she started back towards her rooms, yet it brought a smile to her face. He was right. She had never deep dived into the spell that her father had given her. Didn't understand the true power it. But if she could prove that she knew she was safe, then she could go back out into the world, whether or not Father liked the idea. It didn't matter if someone was actually after her life this time, if that life couldn't be taken.

She could gain her freedom back once she could control the Blessing's power and harness it for her own.

***

This wasn't Owen's first hangover, but the pounding in his head and the ache in his body were not something that he actively sought out. He had been drinking to forget the sights and smells of the night before; it only left him with a morning of bad breath and pain that wouldn't go away. There was a dull ache in his shoulder from sleeping on it wrong, but it was also the same shoulder Vicki had been shot in.

Vicki wasn't shot, remember? Owen pointed out as he stumbled to the bathroom. His reflection had looked better. His skin had a sallow tinge to it, and the five o'clock shadow was looking rough, rather than purposeful. The bathroom lights added shadows to the bags under his eyes.

The pain in his shoulder crashed together with the events of last night, leaving his memories a jumbled mess. Enough so that he had to pull off his shirt to check. There was nothing there. No healing wound, no redness, no bruise—his pain wasn't anything other than a pulled muscle.

This is silly, Owen told himself as he pulled his shirt back on. Splashing his face with cold water, he tried to quell the unrelenting nausea. The longer he was awake, the more firmly the memories settled. He wished he didn't remember any of it. But the screams from last night still echoed through his mind as he reached into the medicine cabinet.

Dad was out when Owen got to the kitchen. An ache filled his chest as he looked around the empty apartment. When he was younger, Dad had to get him a babysitter; that ended as soon as he was old enough to take care of himself. The mornings after the scariest days, Owen spent alone.

Today was no exception as he made his way to the fridge. His eyes scanned through the leftovers that still had his name on them, then the freezer to see what breakfast items were there. Every time he reached for something, his stomach would flip-flop, and he would put it back down. Either the food was too much work to cook and eat, like hash browns and breakfast sausage, or there was too much of a smell, like a breakfast burrito, or it felt like too much work to eat, like cereal.

He settled on a stack of toaster pastries. Not even bothering to heat them, he shuffled to the living room to eat the sweet cardboard. He had to get something into his stomach. This was just as good as the rest.

His phone buzzed in his pocket; it was from the group chat. His eyes went in and out of focus and as he scrolled through a conversation about an upcoming ski trip. Nothing that looked like his friends were planning on going out partying tonight, or actively dying; he could ignore it for now.

The cool leather of the couch was going to be his home for a while as he left crumbs everywhere. He'd clean it up as soon as he was feeling better. For now, that was tomorrow Owen's problem.

His headache had finally eased up when his phone rang. Blinking, he saw Alicia's name. What was she doing calling him? He was behind on the group chat, but nothing in there seemed like it had to be replied to *now*.

"Is this about the ski trip?" Owen answered.

"Oh good, you've seen the messages," Alicia replied, a frown in her voice. "You sound awful. Are you okay?"

"Hung over," Owen replied, pulling himself upright. A dusting of pastry crumbs fell down his shirt.

"Hung over?" Alicia exclaimed; he winced at how loud her voice sounded. "Owen Mills, I didn't know you had it in you."

Owen pinched the bridge of his nose, trying to push down the new wave of nausea from daring to sit up. "Yeah, well, I had to wait for my ride last night, so I might have had one to too many."

"You had to wait—" Alicia started, but she stopped herself. "We can talk about that later. All expenses paid trip to the ski lodge, Mr. Townsend's buying. You in?"

That didn't sound like something that Mr. Townsend would do. From what he could gather from his dad, Vicki would be in lockdown at the family mansion until the threat had was cleared. Why would he send all of Vicki's friends to the ski lodge without her? Especially after an attack like last night? Sending Vicki's friends away would only cause her to act out and do something reckless. Owen wanted to pull the pillow back over his head as he considered the impending fallout. Would it be like the time that the guy Vicki liked had asked Brooke out during their senior year of high school, so Vicki had totaled one of her father's cars?

"Vicki going?" he asked. "And when?"

"I'd expect she'd be there. Her dad's paying for the whole thing," Alicia replied, a smile in her voice. "It'll be Sunday through Wednesday. Come on, it'll be fun."

"No thanks," Owen replied, flopping back against the cushions. He started picking and brushing the crumbs off of himself and the couch, dropping them to the floor where a vacuum would get them later. "Not looking to get another injury this year."

"You've only done that once," Alicia teased.

Owen rolled his eyes; he regretted it when it triggered a wave of dizziness and a sharp pain behind his eyelids. He'd gone to the ski lodge a few times after spraining his ankle, and had never found it that appealing. It didn't matter that he'd gotten the injury over a decade ago; he wasn't looking to repeat the adventure. "Besides, we've all got school," Owen pointed out.

"We saw a friend get hurt. We need a break," Alicia replied, as if that was obvious. "It's for our mental health!"

Owen bit back a snort. They were one week into classes, and he knew his professors. Some of them liked to load in the work from day one. A senior with another year to go, because he didn't have the credits to graduate in the spring, he couldn't just take time off of school to go skiing.

Alicia started talking about all the stuff that she wanted to do while out on the slopes, and Owen stopped paying attention. Alicia had changed a lot over the years. Vicki's best friend first, Alicia had always been right there. Growing up as part of Vicki's household, he'd gotten to know both of them. Alicia had lived with him and his dad for nearly a year, while Alicia's family shattered apart. They'd grown close through that, but sometimes Alicia was too much to take.

It was times like this, when Alicia couldn't hear his refusal, when she continued to push, that he wondered how much longer this friendship was going to last.

"I hope you all have a great time. Bring me back a snowball as a souvenir," Owen suggested.

"For that, I just might," Alicia replied with a laugh. "I hope you feel better soon."

"See you," Owen replied, ending the call. He ran a hand down his face and closed his eyes again. Tried to push down the familiar ache in his chest that he got anytime he told his friends no. It was like a held breath. A hope that the friendship didn't shatter every time he stood his ground. They were his friends, Owen reminded himself. They made space for him in their lives. Today was not the day for evaluating it.

CHAPTER 4

When Levi got the call, he was surprised to find it wasn't Sammy. They'd left to go back to their place a few days ago, but had called to check in several times a day. To check he wasn't bleeding out again, if Levi had to guess.

"How is your shoulder doing?" the Devil asked.

Those few words sucked all of the warmth out of the room. Levi hadn't heard that voice directed towards him since the deal. There had been messages over the years, both in writing and via the Chain sending pain through him. Reminders that Levi was still under this man's control.

"It's healing," Levi replied, waiting for the feeling of the Chain pulling tight. He glanced down at his wrist; the black leather band hadn't been able to be taken off in a decade. He'd more than likely be buried with it. The silver medallion in the center looked as inanimate as always. "The arm is sore and slow, but I can only heal at my speed unless I get a boost. How can I help you today, Mr. Townsend?"

"I need someone to infiltrate Vicki's friend group," Mr. Townsend replied. "I believe that one of them hired a man to attack her. They witnessed the wound being transferred away, which means they have leverage."

"You want me to—" Levi started before snapping his mouth shut. He could already feel the edges of pain from Mr. Townsend's annoyance. Small symbols along the edge of the silver medallion began to glow a soft yellow. "Did you have a plan for how I can achieve that?"

"A member of my security team will be arriving at your apartment shortly," Mr. Townsend replied. "He will give you the necessary information and instructions. I don't need to remind you what would happen if someone goes after my daughter's life."

"I will do everything in my power to protect her," Levi replied. There was only one person who he wanted to protect, and it wasn't Mr. Townsend's daughter. But it was the only way to keep himself alive. He was already digging into his lockbox to double check that everything that he needed was there. The cash was still below the false floor. He paused to count it. Barely enough to keep Sammy safe and comfortable if anything happened, but it would have to do. He returned it locked to the top shelf of his closet; the reach made his arm to twinge.

"Good," the Devil replied.

The burn started as the runes glowed brighter, magic whipping around him. A sensation like scorching flames on his spine drew forth a scream.

"Remember what happens to those that fail me."

"I couldn't forget," Levi hissed through gritted teeth, as a knock came at his door.

Stumbling to it, he glanced through the peephole and found himself face to face with a large, muscular man dressed far too nice for the area.

Tucking the phone between his shoulder and his ear, Levi undid the dead bolt, main lock, and chain. Fingers slipped as he tried to get through the locks with speed, until the door was finally open.

The man was dressed in a suit that was purposefully tailored to hide his firearms. Both of them were about the same height, though the man was a fraction taller. "Carl Mills," the older man introduced. "Mr. Townsend sent me."

"Carl Mills is here," Levi said into the phone.

"Good, follow his command," Mr. Townsend said. "Remember, the Blessing is a secret, even from him."

"Yes sir," Levi replied and hung up. A quick text to Sammy let them know he might be gone for a while, and to check the lockbox for the money. He opened the door wider and let Mr. Mills in. "Mr. Townsend instructed me to follow you on this?"

"What do you know about this assignment?" Mr. Mills asked.

"Mr. Townsend is worried that there's someone after his daughter and wants someone to stick closer to her?" Levi replied. "I'm guessing that I look young enough to infiltrate the friend group and keep an eye out for danger."

From what Levi knew, Vicki and her friends were only a few years younger than he was. What he didn't know was how Mr. Townsend expected him to get close. Maybe that was where Mr. Mills was coming in.

Mr. Mills looked at him with a frown. "It's going to be a stretch, but you'll blend in enough to work."

Levi didn't know if that was a compliment, or an insult. He did not want this assignment and the danger that it posed. But failure wasn't an option Mr. Townsend would let him survive. His wrist still throbbed from the aftershocks of the Chain; he tried to be subtle as he shook out his hand.

"Someone wiped out one of Vicki Townsend's personal accounts," Mr. Mills explained, stepping through the apartment. "An identical sum was then deposited in cash into the account of our dead gunman. While this could be a coincidence, that account is a fund created to share with her friends, granting all of them access. Your goal is to determine which friend took the money and had a motive to set up the attack."

Mr. Mills paused as he looked at the floor. It had seen better days before Levi had set foot in the building. A patchwork of dark stains and bleached spots had only made the tan carpet a collection of colors over the years. Levi never intended to get his deposit back.

"Though, I don't have a clue why he picked you. I've seen your worksheet, and you've never been in the field in your life."

"Miss Vicki doesn't know me," Levi replied. "I'm already loyal, and I won't use this chance to get too close."

"How am I supposed to believe that?" Mr. Mills asked.

Levi smiled, though it was more for show than something that he was feeling. "Some of Mr. Townsend's guard dogs have more of a leash on them than others. I will protect Miss Vicki with my life, but I have no desire for any more favors from the family."

Mr. Mill's eyes crinkled. "Ah, you're one of those. The Chained ones. Well, I always knew that he had a collection of you around the city."

Levi nodded. While he couldn't talk about the Blessing, he could talk about the other power that held him. The Townsend family had sold it as guaranteed loyalty. Others saw it for what it was: obedience. There was no loyalty there. The moments the Chains were gone, every single one that had been bound had turned on the ones holding the leash. He had no desire to push his luck.

Mr. Mill looked over him once again. "What's with the sling?"

Levi looked down to his rig made from the discarded shirt to keep his arm from moving too much. "I had surgery on my shoulder," Levi lied. "It's still healing."

"Well, I'll send a few things for your shoulder when I send up your new wardrobe," Mr. Mills said. "You're going to start college."

Somehow, out of all the options that had run through Levi's mind, college had not been even close to the top of the list. For a high school dropout who barely held a GED, this was going to be painful when he failed.

CHAPTER 5

A few hours after the initial meeting with Mr. Mills, parcels of clothing began arriving at Levi's doorstep. Boxes wrapped in brown paper and shopping bags to stores that did not exist within any income bracket that Levi expected to reach. There were jeans worth more than his rent, shoes that cost the same as two months of groceries, and jewelry whose price tags gave Levi anxiety. Each one came with a note that specified it was to be used as his clothing when he stepped outside of his apartment for the foreseeable future. Any clothing that he owned before this point of time was to be removed from his closet, until the job was done.

The box containing the spell scroll dropped out of his hands when he opened it. It was worth more than every other purchase combined. Unrolling it, Levi found it was one that would help make him likeable to the group. It was reusable, something that he would have to charge every morning, and carry with him every day. There was a case to it, a metal cylinder that could pass for a lipstick if no one looked too close.

Two days later, Levi was going to class for the first time since he'd dropped out of high school. He tried not to bleed on the clothes; maybe he could resell them when this was all over. Everything had scabbed over, but it would be his luck to get another injury while trying to investigate this one. Anything with a god-awful logo he was holding back with the price tags; that way Sammy could get good money for it.

Ice melt crunched under his brand new boots; a blister was already forming as he walked. Sammy's trick to stuff them with socks and throw them in the freezer had not helped. Neither did the trick of wearing two pairs of extra thick socks. These shoes would be sold the moment the Devil's back was turned.

It took effort to not check his pockets for the spell scroll. Any action would draw potential pickpockets' attention. At least it was smaller than a bundle of cash, and potentially less noticeable.

The walk to the subway station revealed just how close the newer parts of the city were encroaching on his own. By the time that he got to the station, he was being greeted by high rises and city cameras without spray paint or cut wires. When he got off the subway near campus, Levi expected to find buildings so tall they blocked out the sun. Instead, he found trees and blankets of untouched snow, over what he could presume was grass. Space between the buildings where people could just breathe. No one had grass on his side of town.

The buildings with classrooms were only a few stories tall. Made of red brick, a contrasting tan stone ran along the windows and the doors. Levi even spotted a building with sandstone columns along the front, but according to his map, he didn't have classes there.

His schedule had already been picked for him, with an array of subjects that lined up with at least one of the group. His first was a management course of some kind, and Levi was already dreading it. He'd known the moment he'd looked over the schedule that there wasn't going to be a single class he understood. Maybe he could have some fun with this. Was this a party campus with a drug scene? Or were the students drinkers? He'd tried to do some research on his phone, but he'd never tried to look into anything like that before; he had no idea how to find it. Maybe he could find out. He only lived once.

The chilly January air broke as he stepped into the building. Within moments, the expensive heavy coat became too hot to take another step in. It was a shock to his system; did everyone else keep their homes this warm? He was glad that he'd had the forethought to button his coat over his arm in a sling. While one of his sleeves dangled empty, it kept his arm safe and warm. It made it easy to slide it off and tuck it over his good one, until he got to the right classroom.

The large auditorium looked more like a movie set. The doors he'd entered were in the back of the room, and up a flight of stairs. Rows of seats gradually got closer to the bottom of the staircase, where the large screen and desk sat, currently devoid of any teacher.

Levi took in the current occupants with a critical eye that he tried to play off as casual. Vicki wouldn't be back until next week, but the others were supposed to be here.

The first one that Levi recognized in the sea of faces was Owen, Mr. Mills' son. The pictures he'd been given to ID them were a mix of social media posts and high school graduation pictures. Owen barely looked like his photographs. Part of that was that Levi had been mentally trying to match Owen with his father, but the two didn't look alike at all. Where Mr. Mills was tall, Owen was short. Where Mr. Mills was bulked out and broad with a military haircut, Owen was thin, with brown hair that framed his face.

Levi found himself glad that he was wearing the most unbranded of the new outfits. None of the students that he could see were wearing items that screamed luxury. At least he'd been given a new warm hat; there was no way that his simple haircut from Sammy could match anyone else in the room.

Picking his way through the crowds that were starting to filter in, Levi tried to find a seat that would put him in listening distance of his target. Thankfully he'd gotten there early enough to spot; if either of them had been late, Levi might not have found him.

"There's room here," a voice said. It was Owen, waving him over to a nearby seat. "A couple of my friends are skipping today, so you can sit here."

That... Levi blinked at the offer. Had Owen already been briefed about what was going on? Nodding belatedly, Levi walked through the rows of seats until he was in the one next to Owen.

"Thanks," Levi replied as he settled in. It was a process taking out each of the items for the class. His shoulder ached every time he leaned down to grab the next one, and there was not enough room on the desk for everything.

His first day of school in almost a decade, he hoped he wouldn't regret it.

***

Owen wasn't sure what he was doing. The man was tall, and he wore his clothes like a model. Even the sling on his arm matched somehow. But Levi had walked in looking like a sad lost puppy. Most of the men his father hired had a cocksure attitude that would boulder into his group with all the finesse of an avalanche. Levi didn't give off that attitude at all. He looked lost, and like he wanted to go home.

The file on Levi Beckett had been easy enough to find by someone who knew where to look. If there was one unspoken security leak in Mr. Townsend's security force, it was how much Owen knew about their work. Finding Levi's file had left Owen feeling conflicted. He didn't want to be the only one looking a little more closely, but how was adding a stranger in supposed to help? Levi's file didn't tell Owen what assignment this guy was doing, only that he had one.

Owen hadn't gone through his files to look for some guy; he was looking for more about what had happened to Vicki. The memories of that night nagged at him, along with the image of the injury that never was. With all of their friends off in the mountains, Owen had gone to visit, only to be turned away. The only person in or out of the Townsend residence since Sunday morning had been his own father. Then came the invoices for clothing, the trips to the other side of town and Owen's college, and other activities that were too out of character to be normal. Worry had fought against his curiosity; he wanted to know what his father was doing. The timing caused a pit of worry. Rather than wait, Owen told himself that it was only natural to be inquisitive. The more he knew, the better he could help.

While his father was out, Owen had snooped through his office and found the file on Levi Beckett. Name, age, address, height, weight, and a photograph were all standard. Owen snapped a picture of the file with his phone. Then came the shoe size and clothing size. It explained the clothing purchases, but not the why. The file contained very little on the man himself. References to middle school and high school, but nothing about graduation or a job. The only other piece was a class schedule that nearly matched Owen's this semester.

But why did his father have a file on Levi Beckett? What had prompted the man to be brought into their space, dressed like he fit in?

Owen had come to two different conclusions: either the man was additional security, or a patsy.

The flinches of pain every time Levi reached down looked real. It was a tightness in his eyes, a bit-off curse. At one point he sat up and leaned back in defeat, before trying again to get a stubborn book from his bag.

"Can I ask about your shoulder?" Owen asked as the management class ended. Most of today's content had been a review from previous courses, so Owen had let his mind wander.

Levi was dropping things back into his bag. His pencil dropped and rolled on the floor.

"Sure," Levi replied, getting up and squatting down to reach for it. "I had surgery, and couldn't afford the healing spells after. Insurance said that I didn't need them, and the hospital jacked up the prices again."

"One of my friends is dealing with that," Owen agreed. Alicia had called him every day while she was out on her skiing trip. Edwin was being a baby about the scratch on his arm and not skiing this time because it hurt. When he'd asked about healing scrolls, that innocent question was met with derision, and a reminder that Edwin's family was having a hard time right now. "He got hurt last week, and healing spells have practically doubled in price since the last time he pulled something dumb."

"Doubled? How long has it been since he needed them?" Levi asked.

"Over summer," Owen replied. Back then, Edwin had been rolling in dough, so his parents had paid out of pocket for Edwin's sunburn to be healed in an instant. A frivolous waste of a spell scroll, in Owen's opinion.

Levi's eyes bugged out. Whatever was going on with his shoulder was not something that happened often. Or he'd never had the money for a healing scroll to begin with.

When he got home tonight, he would reread that file. Maybe there was a page he'd missed that would tell him what had happened to Levi's arm. With how little was in the file, there might not be, but Owen would have expected to find hospital records, if there were also middle school transcripts. There was something about Levi that was bothering him, and Owen planned to find out what.

**

It was a few more days before Levi was able to meet more of Vicki's friends. They had been missing from Monday and Tuesday classes, but by Wednesday three more sauntered in. Levi didn't even recognize them until Owen called them over. They were just a few more faces in a sea of strangers.

Alicia was the one that Levi recognized first. From the files that Levi had read, she was supposed to be Vicki's best friend. Tall, thin, blonde hair and green eyes, Alicia seemed to be everything that her file had said. The probability of her being the one behind the attacks was slim to none. That assessment had struck him as odd. Levi wasn't sure why Alicia, out of all people, got such trust. That was until he met her. She was Chained, like him. There was a look in her eyes, and a weight to the locket around her neck. He was curious who held the other end, if it was Vicki or someone else. It had to be a Townsend to mark her off the suspect list.

With one arm around Alicia, was Edwin. The only other guy in the friend group, and the only other person injured in the attack, Edwin's file had made him out to be someone to look at twice. From where Levi was sitting, he'd already caught a few discrepancies. It seemed that Edwin was dating Alicia, not Vicki. Either the wound on his arm had been larger than the file suggested, or he was exaggerating. A sling that almost matched his own was on the arm that wasn't wrapped around Alicia.

Janie was the only other one present, which meant that Brooke and Vicki were still missing.

Out of everyone, Janie was the outlier. She'd joined later than the rest of them, but also had the least motive. Her file was the smallest, but it didn't miss any of the details. Owen had been the one to introduce her, and within a week, Janie and Vicki had gotten incredibly close. The file hadn't told him if Janie and Vicki were simply fast friends, or if they had slept together. Either way, the only way that Janie could try to get Vicki killed was through alcohol poisoning. Alcohol poisoning was also the reason that Levi guessed that the Blessing wouldn't work against poisons, or anything that had repeated effects like drowning or suffocation. It was a hypothesis that Levi didn't feel safe sharing. Either Mr. Townsend already knew, or he'd learn the hard way. Levi only hoped that he was long gone by then.

Unlike Owen, the rest of the group completely ignored Levi. He'd taken the same desk as before, directly next to Owen. Alicia and Edwin sat next to each other, with Alicia helping Edwin get his laptop out for notes. Janie took the seat on the other side of Owen from him.

"We missed you at the slopes," Janie said, not seeming to care that her voice could travel. The room was loud with other ongoing conversations; even though he was only a desk away, Levi had to strain to listen.

"You know I don't ski," Owen replied. "Did you have fun?"

"Got my mind off of Saturday," Janie replied with a shrug. "Brooke got food poisoning. Stress eating. The guess is that she ate something that was left out too long."

Owen scrunched his face.

"How was Vicki?" Janie asked, looking around.

"Stuck at her dad's still," Owen replied. "I'm going to see if I can visit her after class today."

"Good luck," Janie said, a smile playing at the corners of her lips. "Last time I visited while she was on lockdown, I got thrown out while being yelled at that I should have visited sooner."

"Oh shoot, you're right," Owen winced.

"Bring flowers," Janie suggested. "Maybe they'll soften the blow."

"Don't bring roses," Edwin added to the conversation. "If they're thrown at you, you want them to be as soft as possible."

Did Vicki's friends even like her? Maybe he should revise those files to say that everyone had a motive, other than Owen.

Levi noticed that Alicia was staying out of it. If he hadn't known that she was Chained, her lack of participation would seem odd. But Levi knew what kinds of restrictions those bindings could have on a person.

He must have been staring at them for too long, because Alicia called him out on it.

"Who are you?" Alicia asked.

"Levi," Levi said, embarrassed at being caught. He wasn't cut out for the sneaky stuff. "I'm new."

"I invited him to sit with us," Owen said. "Levi's been my study partner while you all skipped class."

"Nerd," Edwin said, like it was a fact. There wasn't any of the teasing tones that Levi always put into his insults towards Sammy. Owen didn't seem to care.

"I'm Janie, that's Edwin, and Alicia," Janie said, cutting through any dismissal that the others might have had. "We're still missing two of us, but you should meet Brooke tomorrow. Hopefully Vicki's back by next week."

Levi nodded, giving the others a wave. As the class started, Levi found himself hoping that the rest of his introductions would go as smoothly. No one seemed to suspect anything. As soon as he could prove which of Vicki's friends was behind the attack, he could go back to the world that made sense to him. He'd wanted a hobby, but this was not it.

***

The week stuck in her house dragged on and on. The first few days brought no visitors, and no opportunities to escape. Vicki didn't even get a break from school. The switch from all in-person lectures, to ones that were attended virtually, left her dreading class. The management degree was one of her father's choosing: a requirement before she could step into a role in one of his companies. As long as she put in enough effort to pass, there wouldn't be a problem. She might skirt by, barely, if she could get back into the classroom. Or get the professor that read the PowerPoint slides word for word fired.

Her only consolation prize, if it could be called that, was the time to research the Blessing. There was nothing on the internet about it; her only results were religious miracles.

Asking around inside the house resulted in the same— nothing. The Blessing was a secret, even amongst staff. Not even Mr. Mills, the head of security, was privileged enough to have any information about it. When she asked about Saturday night's shooting, the answers she received were inconsistent.

"The blood wasn't yours, it was Edwin's," the maids that had taken her dress to get incinerated reminded her. "You didn't get hit that night."

"We burned through a healing scroll in the car," the bodyguard that sat in the back with her explained. "You got a clean bill of health after that."

"Edwin was the only one shot that night," Mr. Mills said, looking through the status report. "By the attacker, at least. Did you want to know the names of your security that were killed that night?"

She'd left that conversation with an excuse about getting to class. Her focus was on the Blessing, not on the injuries and deaths of others. They knew the job they'd signed up for.

The only information she found was through omission, rather than through confirmation. The Blessing was a secret. It was never sold to anyone. The power to walk away from a gunshot wound without even a scar hadn't gone to auction for the highest bidder. Her father didn't even have a Blessing. How had she gained one?

Those questions plagued her until her first visitor came, almost five days since she'd been stuck inside. Of all the people that she expected to stop by in her solitude, Owen was the furthest from her mind. The son of the head of security brought a bouquet of flowers with him. The paper holding them was crumpled, and the string not as tight as the florist would have attached it. Intermixed into a collection of white and pink roses were smaller white flowers and large green leaves. Owen must have enlisted help from a maid; the bouquet was a fresher version of the flowers that were already in her room. Thankfully he had, because none of these gave her headaches.

"Your father insisted that the flowers were searched," Owen explained as he offered them to her. "I think Saturday freaked him out."

"No kidding," Vicky grumbled, motioning for him to set the flowers down on the coffee table. "What brings you by?"

"Alicia and the others got back from their mini-vacation and told me that you didn't end up skiing with them," Owen replied, dusting his hands off on his pants as he looked around.

"Skiing?" Vicki asked, her eyes growing wide. Her friends went skiing while she was grounded? Anger burned in her gut at the thought of the traitors that she called friends, out on the slopes without her. If Alicia, Edwin, Janie, and Brooke thought that they could have fun without her, without her money, she would like to see them try.

It would only take a phone call, a quick word with the bank. All of that fun money that she'd been providing could be gone in an instant. Revoking their access to the account would only take a word.

"I got an invitation on Sunday, but I turned it down," Owen explained, speaking as he glanced her way. "Supposedly, your dad paid for it?"

Anger bubbled in her at the thought. Not only was her father keeping her locked away, but he was the one paying for her friends to have fun without her? Her hands shook, and her acrylic nails bit into her palm.

"I could have been wrong," Owen continued, rushing to get the words out. "Usually, when your dad sets something up, I hear about it from you, or his secretary. Though, it might have been a good thing that we didn't go. Alicia claims they would have stayed longer, but Brooke got food poisoning."

"Of course you stayed home," Vicki grumbled. She ignored the flowers, instead looking at her kiss-ass friend. Did Owen think he was getting brownie points for staying back?

He didn't rise to the bait. "So, what happened Saturday?" he asked instead. "Security rushed you out of there before I could blink. Were you hurt?"

"It's been days. Why are you asking now?" Vicki spat. Owen could have gone skiing too and lied, or he could have gone on another trip.

"I wasn't allowed in until now," Owen replied, holding out his hands in surrender. "None of the staff was allowed in or out this week, while people were being vetted. My Dad got stuck here vetting his own personnel."

"Why?" Vicki asked, dropping into a chair. After so many hours alone, she was feeling stir crazy. Maybe Owen could be useful after all. Owen had the inside scoop when it came to her security, both the good and the bad of it.

Owen looked around the room and kept his mouth shut, like always.

Vicki moved closer. She should be part of the loop. She was the one that had been locked up. Temper flaring, she opened her mouth to order him to explain, but Owen spoke first.

"I shouldn't be telling you this," Owen started, taking a seat in one of the other chairs and leaning in close. His voice was low, like it was a secret.

"Rumor is, your dad thinks it might be an inside job," Owen glanced around the room, and Vicki followed his eyes. There was no one else in here. "Or that someone accidentally slipped information to the wrong person. About a third of his cleaning staff are currently being paid to stay home until he finishes properly vetting everyone. Several of the office personnel are out, too."

"But the guy that attacked me wasn't any good," Vicki pointed out. While it had been an attack on her life, even without the Blessing, she would have been healed by morning.

"Sure, but someone killed several security personnel and got into your private garage, so that counts as something," Owen replied. He chewed on the corner of his lip as he looked around the room again.

Vicki didn't know what he was looking for; nothing had changed in the last few minutes.

"Besides, like I said," Owen continued once he was satisfied with his search, "your dad is paranoid about your safety. I'm surprised that he's only done this much. I would have expected all of us to be under house arrest this week."

"That's excessive, even for him," Vicki replied.

"Someone shot at you," Owen countered. "Whether or not it hit, that had to be too close for comfort."

Once again, Vicki was reminded how no one knew what had happened. Everyone was walking around like she was fragile or human, like the rest of them. There was only one person besides her father that knew about the Blessing. A decade old Chain prevented that person from revealing the secret.

The idea struck like lightning. It was so obvious, she didn't know why she hadn't thought of it when Owen walked in. She couldn't research the Blessing, locked in the house as she was. But Owen was always poking his nose where it didn't belong.

"I was shot," Vicki said, pulling her shirt collar over to show where the skin had healed and the scar had vanished in an instant. There was nothing there, nothing to show; would Owen even believe her without proof? "It doesn't matter. I'm fine. Shooting me does nothing."

"What?" The word seemed to slip out of Owen before he had a chance to call it back. He looked surprised at saying it. "What does that mean?" Owen asked.

"That's it," Vicki bragged. No one else had been listening to her. At least Owen was smart enough to keep up and keep his mouth shut. "It's something that my dad invented. Even if I get injured, I heal instantly. I've never had a paper cut, a broken bone, or even that bullet wound last for more than a fraction of a second."

"You did bleed," Owen breathed. He reached up and rubbed his shoulder, the same one where Vicki had been shot. "I thought I had imagined it when you didn't get taken away by the ambulances."

"I want you to look into it," Vicki said. "My father said that I didn't know enough about it. I should. I'm the one who lives with it. Will you help me?"

Owen's mouth dropped, and he cast his eyes around the room again. It was getting annoying. She wasn't being watched in her own home. Finally, he gave a small nod.

"You'll report your findings to me. And you can't tell a soul about it," Vicki threatened. "No one knows about it except my dad and me."

Owen pantomimed crossing his heart. It was good enough for Vicki.

"There's someone new at school," Owen said, changing the subject. "He was supposed to start at the beginning of the semester and got hurt, so he's joining our classes now."

They were only a few weeks in, and Vicki had already missed a week of hanging out with her friends in class. It still seemed odd though; why would anyone wait for weeks when they could be instantly healed? "Alicia's type?" she asked.

"Honestly, he's probably yours. Tall, permanent scowl, enough money to pay for your meals, but not enough to think he's better than you," Owen replied, leaning back into the chair again. "Alicia pointed it out and I can't stop seeing it."

Vicki hummed. Alicia hadn't been wrong before. Maybe a new man to drive Edwin crazy would make up for being stuck in her tower.

***

Mr. Mills had called this morning to let Levi know Vicki would be back in class today. Levi still looked and felt terrible. His arm was still in the sling, and he expected it to be for at least another few days. The pain had gone down at least; he didn't need as many pills to function. Though as he made his way to campus, Levi hoped that the medication would kick in before he got his first look at the pampered princess.

Frost covered the ground, and the sidewalks crunched with ice melt. He had yet to figure out how people could navigate the cold like this without extra layers. So many of them wore almost nothing, coats with short skirts and ankle boots, and seemed fine. The number of guys wearing shorts made Levi shiver.

At his first class, he took a seat near Owen. Thanks to that first conversation, he'd settled into his place beside the group. Levi had no illusions of being one of them, but he was close enough to do his job. He could hardly imagine finishing high school with friends like them, with a girlfriend like Brooke or a boyfriend like Owen. Hanging out after school with Alicia and Janie. He might have bullied Edwin, but the man was a wimp and a cheat. Levi's divide between them had little to do with his lack of education. None of them bore the look of someone that had to wonder when they'd get their next meal, or if they'd see spring with all of their fingers and toes.

The class divide between the groups only grew when he pulled out the notebook and pen to take notes, while the other students around him pulled out laptops. Technology like that was unaffordable to him, even at pawnshops and secondhand stores. One of Sammy's coworkers had a laptop as a status symbol, along with luxury bags, watches, and jewelry. Items with branding that Levi didn't even see on this campus.

The pain in his shoulder at once became burning hot, like he'd taken another bullet all over again. Tears stung his eyes as he tried to breathe. In his focus, he'd missed Vicki's entrance.

"Are you okay?" a voice asked.

Levi looked over to find Owen staring at him. Concern filled those warm brown eyes.

"My shoulder is acting up," Levi replied, his voice not all the way back yet. "Thanks for checking." The pain was receding, so he kept talking. "Sorry about that."

"Do you need something for it?" Owen asked, sliding into the seat next to him.

"I already took something. Hopefully, it'll kick in soon," Levi replied as Vicki stared him down.

Her blonde curls looked like they belonged to a movie star, not someone walking into a college class. She was far more awake and alert than anyone else in the room, teacher included. Shorter than him, even in heeled boots, her outfit looked like it was right out of a catalog. A long caramel coat that dusted her knees was paired with a dark-colored skirt that didn't come close. Sheer black tights that looked too thin to be comfortable at this time of year. A chunky turtleneck was enveloped in layers and layers of necklaces.

Pictures didn't do her justice, and yet, Levi was more focused on the false bond fighting between them. That had to be why his shoulder was acting up again, now that they were in the same room. An echo of the last wound between them. He briefly wondered if she felt the same, but there wasn't anything like that on her face. One-sided then.

A little behind Vicki was the last member of their group. Brooke seemed to be the same height as Vicki, though as she got closer, Levi could see that she was wearing flats, not heels. Her blue eyes landed on him and lit up. She took the empty seat on his other side.

"You must be Levi, right?" Brooke asked.

"That's me, how did you guess?" Levi asked. Other than Owen, she was the only one to acknowledge him.

"Janie and Alicia told me that you had joined the class. I'm Brooke," she said, moving to hold out her hand. She paused as she caught sight of the sling. "Right. I heard that you and Edwin were matching. Though, between you and me, I didn't see Edwin wearing the sling at all while he was skiing."

"I've never gone, but my understanding is that a sling might make the whole thing difficult," Levi agreed. He was surprised how friendly she was.

Then he caught sight of the locket around her neck. At first, he thought it looked like Alicia's, but it didn't have the same weight. If that was the case, Brooke would have more freedom to act.

Brooke continued to talk with him until class started, and then again as soon as the lesson ended. Levi had to cut in to ask his pre-planned question.

"Do any of you know of a good tutor to help me get caught up?" he asked. He had to feign surprise when everyone pointed at Owen.

"Well, most of them have been out a week themselves, so we're going to be doing a study session later, if you wanted to come," Owen offered.

Once again, Levi wondered if Mr. Mills had instructed Owen to help, or if he was letting Levi join for other reasons. A bundle of nerves tightened in his stomach at the thought; it gave them more time to see that he was a fraud. Whatever came next, Levi had an invitation and a chance to figure out who among them had tried to kill Vicki Townsend.

***

Vicki had only been gone a week and already her friends had accepted someone new. Something pinched in her gut. Could her friends so easily replace her at a moment's notice? Their attention should have been on *her*. She was the one that had been stuck in her house all week after nearly getting mugged! But the moment she'd walked in, Owen had focused on the new guy. *Levi*. Mr. Friends-stealer.

What's worse was Alicia had been almost right: Levi did fit her standards. Tall, a little older, with a smile that slipped into a scowl when no one was looking. Talked easily with her friends, yet didn't pull attention to himself.

But, Levi wasn't her type. Cropped short hair and a five o'clock shadow that looked like a beard that wanted to grow in too fast, rather than a fashion statement. Not the dark curled hair kept perfectly in place, like Edwin. Vicki wanted someone that looked at her like she was the most important person in the world; Edwin did when they were together. Levi didn't want to look at her at all.

There was something about him that made her want to run as far away as possible. Like there was something hazardous about him, and if she stuck too close, it would spread. Without knowing what the Blessing was made from, she didn't know if she could trust it when this guy let loose.

Did he have some sort of Anti-Blessing? Her skin seemed to crawl as she watched him and Brooke talk. If he did, was it messing with her own? She pinched herself to be sure. The pain bit into her, then faded the moment that she let go. Huh. Well, that was reassuring at least.

Still, there was something about this guy. Maybe it was the wards, warning her of the dangers Levi carried. That had to be it. She would have to warn her friends as soon as they were alone.

Over the next few classes, Levi seemed to charm the others with no effort. It annoyed her, watching Levi flit between all of her friends and ignore her. Her mood soured with every interaction, and the glare that she shot at the back of Levi's head promised a warning when she thought of something suitable. Something small at first, like getting his parking pass revoked so he couldn't park on campus. She didn't want him to talk to her, but she should have gotten to turn him down first!

"What are your socials?" Brooke asked as they were about to split for the day.

"I don't have any right now," Levi replied. A flash of an unreadable emotion faded away before Vicki could figure it out. "I had to delete them because I had a stalker."

"A stalker?" Janie asked.

"Yeah, someone that I thought was my friend turned out to be a little too obsessed with me," Levi replied, explaining that they'd broken into his house and stolen some of his things. The story sounded truthful enough. "I ended up having to move states, change my phone number, delete my socials, and start over. The police still don't think she's a danger anymore." He motioned to his arm. "The surgery was to correct the damage."

Vicki wanted to roll her eyes. Her friends, on the other hand were eating it up.

"Oh shit," Owen replied.

"If your stalker shows up, let us know," Janie said. "I know a few people that could fix it better than the police."

"Thanks," Levi replied, running the arm that was not in a sling through his hair, a flush of color on his cheeks. "I don't know many people in the city, so it's cool to know that I can count on you." He dropped his arm and glanced at his watch. "Study session tomorrow?"

"Yeah, I guess we'll see you there," Vicki replied, giving him a wave as Levi walked off.

She waited until he was out of earshot before glancing at her friends. Who was going to be the first one to call out how weird that was?

"He's nice," Owen said.

"That because he's your type," Janie teased. "I saw you. You wanted to climb him like a tree."

Owen sputtered, as Edwin shrugged. "Not my type, so I can't tell you."

"I'm not even straight and I wanted to fall into bed with him," Janie replied, watching Levi walk away. She seemed to frown at his limp. "I wonder what I can dig up on the stalker, though."

"Are you doubting his story?" Vicki asked, hoping for another person on her side.

"Nah, I just like scaring people that deserve it," Janie replied, her voice growing dangerous. She flashed the group a smile, as if reassuring them she'd been joking. "What about you? You're like the only one that seems suspicious of him."

"Because none of you are," Vicki pointed out. She glanced around at her friends, but none them seemed to get it. Still. "Most of you met him in the few days I was gone, and you're already like best friends. That has to be weird, right?"

"He was really nice," Alicia pointed out. "Besides, if he turns out to be a douchebag, we've dealt with those before. Hell, one of them is in this group."

Edwin grinned, as if it was a compliment.

"Levi checks out," Owen said, tucking his hands into his pockets. "I looked into him while you all were away. Best I can find, he's legit."

"Which means, if he's not legit," Janie filled in when Owen stopped talking. "Basically, the only person with the power that could plant him here like that would have to be your dad."

"Maybe he's someone spying on us from Mr. Townsend. At least he fits in on campus," Brooke pointed out. "You could have Owen's dad, stalking us and watching for danger. What would happen to our social life then?"

Vicki shook her head. There was still something off, but none of her friends were taking it seriously. Why was it when Owen called for danger, everyone else seemed to listen, but when she did, everyone brushed her aside?

Maybe Alicia would be up for talking about it later. She was the one that knew the most about the Blessing. Maybe she could help Vicki figure out how to get Levi far away from them.

CHAPTER 6

If Levi thought he could tell Sammy to stay away, that his current job was dangerous—well, he must have been high on painkillers. No sooner had he walked through his door after a long day of tedious socializing, did Sammy step in after him.

"Nice kicks," Sammy complemented as they toed off their shoes, eyeing Levi's designer sneakers. "Do you think your sugar daddy would get some in my size is you asked nice?"

"Ha ha, very funny," Levi grumbled, pulling off the sling and tossing it onto the counter. Gently peeling away the layers of luxury clothes, he checked every inch for stains. "I hate this. I don't mind the work, but with the borrowed clothes in my closet, I could pay for both of our apartments for a year."

Sammy laughed at his grumbling. "Play nice. Maybe you'll get to keep them when the job is over, and we can sell them at a discount. Or make a quilt with them."

"Can you even imagine," Levi replied, pulling on a cheap plain T-shirt. It didn't feel any different from the expensive ones, which annoyed him even more. The act of wiggling in and out of clothes only set his shoulder off again. He'd hoped for a break from that contraption.

"I thought I told you this job was dangerous," Levi added, pointedly over the kitchen counter. He gave Sammy a knowing look as he put the sling back on.

"And I told you that if your butt is out there in danger, I'm going to hang around and watch your back," Sammy replied. "You don't have the best track record for safety." They rifled through the fridge and frowned. "Think we could sell your shirt to get takeout for dinner?"

Levi rolled his eyes. While it was possible that someone might trade the shirt for a half and half pizza, he didn't know if it would be worse if people thought the shirt was fake, or real. If the people around here thought the clothes were fake, he might not get robbed.

"Speaking of cash, there's some emergency funds for you in the lockbox," Levi said, nodding to where the safe rested.

Sammy glanced towards the box and frowned. "Why?"

"Just in case money," Levi replied. He didn't want to talk about it, and he hoped Sammy would leave it at that.

It was almost a surprise when they did. This was drifting towards the uncomfortable conversations about his mortality again, and Levi hoped he could deter them.

"Though, since I just gave you all my money, you can use that for dinner tonight," Levi teased.

"It's emergency cash. You can't buy pizza with emergency cash," Sammy teased. "But, lucky for you, I have pizza money myself. Do you want your terrible mushrooms and olives?"

"Yes please," Levi replied, falling onto the couch as he scrubbed his face. The only one in the friend group that had held back was Vicki, which meant that his anger towards her had to be transmitting through the spell he'd been given. He would have to work on controlling it before tomorrow. There were only so many times that he could try to get close before the trustworthy spell failed entirely. Then he'd be left to face the Devil's displeasure.

He could hear Sammy on the phone, calling the pizza place just down the block. The walls were thin, and the space was small; he could hear every word on this side of the phone, and some of the voice through the speaker.

Levi grabbed any laundry in sight and moved it back to the bedroom. There were too many designer logos. People around here were desperate enough that it could be a temptation. Bringing even a fake designer piece to the pawnshop would have guaranteed a meal.

While Levi tidied, Sammy pulled down the safe to look. He didn't watch their expressions; he kept busy and out of their way. Though he didn't own much, which meant it didn't take long before he sat back down on the couch, apartment clean and his arm aching.

"So…that much cash you've been saving up," Sammy said, sitting down on the arm of the couch.

"I don't want you to be in a lurch if something happens to me," Levi explained. "I know you can take care of yourself, but I can't afford real life insurance, and I don't think my boss is kind enough to give you a payout."

"Yeah, I saw your will. Nice touch suggesting that I could toss you in the river with some weights, instead of paying for a funeral," Sammy said, with some bite to their voice.

"If something happens to me," Levi tried, remembering the mood he'd been in when he'd left that letter in the bottom of the lockbox. That hadn't been the one that he'd meant for Sammy to read, but he hadn't had the motivation to write something better since. "If something happens, I trust you to take care of me in whatever way is best. Best for you, best for me, doesn't matter. I want nothing fancy. I don't need my ashes on the moon, or dumped in a volcano, and I don't need you to feel obligated to hold a celebration of life with the people I work with. It'll be their fault that I died."

"I had it all planned out," Sammy replied with a smirk, their tone light. "I was going to invite your boss and coworkers and everyone else complicit in your death…" They let out a deep, dramatic sigh before continuing, "And then I was going to figure out how many of them I could send to the grave with you. After your boss wrote the check for the party, of course. Oh well, I guess feeding you to the sharks will have to do."

"Thank you," Levi replied with a quirk of a smile. Reaching for Sammy's hand, he gave it a squeeze. "I'll do my best not to make you find a boat anytime soon."

"You better," Sammy replied, squeezing back before they went to wait by the door. "I need a few more of these emergency cash payments so that I can afford the yacht."

"Yacht? What yacht?" Levi asked.

"Mine, of course," Sammy explained. "I can't wear a sheer dressing gown with fur lined sleeves and a train in my apartment. People would point fingers."

That got Levi to laugh, and the conversation derailed from there. By the time the pizza arrived, Levi and Sammy were designing the specific robe Sammy wanted: black sheer netting, a faux fur trim or maybe feathers, it needed to trail at least three feet behind them as they walked.

There was a strong possibility that this job ended with Levi no longer in the land of the living. He didn't see the harm in playing into Sammy's fantasy of his funeral today.

***

When Vicki caught up with Alicia, she wondered if her friend was avoiding her out of a guilty conscious. It was obvious that Alicia and Edwin had gotten back together over that damn ski trip. The betrayal could have been excused, had it not come at Vicki's expense. It left her single again at a time when she did not want to be alone.

There was also something bothering her about her recent interactions with her friends. What was it that Owen had said? That's right. Alicia thought Levi was her type. He wasn't. Vicki needed to correct that misunderstanding.

Vicki pulled Alicia into the back of one of the Townsend cars and told Edwin to find his own way home. There was a privacy screen up between them and the driver's seat; she could talk freely here.

"Vicki, I was going to go home with Edwin today," Alicia started.

"Did you mention to Owen that Levi was my type, so that I wouldn't notice that you got back together with Edwin?" Vicki asked as the car started to drive.

"That wasn't something that we planned," Alicia started to explain. "Edwin said that he was free to date again, and we clicked. You know how Edwin and I are. I was going to tell you about it. But Levi is your type. Tell me I'm wrong."

"You're wrong," Vicki replied. The annoyance of the day had built. The man's lack of a car had only frustrated her earlier thoughts of warning him away by causing a string of bad luck. Now Alicia was trying to push this again, and she crossed her arms in a huff. Levi was closer to her type, but there was something about him that was a turnoff.

"Is this that whole thing about something being off about him?" Alicia asked.

Vicki knew Alicia was trying to guide the conversation away from her and Edwin; this time Vicki let her.

"There *is* something off about him," Vicki replied. "For a moment, I thought he had something that messed with my Blessing."

"And, was there something weird with your Blessing?" Alicia asked, glancing towards the front of the car. There was a sound barrier that would protect the conversation, but Alicia still dropped her voice to a whisper all the same. "Is everything okay?"

This was why Alicia was her best friend. Out of everyone, Alicia always knew when to pull the attention back to the important things.

"I pinched myself earlier and the pain and the mark vanished, as it always does," Vicki replied. She pinched the arm again to prove her point.

"So, he made your wards go off instead?" Alicia asked. "Considering that Owen's the one that introduced us to him, that does seem odd. Normally, he's really good about screening out dangers."

Vicki wanted to roll her eyes. It was obvious why Owen wasn't running to tell his dad about the dangers of *Levi*; even the golden boy could think with his dick sometimes.

"Talk to your dad about it," Alicia suggested. "If Levi's a problem, he'll get escorted off of campus and banned from the city before class tomorrow."

That was a good idea, even though it wasn't her favorite. "What read do you have on him?" Vicki asked.

"He's just a guy in class that Owen latched onto," Alicia shrugged. "I don't have any of the same wards you have, so if there is something dangerous about the guy, I don't get that read. Owen likes him, Brooke likes him. Maybe he's got some of the same wards you have and they're giving a false signal."

"If you think he's so great, why don't you date him?" Vicki grumbled, trying to understand how Alicia managed to miss the point *again.*

"I've got Edwin. Besides, I think Brooke is going to make her move soon," Alicia replied, a smile crossing her features. "Or Owen. I don't think I've ever seen him blush like that."

"I swear, Brooke needs to cool it," Vicki grumbled. Her self-proclaimed best friend, Brooke tried too hard all the time. Sometimes it was funny, but mostly it was just sad. Still, it might have been better to grab Brooke and talk to her about her issues with Levi. At least Brooke would agree with her, and finally stop "accidentally" knocking Levi's pencil on the ground just to watch him pick it up. In all of their years of friendship, Brooke had only sided against her once. But that had been in high school debates, and the teacher had put them on opposite teams.

"Besides, you heard Janie. She might ask him out first," Alicia teased.

Vicki shook her head. There wasn't enough magic in the world to convince Janie to date a man. The teasing had just gotten out of hand. She opened the privacy screen and told the driver to drop Alicia off first.

Once Vicki was alone again, she leaned her head against the window. "Why does everyone want to fall into bed with Levi? He's just a guy," she grumbled. Maybe all of her friends were still oxygen deprived from the mountains. That had to be it.

CHAPTER 7

Since no one else was calling it out, it was up to Vicki to deal with Levi herself. The moment she got home, she went to her father's office. Though he had several in the half dozen different companies that he ran, she had no doubt he was home today. He would want to be there to watch her like a hawk after her first day back. Art lined the hallways leading to it. Large abstract paintings in monotone grays, greens, and blues that Vicki paid no mind. The paintings were displayed to impress someone, though Vicki didn't know who that person might be.

Her father always said someone in power should never rush about. People should come to them. Well, that didn't work when she was going to talk to her father, but the quick walk through their home to his office was as fast as she wanted to go. She wanted this conversation over with, so she could turn her attention to more pressing items, like planning the weekend with her new found freedom.

Her father was on a phone call when she stepped inside. His fingers were flipping a silver-coin-sized medallion between them. Even from where she was standing, the carved disk radiated power. The Chains that her father controlled were far more powerful than anything she could imagine. Vicki knew better than to interrupt her father while he was on a call with one of them. But she could lean forwards to catch the name engraved on the coin.

Her father hung up and tucked the coin back into the tray, before she could identify more than the first letter: L.

"Vicki, how was school today?" Father asked.

"That's what I wanted to talk to you about," Vicki said, taking the chair across from her dad. "We had someone new in class. Someone…suspicious? He made my wards go off."

Father nodded and motioned for her to continue.

What was there more to say?

"He joined most of the same classes I have while I was gone," Vicki said, counting the reasons off on one perfectly-manicured hand. "He's made friends with my friends. And, while he recognized me, he didn't seem to care that I was in the room. That, by itself, is suspicious."

"What's his name?" Father asked.

"Levi. I don't know his last name, but I bet *Owen* does," Vicki said, crossing her arms. "Or Brooke might have asked, because if we were in middle school, she would have been doodling her first name with his last name in her notes with hearts."

She didn't know why her father seemed to hide a smile. "Levi is not a danger to you," he stated, giving her a reassuring look. He leaned forwards and grabbed his notepad, scratching something down. Something that Vicki had seen him do when he was trying not to lose something important for later. "Though I must ask Mr. Mills if he gave Levi any influence spells."

"What are you talking about?" Vicki asked.

"Levi is one of mine," Father said, motioning to the medallions on display. "I sent him to keep an eye out for anyone on your college campus that might look to cause you harm, or make a quick buck from last weekend's attack."

"You didn't think to warn me?" Vicki asked. Her breath tightened in her chest as she thought about how little trust that her father had in her. She should have known that the stupid new guy was part of his protective team.

"The goal was that no one suspected him as being one of mine, including yourself," Father replied. "His job is to identify and react, so that what happened over the weekend does not happen again."

"So, I can't know, but *Owen* can?" Vicki asked.

"Owen has the same knowledge of this project that you have," Father replied. "This is a need-to-know, and none of your friends need to know."

Vicki fought the urge to roll her eyes. There was no way that Owen didn't know that Levi was a plant. With how Owen tried to include Levi, and how close they were sitting. Which begged the question: why did Owen know about Levi, and not tell her?

Fury lashed through her. Owen's loyalty was to her first. He was the one that gave in and told her about the inside job, and that there was a new person in their classes in the first place!

She frowned at that. Had he tried to tell her? That day when he'd visited the house, he had been looking around before giving her information about the attack. Maybe his segue was supposed to be a clue.

She shut down that line of thinking for now. It would be easy to get caught up in that with no proof, and it wouldn't do anything here.

"Now that I know, can you loop me in more?" Vicki asked, trying to guide the conversation back to its original point. "Has Levi noticed anything?"

"Nothing stands out to him," Father replied. "But it may take a few weeks for the dust to settle and another attempt to happen on your life."

"But we don't have to be friendly to him, do we?" Vicki asked.

"If you want this to work, act friendly when you are around others," Father replied. "If you push him out, your friends will too."

That was the point, Vicki thought bitterly. She didn't like how quickly her friends all seemed to *like* him. It was like her friends were replacing her. First, Alicia had taken Edwin from her, and now Owen and Brooke were acting like Levi had hung the sun.

"Then I'd have to send another," Father continued, clearly reading her annoyance with ease. "Or I will pull you out of college. That space is too much of a risk for you to continue going to daily without additional resources."

"What? No! The shooting didn't even happen there," Vicki shot back before she could phrase it better.

"The club is getting retrofitted with more security, but if the attempt could happen there, it could most definitely happen at your college," Father replied, his eyes hard. "Allow those that work for me to do their jobs."

Vicki wanted to scream, but she pulled it back. Those emotions wouldn't do anything here. Besides, he hadn't dismissed her just yet.

"Thank you for trusting your gut and bringing this to me," Father continued, his eyes softening. "Had Levi been a plant by someone else, you would have been the first to call that out. I'm proud of you for bringing it to me."

Just like that, the anger she had for him melted away. Vicki gave her father a smile. "I wouldn't keep something like this from you."

Father dismissed her after that, and some of the glow of the compliment vanished with it. The long walk back to her room gave her too much time to think. Owen got a pass for trying to warn her about Levi, even if it had been useless at best. She didn't know why she expected more from him.

Father had told her to play nice while Levi was around her friends, but nothing was said about when it was just the two of them. He had a job to do, to watch out for those that might hurt her, but flirting with Brooke wasn't part of it.

***

Levi kept waiting for the other shoe to drop. Someone was bound to have a problem with a stranger stepping in and taking a spot in their tight-knit circle. According to the files from Mr. Mills, the last one to join the group had been Janie, and she'd been friends with Owen for a while before that.

He expected one of the guys might feel threatened he was taking their place, though Owen had been the one to invite him in. Edwin, though, he seemed the type for it.

But no. The person with the highest objection was the last person he expected. In retrospect, it made a sort of sense.

Levi had gotten to class early today to get in some last-minute studying before the group session later. He'd been dropped into the middle of a business degree, and none of the courses made any amount of sense. Long hours were spent researching terms and reading through textbooks, so that he didn't out himself as a fraud. Levi hadn't sat down to read anything for years. The only books that he'd enjoyed previously were part of Sammy's library, since books were expensive and Levi rarely left his house. If Sammy were here, they would joke about making sure that he was reading the textbook in the right direction.

He hadn't noticed that Vicki was in the room until her shadow fell over his notes. The soft pink acrylic nails of her right hand rested on the textbook. When he glanced up, there was a dangerous look in her eyes that sent a shiver down his spine.

"Good morning," Levi started, trying to cover how he felt. The curls in her hair were unexpected, since Levi didn't have any fresh burns to show for it. He hoped that was a sign that she had gotten better at it, so he would have less of those in the future.

"I know you're a mole for my father," Vicki said.

Oh. That was how today was going to start. His first instinct was to sigh and put away his books. Someone else could have the joy of hanging out with these spoiled rich kids. It had been fun getting out of the house, and Owen had been interesting to talk to, but maybe it was time to pack it in.

The memory of Mr. Townsend's instructions and the Chain forced him to rethink that plan. The feeling of fire along his spine that sent tears to the corners of his eyes and made his knees weak was only the tip of the iceberg.

"What do you mean?" Levi asked, blinking up at her. He was a terrible spy, but he could at least pretend. "You think I'm a mole?"

"I know you are. Father confirmed it," Vicki replied, her eyes sharp.

"Well then, what do you want from me?" Levi asked, closing his books and sliding them out of the way. He wasn't sure what her goal was, but he could hopefully hear her out without going against his directives. Keeping Vicki happy would make his life easier, even if Vicki was half the problem.

"Stop acting so friendly to my friends," Vicki said. "If you've got a job to do, do your job."

What? Stop acting friendly? He was being polite, trying to keep up with the conversation so that he could stay close. Get to know each of them, so that he knew how to prove that the friends were either being suspicious, or could be exonerated from Mr.

Townsend's witch hunt. Sure, he was running a spell that made himself more likeable, but that was under Mr. Townsend's orders too.

"I'm not trying to get between you and your friends," Levi promised, trying to placate the moody heiress. She had as many opportunities to ruin him as her father, without knowing that she would only put herself in danger in the process.

"Your job is to keep an eye out for anyone on my campus that might cause harm. My friends are not causing me harm," Vicki snapped, her eyes flashing.

Levi opened his mouth to reply, but magic curled around his words. In the space of a breath, barbed wire filled his mouth, shoving itself down his throat. He could try to push the truth out, but in return he'd lose his tongue. "What I'm doing," Levi said, picking his words carefully, "has been outlined to me. I'm willing to follow what you want as long as it doesn't go against the other stuff."

Vicki rolled her eyes at his attempt.

There had only been a few times that Levi had to talk about his orders, but this was the first time that it had been such a struggle. He didn't know if that was because this was Vicki or not. Old rules about not seeking out or talking to Vicki had been overwritten with this current assignment, but not as well as he would have liked. Talking with Owen or Brooke or Janie had given him a free tongue to weave together his excuses and information as he pleased, but not Vicki.

"Chained are pathetic," Vicki spat. The tilt of her head and the crossing of her arms as she leaned away in disgust, showed how little she thought of him.

Did her statement exclude Alicia, or did it include her too?

"Can I get back to studying?" Levi asked, moving to grab his books. He really wanted to get back to his work before class started.

"That's the other thing. Skip the study session," Vicki said.

"Um, why?" Levi replied. He still had a job to do, and interacting out of class was part of it. Otherwise, he would be stuck in school long enough to flunk out. He wanted to be back to his normal life by midterms, hopefully before finals. Tracking them over the summer would be impossible. There was a time limit on what he could realistically do, before someone noticed Vicki's injuries showing up on his skin.

"Because I said so," Vicki replied.

"What did you say so?" Janie asked, strolling up to them.

"Vicki was just letting me know that I have been dis-invited from the study session today," Levi replied. "I'll have to schedule something with Owen when you guys aren't busy."

"Vicki, don't be ridiculous," Janie replied, giving her friend a grin. "Of course Levi's invited. We're already going to be studying. Do you drink?" Janie's question was pointed towards him.

"Not with the pain meds," Levi replied. A lie, but one that he needed to maintain. "That combination makes me pass out, not black out."

"Next time then," Janie replied. She seemed to ignore both Vicki's frustrated glance towards the back of her head, and the glare that Vicki sent his way.

This study session was going to be great.

CHAPTER 8

After her failed attempt at getting Levi to skip out, Vicki had shown up in a mood. Not a drop of liquor had been pulled out of the cabinets of Janie's apartment. Textbooks took up space on the tables.

It was strange. Janie's apartment looked like it had come directly out of a home decor magazine, though it looked like the inspiration picture, rather than a copy. The soft colors dancing around bled from one space to another, allowing each room to have its own theme and not clash with the one next to it. Blues and greens in one space, yellows and pinks in another. Vicki envied Janie's freedom. How everything matched with the woman who lived there. Vicki could only do so much.

Most of her friends had paired off into little groups already.

Alicia and Edwin were sharing the same chair, Alicia on Edwin's lap, and Edwin whispering sweet nothings into her ear. The textbook on Alicia's lap was open to the wrong chapter.

The couch had been taken up by Owen, Brooke, and, of course, the mole himself, Levi. Unlike Alicia and Edwin, those three were actually studying. Owen and Levi were leaned against each other, talking through a section of the textbook. Annoyance ate at her. She didn't know what Owen's play was, pulling Levi's attention like that. Was he covering for Levi by making him do homework? Or was Owen taking one for the team and trying to distract Levi away from her friends?

As expected, Brooke was sitting at Levi's other side, but that was the side where his arm was in a sling. She couldn't get into his bubble as much as Brooke would have liked.

Janie was the best at putting together a party tray, but there was nothing that could drip or get their assignments covered in cheese dust. Had Levi turned her friends studious? Was this another part of her father's plan? They were all graduating in the next year or two anyway. No need to rush or try too hard.

Sitting in her favorite chair, Vicki sipped at a can of soda as she watched. As one of the only ones that had gone to class and knew the material, she didn't have much to do other than stare daggers at Levi. A look that Brooke seemed to think was part of a weird crush. Vicki's denial had only made the teasing worse.

Janie returned from the kitchen with a glass of water in her hand. Perching on the arm of Vicki's chair, she gave her a smile.

"Once they get caught up on the homework from last week, I'll pull out the booze," Janie promised.

"I didn't know you turned in homework," Vicki said, looking up at her friend.

Janie let out a laugh. "Yeah, well, gotta impress the new guy, right?" Janie said with a wink. She set her glass down on the coffee table and leaned into Vicki's space. Her lips brushed against Vicki's ear as she whispered, "If you're bored, you know my bed's always open."

The offer sparked a shiver of excitement. When she'd first met Janie, it had been after she and Edwin had broken up the first time. All alone and swearing off men, Janie had swooped in and offered to show her something different. Janie was the first woman she'd been with and her first girlfriend, introducing Vicki to a whole other world of dating. Inside the bedroom, they were compatible in ways that no one else had proven to be, but they were too different to stay a couple.

"Okay," Vicki replied, allowing herself to be guided up from the chair. A private party and a romp in the sheets might be exactly what she needed.

***

After their morning confrontation, Levi was trying not pay attention to the glare the Vicki kept sending his way. While he knew that the study session was going to be at Janie's place, it still surprised him to learn that the study session was not at a dorm, but at an apartment. And by apartment, he meant a million-dollar condo overlooking the city. The place was huge, with tall ceilings and lots of natural light. The views were incredible. He had to stay back from the windows; he'd never had a fear of heights until he'd walked into this building.

There was so much color too, light blues and greens on the walls, and yellow and pink furniture in the living room. A wall covered in artwork made him wish he could show it to Sammy; they would appreciate it more than he could.

The moment they arrived, Janie pulled out prepared trays of food and drinks, and invited them to sit in the living room and use the oversized coffee table as a study station. It was for more hospitable than he'd ever taken any of them for.

Between Owen and Brooke, what pulled his attention first was the food, and then the material they had to work on. The way Alicia was leaning against Edwin suggested that the book they were looking at might be a cover for something else. A few giggles from Alicia and hushed murmurs from Edwin seemed to confirm it.

Then it got quiet. Levi looked up to find that it was just him, Owen, and Brooke in the living room. Edwin, Alicia, Janie, and Vicki had all left.

"What?" he started.

"Don't worry about that," Owen replied. "They're probably in the other rooms."

"Reviewing anatomy," Brooke whispered conspiratorially.

Levi did not need to know that. He looked back down at his book and tried to focus on words that were made even harder to understand. It was one thing to know that people were couples, and they were dating; it was entirely another to know that there was sex happening in the apartment that he was in right now. Either there was a foursome going on, or there was a friend with benefits, or a new couple he had not been informed about.

"Are we good to keep studying?" Levi asked, looking between the other two. They were both as close as they could be on either side without touching.

"Yeah," Brooke grumbled, snagging another cracker topped with cheese and jam.

Levi had been very careful not to try it. He knew he would eat half the tray without trying, and then his stomach would be upset later.

"I wanted to check when you might want to take a break," Owen said. "I'm going to need to stand up and stretch my legs soon, and let the information settle for a bit."

"I'm just waiting until we've done enough studying so that I can think about what parties we might hit up tonight," Brooke replied.

"Party?" Levi asked, glancing at Owen. Owen's face was closed off. None of the excitement from Brooke was mirrored there.

Owen caught him looking and shrugged.

"We haven't been back to the club since the attack," Brooke continued, as if Levi hadn't spoken.

"Attack?" Levi asked. He didn't need to fake his surprise there, even if the answer seemed obvious in hindsight.

"Last week, a mugger got past security and nearly shot us," Brooke explained. "He was waving a gun, and even fired it towards Vicki. It's lucky that he missed."

"Yeah, lucky," Levi echoed, feeling the ache build in his shoulder again. He should have known that it would come up. The night that Vicki had been shot. It happened right in front of her friends.

He wanted to ask them what they saw, what happened when the Blessing/Curse pulled the wound from Vicki's flesh to his. How long did it take for the spell to take hold? How much blood was there? What happened to the wound after it was gone from her skin? Did anything remain?

But Levi couldn't ask any of those questions. He couldn't even hint at them. "That's intense. Is everyone okay?" he asked.

"The mugger killed a few security guards, then the remaining team killed the mugger," Owen replied. "My Dad works for the security company and he's not happy that his employees were jumped like that. But all of us are okay, thankfully."

"Edwin got scratched on his arm here," Brooke said, motioning along her forearm. "But that's already healed up. His family bought a couple of healing spells and all that's left will be a scar."

"There'll be a scar?" Levi asked. The healing magic offered to the rich and famous was far beyond anything Levi would ever find. They were performed in person by someone that had a healing ability, like Sammy. It was why it was so important that Sammy keep their powers secret, because they would end up stuck in that job for the rest of their life, using up their limited powers to heal away plastic surgery scars and assassination attempts.

"Yeah, I guess Edwin's family is a little strapped for cash right now, so he was given a spell instead of a Healer," Brooke replied, snagging another cracker from the tray. "You should try these. They're really good."

Levi filed away Edwin's money problems as he snagged one of the treats. If they were strapped for cash, an attempt at Vicki's life might have been a way to fix it. Or he might have guessed about the Blessing and was proving it to someone that was watching, for a substantial fee.

As tempting as it was to hand over Edwin's name and be on his way, there wasn't enough proof yet. Gossip from one of the other friends in the circle didn't count as enough proof to sign away another person's life.

His mind was so wrapped up that Levi nearly spat the cracker topped with soft cheese and jam back out. What was that? Sweet, creamy, salty, and also spicy? "What did I just stick in my mouth?"

Brooke grinned as she explained the flavor combination. The answer that he was looking for was jalapeno jam.

He ate a second one to be polite, still trying to figure out if he actually liked it. In the end, the answer was the same. Nope. Not a fan. Sammy would probably like them, but Sammy wasn't here to try them. This didn't seem like a place that allowed to-go bags.

"Good, right?" Brooke asked.

"Yeah, I'm not a big fan of spicy things though," Levi replied. "It gives me heartburn, so I only eat a little."

"That's too bad," Brooke replied. "It means that I couldn't take you to my favorite noodle place. Everything there is spicy."

"Sorry," Levi replied with a shrug. He forgot how much that hurt when he struggled to hide a wince.

"What kinds of foods do you prefer?" Owen asked.

"My friend would say that I'm pretty picky, but I disagree," Levi replied. "I prefer pizza with veggies over meat, since a lot of meats end up really oily. If I have to pick a ramen, it's going to be pork. You know, stuff like that. I know what things that I like."

"Stalker friend or other friend?" Owen asked.

"Other friend, thankfully," Levi replied, with an easy smile. It was surprising how easy it was to hold a conversation with these two. Levi hadn't talked at length with anyone since he'd dropped out. His neighbors barely got a passing hello in the hallway. He could hold his own at the grocery stores and bodegas, but the small talk was short and inconsequential. Maybe the spell in his pocket worked to ease him through the conversation too. "They know me like the back of their hand. If they were a stalker as well, I would be in so much trouble."

It felt weird talking about Sammy to other people, but he'd been instructed to pretend that there were people in his life outside of this group. It would be weirder if he was just a loner, threw up too many red flags. He'd only written down just enough information for the friend that matched Sammy for it to be easy to remember, not identifiable. The Devil already knew that Sammy existed. He didn't need anyone else to know as well. The stalker was based on a version of Vicki that he'd made up in his head. At least an abuser would give him a reason if anyone saw his old scars.

He ended up talking about food and Sammy, until a disheveled Alicia and Edwin returned and fetched glasses of wine. The homework assignment that he'd started was still incomplete, but Levi planned to turn it in that way. The subject at hand was still murky at best. But after looking over Brooke's attempt, Levi didn't feel like he was that far behind.

"Vicki and Janie are going to be gone a while," Alicia explained, sounding out of breath as she sipped. "So, I'm thinking that the study session is probably over?"

Levi looked down at his notes, trying to finish up his thought, and doing his best not to think about the implications. He could feel his cheeks start to heat up. Sex didn't make him uncomfortable. Years of living in shitty apartments with thin walls, and having a friend that was a sex worker, had left him pretty nonchalant about the subject. But none of what was happening here felt normal to him.

He was glad when Owen didn't mention the red turn of his face, or the way his shoulders had pulled closer to his ears.

"Do you want to take some food back with you?" Owen offered. "You can give it to your friend to prove that you're not picky?"

Levi laughed as he agreed. Owen seemed at ease, picking through the cabinets and pulling out a few trays. There were little sandwiches that Levi hadn't tried yet, more crackers with cheese and jam, some chips and fancy cheeses. Owen easily packed it away into a couple of different containers, taking one for himself and giving one to Levi.

"The others can figure the rest out," Owen explained, offering a couple cans of soda. Levi never turned down free food; he agreed to all of it.

"Want to walk me out of here?" Levi asked Owen once he had everything in hand. "I feel like I could get lost finding the elevator."

"I've done that, and the elevator's been right in front of me," Brooke agreed, but she wasn't moving to get up.

He was fine with spending time alone with Owen. While he needed to integrate with the rest of the friends' group to see if someone was trying to steal the Blessing or simply hurt Vicki, Levi was not comfortable around all of them. He'd work his way through the friends one and a time. Starting with Owen. Though, out of the list, Owen was the least likely to have sold Vicki out.

He was trying to settle on the right question to start off with, when pain radiated down his back and neck. Without thinking, he reached back and ran his fingers over the source. Something wet hit his fingers; Levi groaned at inevitable stain. Sure enough, he brought his hand back, and the dark red of blood greeted him. It had felt like taking a risk to wear the off-white shirt today.

Owen's wide eyes flicked from Levi's hand to the back of his neck.

Shit.

***

When Owen caught the flash of pain on Levi's face, he didn't comment on it. The expression had been gone in a moment. Of course, the long study session must have aggravated his shoulder worse than usual. Levi was putting in a lot of work to get caught up.

Then Levi reached up and brushed his fingers along the back of his neck.

Blood.

There was blood on Levi's fingers. A frown scrunched his face. Owen could see the source: a long scratch stretched fresh below Levi's collar.

Owen blinked. Levi had been by his side almost the whole day, and he hadn't been bleeding once. In a shirt that pale, he would have noticed.

"You're bleeding!" Owen said, unable to keep the exclamation out of his mouth. "How-?"

Levi shrugged; the motion only made him wince. Why wasn't he surprised? It was almost like he'd expected it. But how could anyone expect an injury that seemed to appear without any cause at all?

Owen stepped closer to get a better look. Maybe it was just something that had reopened? A cat scratch from this morning?

Levi took an awkward step back. "It's fine?" His upward inflection had turned the statement into a question.

"I should go back and grab a Band-Aid," Owen said, turning towards the apartment.

He hadn't expected to Levi lunge towards him. "It's fine," Levi insisted. "Nothing but a scratch, I'm sure. We don't have to-" Levi's voice faltered as pain flashed through his face again. "-to bother them."

If Owen hadn't been staring at Levi, if the sling hadn't made the collar bunch awkwardly to expose so much of his shoulder, Owen wouldn't have believed it. But as Levi winced and struggled to speak, a cluster of three long, thin lines appeared on the man's skin. Scratch marks. Owen suspected that if he pulled back Levi's shirt, there would be more hiding beneath it. Specks of red began to peek through the light fabric.

"How-?" Owen repeated. "Dude, you look like you lost a fight to a racoon."

"That's not hard to do. Those buggers can fight," Levi failed to joke as he took another step back. The way he'd gone higher pitched and breathless wasn't funny at all. "Really, it's no big deal. You were going to help me figure out how to get out of here, right? The elevator should be somewhere?"

None of this was adding up. His father's file on Levi. The arm in a sling, so obviously painful that Owen knew that it wasn't being faked. How Levi stumbled over his story about the stalker. He'd found Levi's social media account after their first class together. He had hoped for a clue to what Levi had been hired to do, but there wasn't really anything there. A profile with two people for the picture, and no activity more recent than a few years ago. It looked just like any other abandoned account, but the little that was there didn't match the person standing in front of him.

"How is this even possible?" Owen asked, grabbing Levi's good arm to keep him there. Owen had a sinking feeling that if he let Levi go, he might never know the truth about any of it.

"It-" Levi started, his shoulders dropping as his expression closed off. The absence of any answer stretched on.

Two could play at that game. Even as the silence stretched past comfort, Owen waited.

"It's just something that happens to me," Levi finally said. "It's not a big deal."

"Not a big deal?" Owen sputtered. Scrapes and scratches appearing on his skin wasn't a big deal? Was this some kind of experimental magic? A spell that could transfer or delay injuries at will? If this was some new kink scene—

"It's acrylic nails, it's not like it's a knife," Levi tried to brush off. Even as he spoke, his eyes grew wide. His attempt to shrug it off didn't help.

It was almost like Levi was trying to make Owen feel better about this. Instead, a sick, twisting weight settled into Owen's stomach. A knife? That could have been *a knife?*

The next scratch appeared down the front of Levi's chest, dragging towards the wound on Levi's arm as the man himself tried to breathe through it. Fresh beads of blood speckled the shirt. The injury that Levi had explained away. Was that a knife injury to his shoulder? Did the stalker even exist at all?

The screams and blood from that night came roaring back. Levi had asked about it, hadn't he? The injury that didn't happen. No. The injury to Levi's arm wasn't from a knife. A bullet had caused that.

Owen's face paled. His eyes cast back to the apartment behind him. Levi sucked in a breath.

"Owen..." Levi started, his voice uncertain.

"So, either you've got the shittiest Soul Connection to someone who is having sex without you..." Owen nodded his head back down the hall. If the topic wasn't so serious, he might have laughed at the disgust on Levi's face.

"Owen, stop poking into this," Levi said, his voice almost a whisper. "You're right, it is a shitty Soul Connection. Nothing else I can do."

Owen almost bought it. Could have believed it, once upon a time. But that was before he'd witnessed the magic that protected Vicki Townsend. If Vicki and this guy really shared a Soul Connection that powerful, her father would have never allowed Levi to walk free. Whatever this was, it was one-sided. Owen already knew the name for it too: the Blessing.

What a poorly named spell.

***

Levi had never felt more exposed. They were still standing in the hallway of the ridiculously expensive condo building where Janie lived. Without a single word, the secret of the Blessing was slowly being taken from him. Levi didn't even know how. Mr. Mills wasn't in the know; there was no way for it to slip from father to son. But somehow, there was a leak, trickling out as helplessly as Levi's own blood.

Owen had stopped talking. Those knowing brown eyes were silently searching his face instead. He opened his mouth to ask a question, and then his eyebrows raised at a thought. Finally, he settled into a grimace.

Levi braced for impact, whether through Owen's next words, or from the Chain pulling tight. He waited for that barbed bright agony to start down his spine, or to wrap around his tongue. None came. Not a single lick of magic thrummed from the medallion on his wrist.

Still, he waited.

"You're trying to protect..." Owen started, then stopped and tried again. "Are you trying to protect me? Or are you trying to protect yourself?"

Too smart for his own damn good.

Maybe he should have asked Brooke to walk with him instead. She would have had no idea; she'd have bought his lie in a heartbeat. If he tried any harder, Owen would only dig deeper until neither of them could ever get out.

"Yes," Levi replied, surprised that the compulsion didn't keep him from talking. "Yes, to both."

Pin pricks of nerves started along his spine. It wasn't like the scratching sensation from before, but this conversation felt dangerously close. He needed to get out of here, before this got so much worse.

"Is there somewhere we can talk?" Levi asked as he looked around. There were no visible cameras and microphones, but Levi wouldn't trust a building like this not to have them for insurance.

Owen's eyes widened, and a startled smile stretched across his lips. He licked them nervously. It was a motion that Levi vaguely wondered was a habit. His own weren't much better; Levi had been anxiously chewing them since this assignment had first started.

"Yeah, no, yeah," Owen said, running a hand through his hair. "We could go to my place? It'd be easier to talk there." He flashed a nervous smile at Levi.

Wow. When was the last time someone had looked at him like that? That nervous smile that went all the way to Owen's eyes, crinkling them in the corners. Calming the nervous butterflies that had sprung up in his gut, Levi smiled back.

He let Owen lead the way.

It really was a good idea to follow Owen out. There were a few turns to get to the elevator, with no clear line of sight from Janie's door.

But once Owen and Levi were inside and headed down, it seemed like a very bad idea. He could get home on his own from here. A lie about a call or a text would be easy enough; he could just reschedule for another time and never show.

A fresh wave of aches radiating from his shoulder was all the reminder Levi needed. Death wouldn't come easily, but it could happen to him at any moment. No matter how much of the truth that Owen knew, Levi had no obligation to confirm. All he needed to do was look after himself, and that meant abiding Townsend's painful commands.

Still, there was an ache, a longing, to tell someone about this mess. For someone to know the truth of what Levi had gotten himself into. He had been forbidden to talk about it. Felt that magic burn through him every time it locked his tongue. But Owen already knew. The compulsion to keep it a secret, to not even hint, didn't seem to work with him.

Levi had long learned to live with the ache of loneliness. The person who was closest to him in the entire world, Sammy, had to stay in the dark for both their sakes. The notion that he could turn to Owen was a balm for wounds he'd long given up on.

But every small comfort that Owen offered was in turn a deadly blade to Levi's throat. If there was so much as a hint that Levi was out of line, Townsend would pull the Chain tight.

But maybe, just maybe, Levi could still make this work. If he could talk openly about the attack on Vicki, maybe Owen would give him some answers. That was his job, and the Devil would want him to do it however he had to.

Levi pulled his coat tighter around him as he and Owen walked out of the picturesque lobby to the street beyond. This part of town always made him nervous. He could handle the noise and the smells, the dirt and the trash and the catcalls. But here, the snow had been melted completely off the sidewalks and roads. People weren't sitting on every corner. Street cameras weren't shot out, or spray painted over. Mr. Townsend might not know the goings on of Levi's side of town. But here? Where the white granite was bright, and the steel didn't show any signs of rust? The Devil had all the tools he needed to know *everything*.

Levi walked with his eyes on the ground, trying to ward off even the hint of a conversation. Out of the corner of his eyes, he logged sight of every camera and tried to stay buried in his coat. If Mr. Townsend was watching, Levi didn't want to be seen. Still, there were signs he couldn't hide. His limp from an injury that would never have healed wrong, if he had got professional help with it. All signs that he didn't belong here, no matter what clothes he was wearing.

Owen walked like he fit right in.

The building that Owen stopped in front of stretched towards the sky. It was as impressive on the outside as Janie's place had been. Owen continued carelessly past a doorman that fixated Levi with a look.

"He's with me," Owen promised, and swept Levi onto the elevator.

The ride up was brief. Owen chattered to fill the silence. "Hopefully, my dad's not home, or else he's going to get the wrong idea," he said, like the thought hadn't occurred to him until that moment.

"You live with your dad?" Levi checked. Everyone else seemed to have their own place. Janie had the off-campus housing, and he'd heard Edwin talking about taking Alicia back to his in the middle of class today.

"Yeah," Owen replied. "It's easier this way. I don't have to worry about cooking and cleaning, since he has a service for that, and he's usually away for work if I want to bring someone over."

"If I had someone that I could mooch off of for food, I'd do it too," Levi agreed, trying to ignore the nerves kicking in. He also hoped that Mr. Mills wasn't at home, though his reasoning and Owen's might be different. Owen may have to do with embarrassment, but Levi wasn't supposed to be here at all. Mr. Mills was the one that had outfitted him with everything. Getting caught at Owen's place might mean that Mr. Mills would have to react.

"Thank you," Owen replied. "No one makes any comments about Vicki still living at home, so that I'm still living with my dad shouldn't be a big deal, either."

Levi liked that the elevator and apartment door were close: it meant that he could get home on his own. The place was nice and clean and expensive, but there was something about it that differed from Janie's place. A lived in quality. The couch was nice, but it didn't look new. It looked worn in and comfortable. The television was prominent on the wall, and so were the game systems and DVD collection. The place felt smaller because the ceilings were lower and the walls were darker. Still, it was a large, expensive apartment.

There were only a few lights on; Owen motioned for Levi to follow him quietly to the side of the apartment that was dark. A single voice cut through the quiet, one half of a conversation too muffled to make out.

"Sounds like my dad's still working," Owen said, his voice quiet, but without the forced secrecy of a whisper.

Levi frowned as Owen flicked on a few more lights. Klaxons rang in his mind. Talking with Owen was so easy. It shocked him how often he could forget the danger that he was in, interacting with the son of Mr. Townsend's security chief.

That concern only grew worse when Levi followed Owen through a door and found himself in a bedroom.

The room itself was spacious and a little cluttered. It was obvious by the way that Owen seemed to notice at the same time that Levi did. The laundry hung out of the hamper. Owen hurried to pick up some wadded garment off the floor, shoving it and everything that was falling out of it deep into the basket. There were paper notes on the desk, a laptop open but the screen dark. A piece of yellow paper curled in the corner covered the web camera.

Levi's skin prickled as Owen belatedly tapped a set of wards on his wall to allow Levi's presence within. It could be seen as paranoid, but none of the security precautions that were obvious in the room seemed over the top. The alarms and extra locks on the windows. Protection wards in easy access of the door and another set near the bed.

"So...need something to drink?" Owen asked.

"We both know this isn't a social call," Levi replied, setting his bag of food down on the corner of Owen's desk. Hopefully nothing leaked.

Owen let out a sigh. "Where did we leave off?" He pondered, and Levi left him wondering. "Shitty Soul Connections, and you trying to protect me?" Owen answered for him; his easy grin that did not match the tone of this conversation.

"I was doing no such thing," Levi replied, trying to keep his voice playful. He didn't want to set Owen on edge and upset any of the wards, and he had no idea what word or thought might get stuck behind the wall of his own leash.

Owen seemed to see right through him as he settled down on his bed. He motioned for Levi to take the desk chair.

"So..." Owen chewed his lip, while his eyes drifted around the room. Seeming to come to an idea, he nodded. "Is the shitty Soul Connection the only thing blocking our conversation?"

Instead of answering, Levi pulled up his sleeve, showing off the black leather cuff on his wrist. A silver medallion sat in the center, engraved with symbols that Levi had no chance of reading without a microscope. Chains weren't created by hand anymore; they were laser engraved instead in small batches. It didn't even have his name, only a corresponding number to the control piece he didn't possess.

Levi could tell that Owen didn't know what he was looking at, at first. Chains were marks of ownership, but most people only saw them as pieces of jewelry. There was a market for magical jewelry, from wards to block malicious spells, to spells that could record conversations or send the location of the wearer to someone else. The question was whether Owen could pick out what this one was.

Owen had gotten off the bed and was leaning close to Levi's wrist, when he startled and jumped back. His eyes were wide. "A Chain?" Owen asked.

Levi nodded, feeling a hint of a smile on his face. Clever boy.

Owen walked a short circle around the room, before settling back on his bed.

"To be Chained binds trust from one soul to another," he murmured, almost like he was reciting a poem. His eyes were looking off towards the corner of his room. "Loyalty stronger than a man to his brother. For those bound, you will find things that they cannot say, or confidants that they cannot betray. Though, guard, a Chain broken can never recover."

"Is that what they teach you in grade school?" Levi asked, raising his eyebrows. After he got his Chain, Levi had done some research on the topic. The more he learned, the less he wanted to know. But the part that stuck out to him, other than the horrible ways that Mr. Townsend could do him harm, was that Chains supposedly had symbols that wrote the rules on them. The phrase Owen had spoken was supposedly the translation of the symbols that he wore on his wrist.

"My dad made me memorize it," Owen explained. "As I got older, he was worried that I might end up getting tricked into one, either by Mr. Townsend or one of Mr. Townsend's rivals. So he made me learn what being Chained meant. How depending on how loose or tight, the forced loyalty that could eventually backfire."

"Impressive," Levi replied. He wished that someone had told him about being Chained before Townsend had found him. He hadn't known anything at all back then. Before he'd dropped out of school, it had been a topic at career fairs. Something that was sought after by those that didn't have anything. It was a promise for food and clothing, a way of life.

"I'm going to guess, then, that the holder of the Chain is Mr. Townsend?" Owen checked.

"Yeah," Levi replied. Something seemed to loosen his tongue. The words were somehow able to slip freely and without pain. "Your dad knows about it, too."

"About the shitty Soul Connection, or only the Chain?" Owen checked.

"Only the Chain," Levi replied. "No one, other than Mr. Townsend, knows about the," he felt his lip curl in disgust, "the shitty Soul Connection. No one else can either."

"Yeah, no, I got that when I saw those claw marks going down your back," Owen replied. "Can I see them? Wait, actually, can I see your back?"

"Why?" Levi asked, turning his injured arm away as he leaned back as far as he could get. "What do you intend to do?"

"That night has been going through my mind over and over," Owen said. "The night that Vicki wasn't shot. Or rather, was shot, for a moment. I want to see what happened to you to make that happen. I want to see the real effects of the *Blessing*."

The last word was spoken in the breath of a whisper. Like saying it aloud would give it power. It confirmed that Owen already knew. Not that Levi had any doubts anymore. Though, him knowing the name was its own set of problems.

Levi considered fighting Owen about it. Not showing the wound. But that wouldn't get him very far. "You tell me what you saw that night, everything, and I'll fill in the blanks," Levi offered. He unclipped the sling.

Owen started talking, beginning at an earlier part of the night to set the scene. Not necessary, but it let Levi focus on getting out of this thing. It dropped to the floor, but neither of them paid it any mind.

The shirt was a bit of a problem. The stupid thing didn't have a lot of stretch; getting into it this morning had been an exercise in patience. Now it was even worse. The blood on the inside of the shirt showed off the newly scabbed wounds. Dark, dried red against the off-white fabric.

It was weird, Levi realized, as his shirt dropped and it was just the bandage left. Owen's eyes were roaming around, but not focused at all on the injury itself. The story he was telling stopped with the gunman stepping out of the shadows.

Levi braced himself for what would come next. He saw that same pity in his neighbor's eyes, anytime he went to the grocery store in short sleeves. When he took out the trash on the bad weather days that made his limp worse. When he had to sit on the floor of the laundry mat, because carting his clothes had taken all of his energy that day.

But the look he found on Owen wasn't pity. Concern widened warm brown eyes, before they narrowed, dashing to each and every scar. The thoughtful, calculating expression made Levi squirm.

Time stretched before Levi realized that neither of them were doing what they should have been. Refusing to be the first one to break it, Levi reached over and peeled back the bandage. The wound was partially healed, the edges scarring over, but there were still stitches that needed to be protected.

"That's the same spot," Owen said, taking a step forwards. Close enough that Levi wouldn't have to reach if he wanted to touch. To push away, or to pull closer.

Levi didn't know which he wanted, so he stood stock still, skin heating under Owen's gaze. No one had been this close to him in so long. No one except Sammy. But even then, Sammy didn't know the truth to what they saw.

"You're taller," Owen continued, "with broader shoulders, but that's the same spot she was...oh shit. You could have died that night."

"Yeah, I know," Levi replied, smoothing the bandage back down, the damage safely out of sight. He'd joked about it with Sammy, but that attitude wouldn't calm the fear in Owen's eyes. But was he afraid for him? Or afraid of Mr. Townsend?

Levi leaned down to grab his shirt. Owen followed with a quick, "I'll get it!"

Levi allowed it. If it left him with less strain on his arm, all the better for it. Their fingers brushed as Owen handed it over, and Levi turned his full attention to the article of clothing. This had gotten way too intimate.

Sliding his arms through the sleeves, he turned to look at Owen. "Are you going to be okay? You look like you're going to pass out," Levi said, as he pulled his shirt over his head again.

"I- I'm processing," Owen replied, swiping a hand through his hair. "It feels like everything I knew has turned on its head this last week. For Mr. Townsend to draw you into this, it feels serious."

"It's serious for someone," Levi agreed. Owen's file had mentioned how smart he was, how he could process information and make connections like no one else. It hinted, without being obvious about it, that every part of the security detail around Vicki that night, Owen had had a hand in. That should have put Owen at the top of the suspect list, but the creator of the file had trusted him. Levi found himself agreeing with that assessment. "Remember, no one can know about any of this."

He didn't think that Owen needed the reminder, but it needed to be said.

Owen seemed to pull himself together as he nodded. "I won't tell. For your safety as well as ours."

The confirmation let the air back into the room, as Levi worked to pull on his coat.

Owen let out a little laugh. "You know, last time someone was undressing and dressing in my room was a lot more fun," Owen said, almost like a self-deprecating joke. It wasn't a come on, or a flirt.

"Yeah, well, pick your suitors better," Levi replied, adjusting his coat to sit over his sling. He bit his lip against admitting that he didn't normally take his clothes off for free. That would have made Sammy laugh, but with Owen it seemed in poor taste.

"Still isn't my worst date," Owen replied, checking over the food that Levi had packed for home. He had a faraway look on his face, and then a full body shudder, as if trying to purge the memory. "You haven't tried to steal my wallet once."

"That sounds like poor decisions on whomever tried," Levi replied. He had seen the cameras on the way here, all the security options. Even if the person had gotten away, they wouldn't have made it far.

"That was poor decisions all around," Owen hummed. He looked over the room, and Levi wondered for a moment if Owen was going to ask him to stay. "Anyway. Want me to walk you home?"

Thankfully, Levi didn't have to come up with another excuse. The day, and the release of secrets, had worn on him. He was ready to leave.

"I can get home on my own, once I get to the street," Levi promised, taking the bag of food in hand. "You can go back, hang out with your friends."

Owen offered again once Levi was on the street, but he waved away the concern. Owen already knew too much; he didn't need this guy knowing where he lived too. The longer he could keep Sammy away from the rest of them, the better. He checked a few times on his route home that he wasn't being followed. If there was a tail, Levi never spotted one.

CHAPTER 9

Walking into his apartment, Levi was greeted with cold silence. He didn't keep the furnace on while he was out, and he'd been gone a long time.

Clicking on the lights, he placed the bag of food on the counter and turned to the process of getting the apartment livable again. Turning up the heat, he listened close for the sound of it kicking over before he moved on. The sling came off next. His keys were put on the hook. The spell scroll to make his job easier was dropped onto the table next to his favorite chair. Then he went back to his room to change into something comfortable. Something his. He reveled in the comfort that came from old sweats and dark fabrics that wouldn't have betrayed him to Owen.

After all of that was done, he focused on getting the treats put in the fridge and sending a message to Sammy.

They were working tonight; it would be a few hours before he got a reply.

Only with his check-in complete, and his food safely stored, did Levi allow himself to think about what had happened. He had been doing this for years, with Sammy constantly in and out of his space, and not once had he given anything away. He should probably look at the new wound on his back and see what mess had been created over Vicki's evening, but he was struggling to care about the small cuts and scrapes. He didn't want to think how the scratches had only appeared after Vicki had taken her friend to bed.

He'd been caught up in the blinding terror of being known, but had Owen been checking him out? No. No, that was out of the question. Owen had the pick of anyone. Why would he be looking at Levi with anything less than horror? The loneliness and forced celibacy had to be getting to him. His mind was adding a filter now that there was someone else who finally knew. It was a good fantasy, though. To feel wanted.

He had only known Owen for a few days. The fact that Levi had gotten that close had to be related to all the magic in the air. Or, Owen had known he was on a job all along.

Levi blinked. He hadn't noticed it at the time, but Owen hadn't reacted to the fact that he'd been ordered to meet Owen. Hadn't commented when Levi had admitted that Mr. Mills knew that Levi was Chained. Owen had known why Levi was really there, but hadn't been told the rest. Why?

Sitting down on the floor, Levi crossed his legs and stretched to sit up straight, as much as his shoulder would allow. Breathing exercises. He needed to work through breathing exercises. This wasn't the time to try to figure out Owen. His job would be done soon, and then he wouldn't need to think about Owen anymore. Deep breath in. Long breath out.

A sharp pain started through his arm, the same side that the gunshot had gone through a week before. He squeezed his eyes shut tighter, trying to ignore it. But it kept coming, and it kept growing, dragging down like a knife. Opening his eyes, he glanced at his bleeding arm in tired frustration. What had Vicki got into now?

***

Dressed again, Vicki walked arm in arm with Janie to find the study session was already over. The only one out there was Brooke, who had gotten into the alcohol and was throwing herself a party for one. The snacks had been raided and Janie found that one of her repurposed take-out containers had been taken.

"Who wants to put money on Owen and Levi, leaving to have their own private party?" Janie asked, her voice alight with amusement.

Brooke shrugged as she sipped from the wineglass. "I couldn't tell when they left. They kept talking about studying, and Owen offered to walk him out." There was a hint of bitterness in Brooke's tone at the end.

Vicki shrugged, placating the lonely drunk. Owen had been pretty open about his opinions about Levi; it was obvious there was a connection there. She still wasn't sure what she thought about Owen, but he'd promised to help her look into the Blessing, and he wasn't the one actively sleeping with Edwin.

"How about we reset this to a party, instead of the nerd party it was before?" Vicki asked, picking up the textbooks on the table and moving them to the side.

"I think you already started," Brooke pointed out.

"You've already started," Janie remarked, looking through the liquor cabinet. "Have you taken a shot of everything in here? Or just moved the bottles?"

"I had to move some things around so that I could find what I was looking for," Brooke replied, raising her glass. It sloshed on the floor, leaving a mark on the table and spilling red wine onto the large rug that filled the room.

"Shit," Brooke cursed, leaning down to pick it up and making an even bigger mess.

"Let me," Janie replied, moving Brooke out of the way, and taking the glass. "I think you need to have some water and cool off a bit," Janie suggested, a look in her eyes Vicki knew all too well.

It was the reason that Vicki and Janie hadn't worked out. Her "mom mode" made Vicki's hair stand on end, made her feel guilty when she had done nothing wrong. Janie could be the life of the party, bringing out the best of everyone. But she could be firm and cold when someone wasn't listening and getting hurt.

For Vicki, who had never had a mother, it drew out uncomfortable feelings. Made sex awkward and weird until those feelings went away.

"Vicki, can you take this back to the kitchen for me?" Janie asked, holding the wineglass out to her.

She did, and she wondered if it was actually time for her to think about going home as well. Janie was going to spend time with Brooke now and get her to sober up. That wasn't any kind of party. "I'm going to call a cab," Vicki said as she returned from the kitchen.

Brooke's eyes went wide and her lip waver like she was going to cry. "You're going to leave already?"

Internally groaning, Vicki didn't know if she was okay with Brooke's expression or not. There wasn't a competition here; Brooke getting attention and ruining the night because Vicki and Janie had gone to have sex wasn't a win. Vicki had gotten what she'd wanted already.

"You don't need to leave yet," Janie pointed out.

"I know, but I'm kind of tired, and it's a long day tomorrow," Vicki replied. She should feel happy that her friends were here without Levi. But the mood was off. She hated to admit it, but honestly, it had been better when he was here. When Brooke hadn't drunk herself silly.

"Well, let me call you a car," Janie replied. "No, none of that look. Your dad would literally kill me if you had to wait downstairs in the lobby for a random cab."

Sitting back down, Vicki started poking through her bag, checking that she had everything with her. She'd left her backpack where Brooke could mess with it for God knows how long. Dammit Owen, he was supposed to watch out for Brooke and her tendency to get into things that didn't belong to her.

The door to the apartment opened, and it was Owen, shrugging off his coat. "Vicki, Janie, Brooke, hey. I had to stop by my apartment," Owen explained. "Levi's home now."

"I was about to call a car," Vicki explained.

Owen shrugged. "I guess that's fair," he said. His gaze drifted over the carpet where the wine stain was already setting. "Well, if anyone wants to hang out, I'm free, otherwise I'm going to go head to a bar or something. I need to stay out of my apartment for a bit."

"Why?" Janie asked.

"My dad saw me and Levi heading out after we stopped by to grab my wallet," Owen explained, his cheeks flushing deep. "It was so embarrassing. He winked at me when Levi and I left together and I just can't go back yet."

"So you and Levi didn't..." Janie asked.

"No," Owen explained with a shrug. "He's still a little skittish from that stalker, you know."

Vicki frowned. Out of everyone here, she thought Owen had seen through Levi's lie. While she hadn't confirmed that Owen knew Levi was a Townsend plant, this was Owen. He had to know. Which meant that he also should know that Levi's stalker story was a flat out lie.

Though, Vicki considered, crossing her arms and studying Owen in the entryway, maybe she was giving Owen too much credit. Owen knew all of that information because Mr. Mills passed it to him. So, Mr. Mills could have fed Owen a lie about who Levi was, or neglected to tell Owen at all.

She could solve this with a simple conversation.

The bedroom that she and Janie had walked out of was Janie's and still smelled of sex. That was not a place that she wanted to have this talk. The guest room was occupied. Which left the living room where they were standing, or the kitchen.

"Owen?" Vicki asked, motioning for the man to follow her. She did not want to have this conversation in front of Brooke.

"Yeah?" Owen replied as they stepped onto the modern tile floor. Even though it was perfectly warm in Janie's, Owen rubbed his hands together like he was cold.

"Now that he's gone, I want to talk about Levi," Vicki started, keeping her voice low. She did not need a drunk Brooke joining the conversation. It was annoying to be whispering, but she wanted to have this conversation where her Dad couldn't interrogate her about it later.

"What about Levi?" Owen asked, his voice clipped.

Vicki blinked in surprise; Owen never talked to her like that. Nervous energy radiated from him. If he hadn't just denied having sex with the guy, she might have guessed otherwise. But this was Owen. He didn't hide things from her. He didn't lie to her. And he didn't have a real relationship with anyone.

"No, you go first. What about Levi?" Vicki replied, crossing her arms. "What are you hiding about him?"

"Nothing," Owen brushed off, tucking his hands in his pockets. He wouldn't meet her eyes. "Nothing important." Tension radiated through his posture. The last time she'd seen him like this, he'd brought her flowers and told her all of her friends had abandoned her to go skiing. "You wanted to talk about him, though?"

"Levi isn't who you think he is," Vicki started, watching how Owen's expression opened up in surprise. Good. She was getting through to him. "I don't know what lies he told you, but he's a plant."

"A plant?" Owen asked, his voice smoothing out as the surprise vanished. Instead of the righteous anger that she expected, there was a calm instead. "From who?"

"My father," Vicki revealed, smugly, waiting for Owen to react. Once he understood Levi was a liar, Owen would stop getting fooled. Stop bringing him around. Her friends could pay attention to her again, instead of the new guy who wasn't even real.

The nervous excitement in her gut dropped like a weight when Owen shrugged. Why wasn't Owen following? Unless…was he in on it? Did he mention that stupid stalker story because he knew it was fake? It had stopped Janie's teasing immediately.

"You don't need to keep bringing him around," Vicki pointed out. "I know he works for my dad. I know that somehow my dad or your dad put you up to bringing Levi around. You can stop."

"No one put me up to anything," Owen cut in. His expression changed to his focused work mode. The one that he got when it was time to leave the nightclub. Or when he wouldn't let her drive, because she'd been drinking. She hated that face. Like he thought he was better than her.

"If he works for your dad," Owen continued. That same know-it-all look on his face. "Then we should let him do his job."

A flash of anger coursed through her. Everyone kept thinking that they knew better than her. Janie telling her to wait for a called car. Her dad and his overbearing protection. Owen, not listening and bringing Levi around. No one believed she could take care of herself!

A magnetic display of knives glinted on the wall next to the stove. That was one way to get Owen to listen.

Snagging a little one, she tested it in her hand. The idea seemed a little scarier now that her fingers were wrapped around it, but she wasn't actually going to get hurt here. That was the point.

"Vicki?" That damn nervous tension of his rose higher. Did he think she was going to attack him? Cute. Maybe then he would listen. "Can you put that down? You're freaking me out."

"Why? You know this won't hurt me," Vicki replied, pressing the tip of the blade so that it kissed her finger, not even breaking skin.

Owen flinched again, helplessly glancing back and forth between the knife and her face.

"You and Levi don't need to protect me, or tattletale back to my dad, or whatever Levi's doing," Vicki continued, pushing her insistence into her words. "I can't get hurt with this."

"I don't know what you want me to say," Owen replied, stepping towards her. "I don't know how this works. I know the injury is there one minute and then gone the next, but that doesn't mean it doesn't hurt. You screamed the night they shot you. Even if it didn't stay, that doesn't mean that the wound didn't hurt."

"That's not an answer," Vicki said.

"It's the best I have," Owen said. His eyes darted back to the others in the living room, and then to the knife. It was like he was weighing options, which meant that she needed to decide before he did. Would he try to take the knife away? Call for the others?

Vicki couldn't see Janie and Brooke from where she was standing, but she didn't care. Why was this a secret, anyway? Her Dad's rules were stupid. The whole reason her friends were acting like she was a fragile child, who couldn't even take a cab on her own or walk to the front door of the building without an escort, was because of those rules. It was just another reason her friends didn't trust her.

"Maybe you need to see it in action," Vicki said and pressed the knife against her arm.

Owen yelped, fear flooding his face. Just someone else that didn't believe her. She could hear his weak pleading, begging her to stop. She should have known Owen was useless.

***

Owen let out a cry for help. The knife was still in her arm; there was no rush of magic swirling to patch things up. The vindictive smile on her face said that she was doing this on purpose. Vicki wanted everyone to see.

Brooke let out a scream. Janie made a similar sound to the yell that had escaped Owen's mouth. But the person Owen was distressed over and the person Janie was concerned about were not the same.

"See," Vicki said, lifting the knife off her arm. The wound stitched shut like expensive healing magic, erased as if it never was. "Nothing can hurt me."

"Don't you ever do that again!" Janie cried. Ripping the knife from Vicki's hands, she threw it to the ground. It continued to spray blood until it skidded to a stop on the tile floor. "Don't you ever trust that stupid magic to protect you!"

Owen didn't have the energy to ask Janie how she knew; he was still pretending that he didn't know already. Janie wouldn't be able to see her scratches vanish in bed and not make a guess about how they never stayed.

While his eyes were focused on the blood on the floor, his mind could only see Levi. Even looking at the wound made his arm ache in sympathy. Another wound that Levi didn't ask for. Anger bubbled in him, and it was a fight to keep the words down. Levi had told him the cost of letting the others know. He couldn't risk Levi over someone that would stab themselves to prove a point.

"Don't let her do anything else stupid," Owen commanded, looking at Janie. His skin burned with frustration and fear. He was the one who fixed things, but how the hell was he supposed to fix this? "We don't know what the magic will protect her from, or what it will decide to let her keep."

The terror that radiated from every point of Levi's being when Owen had found out was enough to convince him not to use the name. But anyone who was convinced that they could cut themselves and let someone else take the injury shouldn't call what they had a Blessing. Vicki might not know what was behind the healing magic, but Owen found he didn't trust her with that knowledge.

"Magic always has a cost," Janie lectured, cleaning the blood from Vicki's arm with rough clipped strokes. Brooke was still sitting on the floor, eyes wide at the red splatters on the floor, the cabinets, even on the stove. There was a wet stain in her pants that Owen ignored.

He didn't say goodbye as he grabbed his coat. The door slammed shut behind him. Levi had told him to stay away. That putting the pieces together had a cost. That if Mr. Townsend guessed Owen knew, there would be a world of hurt.

Fuck that.

If he didn't act, if Levi didn't get some kind of medical treatment, this could be really, really bad. He needed to get to Levi, make sure the man wasn't bleeding out from Vicki's actions. Drag him to the hospital if needed, or at least bandage the man's arm. First, he needed Levi's home address.

Pulling out his cell phone, his fingers paused over his dad's number. Calling his dad for information would come at a cost. He'd only create a paper trail, and lose time coming up with a feasible explanation to trick a man trained in finding lies.

Owen switched tactics as he wiped his face with his sleeve. Scrolling through the photos he'd taken to review the files in private, Owen found the page with Levi's address on it. Bingo.

***

When the cab pulled up to the building, Owen wasn't sure what to expect. He'd seen the route his father had taken to get here, knew the part of town that this was in. In person however, it looked different. The old brick apartment building needed several renovations to get it up to a modern design. There were fire escapes in the alley that looked like they weren't particularly taken care of, and might be used more for sneaking in and out than any emergency.

There wasn't a doorman either. He could walk right in without even pressing a buzzer. The interior wasn't awful, but the ceilings were low and the lights cast a weird yellow glow on everything.

The door to Levi's apartment didn't look any different from the others in the hallway. The numbers plastered above each peephole were the only sign that he'd found the right one.

Knocking, Owen felt his heart thudding in his chest. Had he made the right choice? What was he going to find on the other side of this door? Levi could be perfectly fine, having dealt with the mess. Or his friend might have already been called to help deal with the injury.

"Owen?" Levi asked, opening the door to the chain and staring at him. "What is this? I didn't give you this address."

"Can I come in? I don't think you want this talked about in the hallway," Owen said. While the floor was empty, it took little for that to change.

Levi frowned for a moment before nodding and closing the door. For a breath, Owen wasn't sure if it would open again. Then the door chain rattled, many locks clicked, and Levi let Owen in.

The apartment was cold. The radiator rumbled and hissed as it blasted warm air in its fight against the chill. Levi had changed into comfortable sweats and a short-sleeved shirt. Both already had blood on them. A sloppy bandage was wrapped around his arm, which hung loosely at his side. The same arm that had been in a sling only an hour before.

When they'd parted, Owen had hoped that there'd been a weight lifted off of Levi's shoulders. But now, it was like the yoke was being pulled further down. A bone-deep exhaustion radiated from him as Levi stood there, just as bewildered as he'd been when Owen had first knocked.

"Do you need help with that?" Owen asked, motioning to his still-bleeding arm.

"Why are you here?" Levi replied, as if that was the better question.

Owen's shoulders slumped. "Vicki was having a tantrum, I guess. She decided we didn't believe her about something, or wasn't getting the attention that she wanted, and cut her arm. I saw how much it bled before it healed."

Anger flashed in Levi's eyes, his jaw ticking. Tension radiated through every line of Levi's body. And then it was gone. Like strings being cut from a marionette, Levi slumped where he stood, taking in low and slow breaths.

When he looked up again, the weariness had returned. The light was gone from his eyes. "I told you this was dangerous," Levi pointed out, his voice flat.

Sirens blared at the sudden change. The anger he had braced for. Expected. But this? He'd said that staying away would keep Levi safe. Was this safety? Tucked away in an apartment with no defenses, no guard, waiting to die? Was Owen the only one that knew? The only one that cared?

"I know, but it's also dangerous to be around Vicki," Owen replied, trying to get a reaction. Replace that resignation with...anything.

He wasn't getting kicked out, so Owen shrugged off his coat. The cooler air washed over him as Levi guided him away from the door. There was blood all over the living room carpet; the trail ended at the kitchen sink. A towel was abandoned on the floor in the kitchen, darker and discolored.

"Sorry about the mess," Levi remarked, as if his apartment had normal clutter and didn't resemble an active crime scene.

Horror settled into his stomach. Sucking in a breath, Owen tried to shove the feeling down for later. This wasn't about him. Glancing back to Levi, Owen wondered if this *was* normal mess for Levi, rather than take-out boxes and sodas. How long had this been going on?

"*Someone*," Levi added, "came over before I could finish cleaning up."

"I didn't have your number," Owen replied. "So I couldn't call and make sure that you could handle it, or if you needed medical assistance."

"Now I know I shouldn't give my number. How suspicious would that be? Vicki gets hurt and you immediately call me? Someone would notice," Levi replied, going back to the sink where there was already a full bucket of soapy water. But when he reached in to grab it, pain flashed over Levi's face, stopping him from getting very far.

With a few quick steps, Owen grabbed the bucket before Levi could try again. Carrying it over to the worst of the mess, Owen set it down on the floor.

116 | MC Warner

"I know you've been doing this on your own for years," Owen stated. "I know you *can* do this on your own. But I can't just sit by and go partying with Vicki, knowing that you're dealing with the consequences of her little fit. Knowing that you're cut and bleeding…" Owen looked down, watching the bubbles pop. He didn't know if he could meet the defeat in Levi's eyes right now. He wanted Levi to look alive again. To make those little smiles he didn't seem to give anyone but him. "I dunno, something snapped, and I had to get here as fast as possible." He shook his head, trying to clear away the panic that he'd walked in here with. Instead, Owen looked around for something of use. There was a large scrub brush, but Levi stopped him first.

"If you're going to help, put on a pair of gloves," Levi cautioned. He looked so weary even as he explained it. "There are some rubber ones under the sink. Just because I'm sitting right here doesn't mean you shouldn't take precautions around blood."

"Right," Owen replied, feeling foolish. He stood again to riffle under the sink through the extensive collection of cleaning products. Sliding them on, he took the rag and a scrub brush and got to it. Side by side, Levi worked with his one good arm, while Owen scrubbed with both hands. Together they slowly made progress. The red stain gradually moved from the floors into the bucket, slowly dirtying the water with each dip.

As his arms grew sore over the sections where the carpet refused to let go of the stains, Owen's mind poked at him. What was he doing here, on his hands and knees like this? Levi was safe. He had learned what he needed to know. Owen could be out at a bar, or having an adventure with a stranger from the club, or swiping through a hookup app until he found someone that looked enough like his current crush to get over it. Instead he was here, scrubbing blood off an old floor that would never fully come clean.

Owen froze at the realization. Crush? Casting a look at Levi out of the corner of his eye, he could see the person behind the fancy clothes and the bright lights at school. Instead, he saw how intently Levi focused on the subjects in school. The thoughtful questions of someone that didn't quite understand the topic, but was trying. How Levi's genuine smile was a joy to see and something to be earned. When had his interest in Levi turned into a crush?

Levi must have been caught up in his own thoughts, because he didn't seem to notice that Owen had stopped working. The man was kneeling on the ground, trying to wring out a rag with one hand, before dropping it into the bucket with a small splash. There was a tension to Levi, as he moved to pick up the water bucket. Owen hurried to stand and grab it instead. He heaved it to the toilet and dumped it down the drain, filling it again with fresh water at the sink.

"I just realized," Levi said, looking surprised. "The spell that your dad gave me to get close to your group...I turned it off when I got home." He looked back at Owen. "Are you sure you're here on your own free will?"

"My dad gave you a spell?" Owen asked. A sinking feeling filled his gut.

"Yeah, scroll is over there," Levi pointed to the side table. "Something to make me likeable or something."

Owen took off the gloves and rinsed off his hands. Maybe the spell was still running. That could explain a lot, such as why he was still there at all.

Weirdly enough, he didn't feel angry or betrayed. A spell, a slight compulsion, would explain why most of the group had been instantly accepting of him. Except...

Owen unrolled the spell, looking it over. It was a basic enough scroll, one that Owen had seen many times before. His dad had been very careful to make sure that even though Owen had no practical magic abilities, he knew the spells and their side effects, how to avoid their effects. Wards against the most common ones were kept on his key chain, disguised as little trinkets.

"This spell? My dad gave you this spell?" Owen asked.

"Yeah," Levi replied.

"It doesn't work," Owen replied. "On me, I mean..."

"What do you mean it doesn't work on you?" Levi asked, poking his head out of the kitchen.

"I mean, Dad bought me a ward for it a few years back," Owen explained. "He wanted to protect me when I was going out to clubs and such so that I wasn't getting caught up with guys that were using spells to get to me. Nothing like this works on me."

Levi frowned. "Then why give me a spell that you're immune to?"

"Either he trusts me not to be involved, or he doesn't trust you enough to have a spell that could influence me," Owen replied, rolling the spell back up and turning back to Levi. That same twisting feeling that had been in his gut came back. He tried to put a smile on his face.

"I've never been under your spell," Owen continued, glancing at the charging case. He'd not been under *that* spell at least. The thought made his face grow hot. He looked back at Levi and hoped that his flush wasn't betraying him too badly. "I'm still here. That's got to count for something, right?"

Levi rubbed his eyes, somehow looking older and more tired than ever. The arm with all the bandages was hanging uselessly at his side. It was like an arrow to Owen's heart. Those warm fuzzy feelings from before were extinguished with a bucket of ice. He opened his mouth again, hoping against hope that he could show Levi that this was a good thing.

"Owen," Levi started, turning back to the sink and struggling with the bucket. "Someday, I'm going to get hurt enough that I can't recover. I can't go to the hospital, because no one can know about the-" His words cut off for a moment. "The *shitty Soul Connection*."

He said it like a disgusting curse word. Owen had to agree.

"One day my body is going to give out, or Vicki is going to get attacked in a way that I won't survive," Levi continued. "It gets really old, really fast. That I've survived this long has been from spite, and because I can't abandon my best friend to this world on their own. Not until that choice is taken from me."

Piece by purposeful piece, the wall was building back up again between them. Owen felt like he'd returned to that hallway with the same question on his lips. Are you protecting me? Or are you protecting yourself? Was this years of pushing people away, until there was nothing left but a run-down apartment and a single friend? Or had this always been Levi?

What about the Levi that he had glimpsed back at Janie's apartment, talking about his best friend with a smile on his face? The one that hesitantly tried food and crinkled his nose at it while swallowing the rest down. What about those moments back in Owen's room? Had he glimpsed the real Levi then? Or was that the illusion, while the harsh reality stood bleeding before him now?

Those thoughts whirled even as he took the bucket of clean, soapy water from Levi's hand. It was heavy and sloshed against his pants, leaving a damp line on his thigh. "So, you're just resigning yourself to a life of nothing?" Owen asked. A tight lump formed in his throat.

"It's better this way," Levi replied. "Then there's fewer people that are going to cry at my funeral."

Owen felt a flash of anger, heat radiating down his arms and chest, as he took the bucket over to the living room floor. He took the time to put back on the gloves, wanting to snap them in the silence that stretched in the apartment. It wasn't Levi that deserved his fury.

Strange how quickly things had changed, how his feelings towards Vicki had turned bitter. He had grown up in her shadow. Permitted access to a world he would have never had on his own. He always thought that he gained as much as he lost with Vicki and her friends. But looking at Levi, the loyalty that he held for his single friend and the promise to survive this hell as long as possible, so they weren't left behind? Owen yearned to be cared for like that. To be even half that special to someone.

If that gun had shot down and to the left, he would have never met Levi, never known that someone was out here putting their life on the line, for someone that didn't even know to be grateful. If he hadn't noticed, hadn't asked, Owen might not have known that Levi was here, cleaning up the blood of Vicki's bad choices.

He'd heard whispers of her father's nickname from disgruntled former staff walked out by his father's team, to people trying to get at Vicki and hissing it out like a curse. He had never thought about what that meant until today. The Devil and the Devil's daughter, holding the life of someone else in the palm of their hands, to be destroyed at a whim. How was he supposed to process this? How was Owen supposed to go to school tomorrow and just act normal around the people that he'd called friends this morning?

CHAPTER 10

Sammy sent a message after midnight that they would stop by during daylight hours to raid the fridge for the treats. When Levi read the message the next morning, he was still wondering if he should skip school. The whole mood was going to be off. He was going to need to wear a high-collared shirt, or even a turtleneck, to cover up the mess from Vicki's exciting afternoon. As it was, he was trying to be careful with the bandage and how his arm was laying in the sling, to keep pressure off the new wound.

None of Owen's reactions had been what he'd expected. When he'd figuring out the Blessing that tied Vicki to Levi, wanting to see the wounds made sense. Wanting to walk him home after, finding his address and coming to his apartment because he knew Levi had been hurt and demanding to help, made no sense at all. Nothing could be looked at through the normal lens with this guy.

Telling Owen about the spell was supposed to scare him off, not make him happier about their connection. Telling Owen about how Levi was going to die was supposed to make him get closed off and leave, not stay longer and scrub crappy floors until his knees hurt. It was a good thing the weather was cold, because Levi did not think he could take any jokes about Owen's knees today.

He'd resigned himself to school being awful. What he didn't expect was Owen stepping close and whispering, "I think I know what the spell is."

Levi blinked, trying to ignore the soft breath against his ear. *Spell? What spell was he talking about?* It took him longer than it should to realize what Owen meant. "What?" Levi asked.

"You hinted at it yesterday," Owen replied, his voice still soft. "If you want to hear my theory, meet me after class."

Levi chewed his lip as he glanced at Owen, then the rest of the group that was filling in around them. Owen was standing closer than usual. Their legs touched as they whispered. A hand was resting on his good arm.

"What's this?" Levi whispered, running a finger over Owen's hand, resting on Levi's bicep.

"Revenge for scaring me yesterday," Owen said plainly. "And to stop Brooke's comments. Is it okay?"

Levi sighed and nodded, allowing himself the small moments of comfort. There was a thrill to the heat under his skin. The desire to lean closer startled him, but not enough to push Owen away.

What harm was there in letting Owen have his moment of fun? When Owen had left yesterday, it had seemed that the conversation had about a fifty percent chance of scaring him off. Instead, Levi was looking at the bags under his eyes, and a slightly wired expression. Owen was running on very little sleep, with borrowed energy that had come in chemical form. No use denying him a couple of favors for scrubbing the carpets cleaner than they had ever been.

"After class," Levi agreed. It was almost worth it to see Vicki's scowl. Brooke wouldn't meet his eyes.

There was a lot about Vicki that didn't seem right this morning. She kept turning away from Janie, while Janie kept redirecting her. If Owen's story was true, then Janie also knew about the "magic" that protected the Townsend heiress. If one of the friends was a suspect, like Mr. Townsend said, Janie was now on the list.

Janie, whose apartment was expensive, but didn't have the same family background as the rest. Edwin, who at least pretended not to know about the spell, but whose family had money troubles. Alicia, who was bound as a friend, and had known before this point. There were ways to get around loyalty pledges, Levi knew that already. Owen...

Levi refused to believe that Owen was behind any of it. Not just because of his kindness, but because Owen had nothing to gain. He had more to lose if something happened to Vicki

Townsend. His father would lose his job as head of Townsend's security, or the pair could lose their lives if Owen was found to be behind the attack.

"Soul Connections," Owen told him, once they found some place private to talk after class. "The spell hijacks the Soul Connections."

"You're saying I'm Connected to—" Levi wanted to retch at the idea.

"No. Not her," Owen replied. "It's stolen your Connection, corrupted it, and then attached it to Vicki. If it were a real Connection that was hijacked for this purpose, it would work in reverse, too. There's no way around that."

A stolen Connection? Whose? Had it overwritten a Connection that was already there, or did it add one by latching onto the tethers of someone else? When he closed his eyes and concentrated, he could still feel the magical energy that weaved through the city to Sammy, like a gossamer thread. Not even the Devil had broken that. But he only knew of that singular Connection. Owen had suggested there was another.

"So, I had a Connection with someone else that was taken?" Levi asked, his chest tightening with anger. Did that mean a stranger out there was getting hurt from his choice? Sammy always knew when he was in trouble, but they never felt the pain he was in. What about the person whose Connection was corrupted? It had always been him and Sammy against the world. Who had been stolen from him?

"Yeah," Owen replied. "See, I was doing some digging-"

"Where?" Levi interrupted him. Levi's heart pounded in his chest. If Owen got caught, digging into something Townsend never wanted found-

"Academic resources, research papers, forums," Owen explained with a wave of his hand.

Levi wasn't having it. Could Owen be found complicit through a paper trail? He asked again, worry aching through him.

"Places that I dig through already," Owen replied. "I'm nosy. Besides, these are all places that I already access for my classes. Can I tell you what I found now?"

It didn't feel like it was enough. But it had to be. He was going to have to trust Owen on this, even if he couldn't stop the cold terror from eating his insides.

"You can't just give someone the effects of a Connection," Owen continued. "And yes, there are Connections with wound transfer. There aren't a lot of them, and most don't have the kind that you're experiencing. If that was the case, the ones that did would live shorter lives. Anyway. There are bonds like this, which means this is just a corrupted version of those."

Guilt added to the fear from, so he redirected. "You're rambling," Levi pointed out. As private as the small alcove was, it was still just off the main hall. There was a chill from the window that wasn't completely sealed, and the two chairs barely fit in the small study space. Someone could walk up to them at any point.

"Sorry," Owen replied. He took a deep breath, as if to center himself. He was still leaning into Levi's space when he whispered, "My hypothesis is whatever Connection the Blessing was splintered from, it's a powerful one, something that can handle the abuse that the corruption takes."

"Splintered? Not overwritten?" Levi asked.

"Yeah...I think you still have that Connection," Owen replied, his eyes shifting around the room. "Maybe it's buried or covered up, but it's still there. If it had been severed or overwritten, you couldn't hold this Connection either."

"This is all guesswork," Levi said, flatly. As Owen glanced towards him, he let his eyes focus on the far corner of the room. It felt too intimate to be making eye contact, while talking about Connections with Owen.

"A little," Owen replied. "But I found studies. Actual published research. How people who purposely get their Connections severed find it impossible to create a new one. But people can also find multiple Connections over their lifetime."

Levi shook his head, not sure what else to take from that. Owen seemed to believe it was true, but that didn't actually mean anything. He could have misinterpreted what he was reading and filled in the blanks.

Soul Connections were rare. Not everyone got one. And it wasn't always a romantic thing. A friendship with someone that just clicked, a coworker that made your shitty job better, a childhood friend whose words carried you for your whole lifetime. A Connection stayed with you, even if the relationship came to its natural end. Connections were rarely true love, even if the movies tried to brand them as such. Connections were simply relationships with other people that seemed to be stronger than others. Sometimes there was extra intuition about the other person's day or week. Sometimes it was a small telepathic connection between two people. Mostly it was a person you wanted to keep in your life, who wanted the same in return.

"There's no way to check if you're right or not," Levi pointed out. "I don't know what that gives us- Um, you."

"If I picked right, we could break the false Connection," Owen whispered.

Levi blinked, stunned. Break the Connection? Remove the Blessing. It brought a flash of hope that Levi purposely quelled. Hope was dangerous. It gave root to futures and desires that Levi had so carefully forbidden himself. It gave way to guilt and shame for how he had lived his life thus far, and all the experiences that had been robbed of him. He couldn't allow himself to hope, and in return feel the bitter pain of it being cut short.

"Then what?" Levi asked. "What's the end goal? Someone else gets the spell?" Would it go to a stranger, or worse, someone more evil that the Devil himself?

Owen shrugged. "I'm not saying that," he murmured. "I thought you would be more excited." His head dropped and his shoulders slumped. It left Levi feeling like an asshole.

Reaching over with his good arm, he squeezed Owen on the shoulder. "That's not what I meant," Levi said. "When I signed up for this, he did not offer me an end that wasn't death. If, and that's a big if, something's here, and it breaks, then what? Breaking the spell could put everyone that's involved in danger. Get you and your dad caught up in something that you didn't sign up for. I can handle this. That doesn't mean that the next person in line can, too."

"So what, you're just going to let it happen?" Owen asked, a flash of anger in his eyes. "Just let that man kill you?"

Levi couldn't help but smile. "You'd like my friend. They would have the same reaction if they knew."

Owen's fury wilted into sadness. "I don't like this," he stated.

"I know," Levi replied. He thought about his next words carefully. "I'm not going to try to stop you again. It doesn't look like it would matter anyway," Levi stated. "What I will ask is that you be careful. Protect yourself. At the end of the day, I don't want you to be another casualty."

"Like you?" Owen asked.

Levi shrugged, trying to hide how tight his throat felt. His teenage self had no idea what the side effects would be, never stopped to consider the big picture. "I've been a dead man walking since I was sixteen. A decade isn't a bad deal."

Owen stared, eyes growing wide and mouth parting. Whether it was to gasp or to argue, Levi continued.

"Yes, I was a teenager. You could say it was dumb, but I was cold, starving, and we were about to lose the roof over our heads," Levi said, gritting his teeth to push the information out without being interrupted. "So don't give me shit about this. I got ten years. That's more than I would have had without him."

He shot a glare at Owen, only to find that Owen's expression had softened. Owen's eyes shone with unshed tears as he took in a breath. Resolve settled over Owen like a blanket.

"I'm going to keep looking," Owen promised. "There has to be a way to transfer the injuries to a mannequin, or a cadaver or something. You shouldn't have to trade your life for someone who doesn't deserve it."

Levi couldn't argue that. It was something that he had grown to feel every day since he signed his life away. It wasn't even that he didn't want to be free; it was that he didn't know what it would cost. Whose life would be traded next, if anything happened to him? As long as it only impacted him, he could handle it. If the Connection had been giving someone else a ghost of Vicki's injuries this whole time, he was going to raise hell.

He had stopped looking into Connections years ago, once he understood the gravity of taking Vicki's injuries in an all too painful reality. That was the moment that he'd stopped wishing that someone would come and share his wounds, and started wishing that no one was feeling this, too.

He hoped that Owen was wrong about Levi having another Connection. The idea that someone else was caught up in this mess was almost too much to fathom. Was someone else feeling his pain, getting his and Vicki's injuries through the bond? Or was that Connection fragile enough, corrupted enough, that whomever they were, they were spared the pain too? He knew that was going to preoccupy his mind with university lectures for the next couple of hours, or until Vicki did something stupid again, though he had no way of knowing which would come first.

***

Today was the worst. It sucked even more than the week her friends had abandoned her to go skiing. Owen was being distant and weird; she wondered if she should tell the others that she was kicking him out. Who needed a spineless nobody like him? They could get another designated driver. People were lining the blocks to be Vicki Townsend's friend; replacing him wouldn't be very hard.

Janie was still in her weird "mothering mode" and it was giving Vicki the ick. Just because she'd sliced open her arm yesterday didn't mean that she was going to do it again today. But Janie had threatened to tell her dad, which was the only reason Vicki hadn't pushed her away either.

If anyone was going to report her, it was tattletale Owen. She had waited all night to see if he would. Instead, he was ignoring her.

Brooke looked like a mixture of still drunk and hungover, like she was trying to drink away the memory of yesterday. Useless.

Alicia and Edwin were acting the same, but those traitors didn't even come out of the bedroom when the screaming and yelling had happened. Janie had cleaned up the blood alone, before they'd come out looking freshly showered and ready for the club. A club night that only Alicia, Edwin, and Vicki had gone to.

Then there was Levi. Vicki was almost disappointed that he'd been gone when she cut her arm. Maybe then he would have listened to her to stay away from her friends.

Instead, Levi and Owen could not stop touching each other. They leaned into each other's space, whispered in each other's ears and they couldn't keep their hands to themselves. Owen was throwing himself at Levi, and Levi was returning it like it was second nature. Owen leaned on Levi's good shoulder, so Levi draped his arm over Owen's back. Owen complained that class had taken too long and he was ready for a nap, Levi patted his forehead or shoulder with a teasing "there, there". Levi winced at his stupid shoulder injury, Owen gently massaged his arm.

Vicki had counted a dozen barely decent touches between the two, and that didn't even count the looks from across the room. She needed both of them gone yesterday.

Watching the men sneak away for the second time today, Vicki looked over at her one remaining friend. "What's with the two of them today, do you know?" she asked Alicia.

"They've just been like that," Alicia replied. "Owen keeps denying that they're together though, so I'm wondering if there's something about Levi's home life or inheritance that's keeping it a secret?"

"What home life? He's never mentioned anything," Vicki asked. Maybe she could use someone in Levi's family to make him disappear, since neither Owen nor her father were being any help.

Alicia shrugged. "You'd have to ask the others. They might know more. Why?"

"He and Owen are annoying me. I think we shouldn't hang out with them anymore," Vicki stated.

"Because they might date? Come on, that's shallow even for you," Edwin pointed out. "Let them have their fun. In a few weeks, they'll either have confirmed it, or broken up anyway."

"A few weeks? Why should I have to wait a few weeks to stop dealing with their," Vicki waved her hands at them. It was bad enough before she'd confronted Owen that Levi was working for her dad. Now that Owen knew the truth, it was like she'd gotten rid of the last reasons he was holding back. It was awful. She wanted her friend back. It was supposed to be up to her whether or not people were part of the group. Owen wasn't allowed to ignore her of his own volition.

"Owen's probably just excited that there's someone he can date," Alicia offered. "How often do his dates turn out to be one-night stands with more effort?"

"Why would I care about that?" Vicki asked.

"Because when he's happier, he's more willing to help us out," Edwin replied. "Come on Vicki. I know everything is weird right now, with your dad being sure that there's someone after you. He's been on our case about watching your back, so I'm sure that he's been extra difficult at home."

Vicki pursed her lips. Father wasn't even home right now. He was off on a business trip, trading magic for favors, or trading in favors for chances to do something more. Either way, he was not interested in being here for her.

"Oh, he's gone again?" Alicia asked. She had always could read Vicki's face. "Do you want us to come over? Or we could go out again tonight, party it up."

Vicki shook her head. It felt like pity coming from Alicia. *Look at Vicki, she's so pathetic. Let's give her attention, so she doesn't jump in front of a car.*

"Maybe Owen will find us another hook up, now that's he's happy with his new buddy?" Edwin suggested. "I think I could talk him into paying for it, don't you?"

"That might make me feel better," Vicki replied, as Edwin gave them a wave and wandered off.

Alicia waved before her smile dropped. "God, Edwin is an idiot sometimes," she grumbled. "All I had to tell him was that Owen broke a plate, bled all over the place and left, and he believed it. Even though there was no broken plate and Owen didn't have an injury. You okay though? Owen didn't hurt you, did he?"

Vicki shook her head a moment too soon. If she'd caught the opportunity before she'd replied, she could have split the group without any more effort. Oh well, next time. "I was trying to prove a point, and no one gets it. Everyone is babying me today, and I just proved that they don't have to."

"Maybe they don't understand how long you've had the Blessing, and that you know it works," Alicia stated. "I mean, I also would have been happier if you didn't hurt yourself to show them. But that's because I care about you not getting hurt, even if the Blessing fixes it. Besides, you had to remind me a few times you were going to be okay after I found out."

"But we were little when I got into that accident that should have broken my leg, and you found out because you watched me get knit back together," Vicki replied.

"Well, Janie is used to having to protect our group. That won't stop just because you're invincible," Alicia said. "Brooke, well, it's Brooke. And Owen, you know he's there for us when we need him. Yeah, sometimes he's changing our plans or telling us it's time to leave, but he's better than the alternative of your dad's bodyguards following you around. Right?"

"I was trying to prove a point that I *don't* need that." Vicki crossed her arms in front of her chest with a huff. "Now he's ignoring me. The whole damn reason I cut my arm was so that he could listen. But instead he got pissed off and left, and he hasn't said a word to me today."

"Did he say anything before he left yesterday?" Alicia asked.

"Something about consequences and side effects," Vicki said. "You know, the normal bullshit."

Alicia looked thoughtful, her eyes widening, before shaking her head. Her golden locks swayed as she did so. "Maybe not. You said that you told him about the bond and he was going to do research. What if he knows where the injuries go?"

"That's what I tried to ask him yesterday," Vicki pointed out.

"Well, let me try asking him," Alicia suggested. "He might open up to me."

"More than me?" Vicki asked.

"Well, I have known him a long time, and I was the first person he came out to," Alicia pointed out. "But I can put my phone on speaker, and you can listen in. Just keep your side on mute so that he doesn't know."

Vicki hummed. That actually seemed like a good idea. It would give her a chance to hear what Owen really thought. Maybe she could learn about what Owen was hiding from her. And why Owen thought it was okay to keep secrets.

**

It took a full two days before Alicia and Owen's schedules lined up again. Vicki hated waiting, but Alicia promised she hadn't prepped him about the conversation, and that was good enough for her.

The phone was a little muffled because it was in Alicia's purse, but Vicki could still hear enough.

"I figured," Alicia started. "That we could compare notes about the Blessing."

"Yeah," Owen replied, sounding far away. "You mentioned that when we set up this meeting. Did we really have to meet in your bedroom, though? Edwin's going to get the wrong idea."

"He thinks that you're helping me pick out a lingerie set," Alicia replied. "Quickly, red or black?"

"Did you have to pick such basic colors?" Owen replied, but there was a teasing lilt in his voice. "I don't know what they look like on, and I don't care, but the spider webs on the black one are cool. Not sure about sexy, though."

"It's reminding him I could be a black widow if I wanted," Alicia teased back. "Oh, if only…"

The sound of Owen clearing his throat cut her off. "So the Blessing," he started, redirecting the conversation. "Have you ever seen it in action?"

"A few times," Alicia replied. "When I first saw it, Vicki had just, like just gotten in an accident, and I watched her leg go from broken to completely healed in an instant."

"That had to be weird," Owen replied. "When was this?"

"A few months before my brother died," Alicia said, her voice soft.

There was a lull in the conversation. Vicki leaned close to the phone to hear what she was missing. If Owen spoke, it was too soft to make out.

"I thought I had knocked my head too hard," Alicia continued, sounding like herself again. "Anyway, what about you?"

"Well, I saw the bullet wound, but I didn't pay attention until long after it healed, so the only one I've seen is the arm thing from the other day," Owen said, a bitterness in his voice that Vicki could hear through the phone.

"Vicki said that you got mad about it," Alicia prompted.

"A couple of us got mad," Owen replied. "The biggest thing is that we don't know what's taking the wound away. All magic has a cost, everything has a side effect, so if Vicki doesn't have the wound anymore, where did it go?"

"Maybe it just healed in an instant," Alicia pointed out.

"Maybe, but that's a lot of magic," Owen replied. "An extreme healing spell that is spontaneous and takes just a few seconds? Then it begs the question, is there a charge time between the spells? What if purposely hurting yourself weakened healing at a future time? Those are questions we cannot get answers for unless we dig into the spell first. Find out where the injury is going."

"I mean, we could test that stuff out," Alicia pointed out.

"But what if it's not healing? What if it's going to boomerang back at a later date?" Owen suggested. He sounded a little panicked at the idea of Vicki testing out the Blessing some more. "We're talking about injury. That's not something that you can just take back."

"Oh, I didn't think about that," Alicia replied.

Vicki held the phone closer to her ear, trying to make out more. It had gone silent, and with that silence meant that she was left guessing. Were they writing something back and forth and sharing information without her? What body language was she missing out on? What information did Owen and Alicia know that she didn't?

"So if you don't know where the injuries go, what do you know?" Alicia asked.

"A little," Owen replied. "Vicki still gets drunk, still gets high, and still gets hangovers."

Vicki blinked. Yeah, she did. What did that have to do with the Blessing?

"So the Blessing might only work on physical wounds and not things she ingests," Owen explained. "Or other effects. Those are not things that we should test either," the last sentence added rapidly. "Also, Vicki's arm didn't heal until she took the knife away, which meant that if she were to say get shot with an arrow and it stuck in her, or stabbed and the knife stayed in, the Blessing couldn't heal her until it was out. Both could be bad. Really, really bad."

"Shit," Alicia gasped. "Yeah. She might not be as invincible as I thought."

"I'm only bringing this up because I don't want her to get hurt," Owen continued. "I'm not saying that she needs to be wrapped up in bubble wrap, but unless her dad had given someone else the Blessing and tested these scenarios before Vicki got it... Oh. That's an idea."

"What?" Alicia asked.

"Something unrelated," Owen murmured, sounding preoccupied. "Basically, unless her dad tested it on a bunch of people and knows what is too much damage, or the wrong damage, we don't know what's too much. Please remind Vicki to be careful."

"Owen, what's wrong? You look pale," Alicia asked.

"There's another puzzle that I'm working through, and I think I just found the answer. I've got to go," Owen explained. "We can talk more about this later, yeah?"

"See you," Alicia replied, sounding concerned.

Vicki wanted to lean through the phone to catch anything else, but there was only the sound of the door opening and closing before Alicia's voice came clearer. "Could you hear everything?" she asked.

"Enough. What set Owen off?" Vicki asked.

"Not a clue," Alicia replied.

They chatted for a while, before the conversation dwindled and the call ended. There was something about how Owen talked that reminded her of the night that she'd proved her point. He knew more than he was letting on. Even though was supposed to be telling her everything about the Blessing; he'd promised to help her figure it out! All of this running around and keeping secrets would not do. Owen would need to think about his place in their group, and whether he'd still be useful to her in the future. As it stood, Owen was turning his back on her, despite the opportunities she and her father had given him over the years. Maybe it was time to cut him off. See how long it took for him to come back begging for his place among them again.

***

It had been strange when Alicia called him over to talk about the Blessing. He didn't know how she knew he knew, but with the mess that had happened the other night, just about everyone did now. The suspicion that filled him at her request was quickly overridden by his desire for answers.

He and Alicia had known each other since they were little, when his dad had started working security for the Townsend family, and Alicia's mother had been Vicki's nanny. When they were little, it had been him and Alicia trying their best to be friendly with the newly motherless Vicki. Alicia had gotten in as best friend. Owen had been pushed away and called a weird kid for wanting to play with girls.

Their friendship had stuttered back and forth over the years, sometimes getting close and then drifting away again. Still, Alicia had been the first person he'd came out to when he was trying to understand his sexuality, and he had been there for Alicia after her brother had died.

Now, though, things seemed to be contrived. Alicia avoided magic conversations like the plague; the fact that she'd invited him over to talk about the Blessing set off so many red flags. She hadn't even been present when Vicki cut her arm. If Alicia had been told about it after he'd left, no one told him. Owen had kept his time with the group brief over the last few days, preferring Levi's company instead. Maybe he was being paranoid, but he wondered if this was Vicki's idea. Alicia never said no to anything Vicki asked.

So, he prepared his answers. Listened when Alicia talked about when she first learned of the spell. Was that where Levi's limp had come from? He'd have to line up the dates. It wouldn't be too hard; Owen could never forget that ski trip. It was the only one that he had been on. He'd left early once he'd sprained ankle; his general dislike of the mountains gave him no reason to stay. That had been one of the worst injuries of his whole life, but he hadn't known that Vicki had gotten hurt. There were only two injuries on that trip: Owen's and Dylan's. Alicia had hated how her last fun vacation with her brother had been cut off by Dylan, ending up in the hospital not long after Owen had checked out.

Then, it was back to the talk of the Blessing. To distracting or derailing any attempts at testing it out.

The word had hit Owen like a lightning bolt.

Tested.

The Blessing had to have been tested before it was given to Vicki. There was no way that a man as cautious as Mr. Townsend would hand over a dangerous spell to his daughter, without knowing the limitations.

How many times had it been through trials? How many lives had been destroyed by that man as he checked if a bullet through the head or the heart could be given to someone else? A shooting had been the famous end of his wife, so that had to be the main defense by design. But the rest: stabbing, drowning, poison? He didn't know if drowning could be passed through the bond. Nothing about the spell transferred the physical side effects. Owen had even checked if the drugs passed through the Blessing, but Levi had never once been high. When it was safer, Owen was going to fix that.

Owen had gone over to Levi's apartment yesterday to talk about the effects, and to learn more about the dangers. In return, Owen had presented the information he had gathered so far. The conversation had been equal parts enlightening and terrifying.

But first, before he could help Levi taste what it was like to get out of his head for a little while. Before he could think about taking Levi dancing, or driving, or anything else that Levi had never gotten to try because of this grotesque spell, Owen had something else that he had to do. He had to look up and see if there was anyone that might still be alive from the testing. Witnesses, doctors, family members maybe—anyone that knew about it. Then he had to find someone that might want revenge, or a chance to get their story out into the sun.

Owen didn't know where to start. Obituaries maybe? Employment records that he wasn't supposed to have access to? There had to be something.

Someone was after Vicki, but not for a ransom. The shot that still made Levi flinch at times didn't match what had happened to the security guards. At such close range, a bullet in the arm was too messy to be a mistake. It looked like a warning, or a test. Someone was after the Blessing, and Vicki was the collateral.

CHAPTER 11

When Owen had suggested the idea that someone might want revenge against Mr. Townsend, Levi tried not to laugh. That was the whole point of the Blessing, to keep the Devil's daughter safe from his enemies. But then Owen had suggested that it was because of early trials for this experimental magic, and Levi felt that laughter die away.

Owen had invited himself over to Levi's apartment again. Any conversations about trying another study session with Vicki's friends, or a bar crawl, had died before the night had even begun.

"You think that whomever is after her is going to attack to prove that the Blessing isn't all that it's cracked up to be?" Levi checked. He still didn't have a strong enough motive from any of Vicki's friends. This could mean that none of the friends were involved. But then, who took the money out of the account only their group had access to? And why?

"That's my guess," Owen replied.

"It's not a bad guess," Levi said. "The timing is suspicious, though. It's been a decade since I since followed that bastard into his car. Why now? What's changed?"

Owen hummed and turned to look at Levi. "Tell me about that. Maybe there's a clue in there?"

Levi didn't think there was anything useful to be had, but he told it anyway.

"I was just a kid back then," Levi started slowly. He had told parts of it to Sammy, enough to explain where he had gone and where the money came from. That version had been mixed with enough lies that it didn't trigger any backlash. But he'd never said all of it aloud. "I was young, hungry...desperate, honestly. He was looking for that, I suppose. Someone that didn't have the means to say no."

Levi had given Sammy the last bit of food, before heading out to beg for change. The power had been turned off, and it was only a matter of time before the bank took the deed away too. But the fireplace still worked, which meant that there was some heat to keep out the cold. It was the home that Sammy had grown up in, the one that Sammy's parents had died trying to pay for. Levi didn't know what that was like. He'd been passed around by relatives that didn't want him. That threatened to kick him out for eating too much, or being too loud, or simply existing in their space. It had been a blessing when Sammy's family had taken him in, until they were gone, too.

He'd refused to let his past become Sammy's future.

The two of them had survived that first winter, before Levi dropped out of school to get a job. Then the bills had started piling up, and Levi struggled to keep up. Each month, the pair of them fell further behind. The few hours of work Levi was permitted each week couldn't cover it.

They'd made it that far by pawning off anything they could. The precious memories and clothing that Sammy wouldn't have given up if they could help it. But now there wasn't anything left to sell, other than themselves.

Levi had been desperate when the car had pulled up beside him. The windows were like shadows. Even when the back one rolled down to reveal the occupant inside, he couldn't read his face.

The promise of cash and a warm meal shouldn't have tempted him in that way, but if there had been a chance that it was real, well, Levi couldn't say no. Into the warm car he climbed.

Once inside, a teenage Levi looked at his new benefactor, and tried not to shiver.

"What do you want from me?" Levi asked.

"I have a test that I want to run, and if you pass, I'll offer you a job," the man replied. "If you fail, I'll pay you a good sum of money to keep quiet and send you home."

"That's all?" Levi asked, a mixture of hope and skepticism bubbling up in his gut. "What kind of test?"

"A compatibility test," the man of shadows replied. "I'm looking for someone with the right kind of magical potential."

Levi opened his mouth to mention that Sammy was magical, and they might be a better fit. As far as he knew, Levi didn't even have magical talents. But the shadows of the car and a lead weight in his gut kept him quiet. Sammy hadn't climbed into this car; Levi did.

This could be a trap. But if he was lucky, maybe he could get enough money to keep the house a little longer, or pay for food for the week.

The first lie from the man in the car had been of omission. The magical test had sounded like the kind that some kids got in school. When Levi's height, weight, blood pressure, and every other indicator of physical health were checked, Levi had started to sweat.

When the physical was complete, he was forced into a chair. Leather straps were buckled around his wrists and ankles and around his chest. Electrodes were taped to his chest and forehead. Guards surrounded him, and Levi could only hope that Sammy didn't cry too much when Levi never came home.

Pain whited out his vision and his consciousness along with it.

When he came to, he was still slumped in the chair. The leather cuffs were undone, but they'd left burn marks on his wrists. There were marks on his chest where the electrode had been taped. The room was empty, except for the man of shadows.

"Congratulations. You're compatible," the man stated, holding out a hand as if to help Levi stand.

Levi pulled himself upright on his own, determined to turn around and leave. If that was only the test, anything that happened next would be a thousand times worse. However hard it was to make it on his own, it couldn't be as bad as whatever this man had in store.

Speaking the story aloud left him feeling numb. He had stared at a spot on the carpet the whole time. Even now, Levi didn't want to look up. He could imagine the horror that had to be there. Nightmares that Owen could have lived without.

"I don't know when I was approached exactly," Levi added, trying to get the conversation back on track. "I know it was winter break because Sammy at least got breakfast and lunch from school, and right then we were trying to scrape together pennies for either of us to get a meal."

"This was when you were sixteen?" Owen asked, his voice tight. "So, ten years ago?"

"What about it?" Levi asked, finally daring to look. Owen's eyes were red, and the skin was puffy around them. Had he made Owen cry? He should have kept to the abridged version.

Still, there wasn't any look of horror. Concern filled his features, a thoughtful frown stretched his lips. Was Owen putting together how old he was from that? Levi was only twenty-six, or thereabout. He barely remembered what day of the week it was, never mind whether his birthday had happened. Did Owen think Levi was too old to be hanging out with him? Owen was only a few years younger, at least according to the file.

"It's just, the dates don't line up," Owen murmured. "Alicia told me that Vicki had the blessing in October, but you're saying that it was around the New Year?"

The implications of that weighed heavily on Levi. "What was the injury?"

"Skiing accident, broken leg, maybe cracked ribs?" Owen said.

Levi shook his head, silent in his dread at what this meant. He hadn't been the first one. While he never expected that he would be the last, knowing there had already been others sent a flash of panic through him that chilled him to the core.

"I didn't take those injuries," Levi replied. He took a deep breath and focused back to Owen's original question. "Revenge still fits, right? Even a decade later?"

Whomever it was had been dealing with the pain or hatred of being Blessed for even longer than Levi had. He glanced towards Owen and nudged him to get him to focus again.

"So, we're looking at someone that was too young, too hurt, or too imprisoned to do anything about it until now?" Owen asked.

Actually, that wasn't a bad thought.

"So, a kid who found out what happened to their family member when they turned eighteen, someone that was injured and couldn't get back until now, someone that just passed away from their injuries and the family member is reacting with grief, or someone that was locked up for the last decade," Levi hummed. All of those made perfect sense to him, as long as he ignored the funds that had been taken out of the fun money account. Looking at the friends group for a killer had been like looking for a needle in a stack of needles. He needed to be looking at Vicki's attack from a different angle, and Owen's suggestion was as good as any. As long as he found the person behind the attack and explained the money out of the account, Townsend shouldn't be mad. Right?

That conversation had been a few days ago, and even though Owen hadn't been able to find anyone yet, he still ended up at Levi's apartment to hang out and do his research. Some research got done, especially while Levi was doing his own studying. Though, for every two or three hours that were spent heads down in research, another hour was spent hanging out and learning more about the other. The shows that they watched, childhood games, favorite foods and so on.

So inevitably, Owen and Sammy were going to meet, because while Sammy's visits were sporadic, they would happen.

Owen had settled into what Levi was already referring to as "his spot," the old chair in the room's corner. He always sat cross-legged in it, laptop in his lap, and a tray table that had appeared one day full of drinks and snacks. One of Levi's neighbor's had been getting rid of the chair, so instead of carrying down the flights of stairs and leaving it in the lobby for someone to take, Owen had carried it into Levi's apartment. Levi had added a small trash can there for all the empty drinks and containers so that it wasn't a pain to clean up. Owen's spot caused the television to be pushed against the wall, and there was barely enough room for it all, but it worked, and left Levi's recliner and Sammy's couch free.

"I don't think you've moved from that spot all day," Levi said, stifling a yawn. It was late on a Saturday, the kind of late that Levi usually stayed up through. He would end up getting woken up eventually, with a jolt of pain from whatever hip checks and scraped knees Vicki got while out partying. Owen had avoided them this weekend and kept himself parked at Levi's instead. Levi hadn't seen Owen move in the last hour, scrolling up and down the web page with a frown on his face. "You're creating an imprint in the chair, and I think either you or it is growing a scent."

Owen sniffed himself and shrugged. "It's not that bad."

"If you won't go home, at least grab a shower," Levi suggested. "I know you want to stay until you get this figured out, though I don't see how waiting here is going to make any difference, but you've got to take care of yourself. Up, up, up."

Moving the laptop to the side, he pulled Owen up from the chair. "You can borrow clothes, towel, shampoo, anything you need," he offered.

Owen grumbled before he eventually agreed. Levi was pretty sure that the small bathroom, the short hot water heater, cheap shampoos, conditioner, and towels would be enough to make Owen run back to his luxury dwelling. Or he might feel good enough after the shower to crash and fall asleep. The prospect of the couch might be enough to send him packing.

Fresh from the shower, a towel wrapped around his waist while Levi kept trying to redirect to borrow the expensive clothes instead, was how Sammy found them.

"Levi, you didn't tell me you had company," Sammy said, leaning against the doorway to Levi's bedroom. Levi hadn't even noticed the jingle of the keys in the front door, or the sounds of Sammy's boots on the carpet, yet here they were.

"I forgot to update my social calendar," Levi replied, looking at Owen. "You can borrow whatever you want, but I'd prefer that you be dressed before you officially meet my best friend."

Owen looked at Sammy with wide eyes and then smiled. "I had hoped to make a better first impression," Owen said, grabbing at the towel around his waist and holding onto it, just in case.

Levi had to bite his cheek against saying, "Could this night get any worse?" because it absolutely could. If the universe was kind, he'd shot dead through the bond. But then that would leave both Owen and Sammy to deal with his body.

Patting Owen on the shoulder, Levi replied, "Well, get dressed and we can try for first impression version two." He pulled the door closed behind him. "No free show for you," he told Sammy.

"I pay for my shows, thank you very much," Sammy replied. Leaning on the arm of the sofa, they took the whole space in. "You've redecorated."

"It just…happened," Levi replied, moving some of the empty cans into the trash. He filled it the rest of the way with empty snack containers and then tied the bag off. "It wasn't something that I had planned on."

"And the young man changing in your bedroom?" Sammy asked, their eyes twinkling.

"Was he something that I was planning on?" Levi asked, reaching for the drawer of grocery bags for a new liner.

"No, silly, who is he? How did you two meet?" Sammy asked.

"I'm leaving the introductions for when he's dressed," Levi replied, continuing with the chores and ignoring the ache in his arm from Vicki's stupid knife games.

"That bandage is new," Sammy said.

"Yeah, it took a few butterfly bandages, but it's healing okay," Levi replied. "When I'm out of the apartment, my arm is in my sling, so don't worry about me doing too much and opening it again."

"I told you to call me when you got hurt," Sammy said. A disappointed look mixed with worry spread across their features.

"Owen was here. He helped me with it," Levi replied. He stopped with the chores and just looked at them. "You were working, and I didn't want you to worry while you were on shift. Then I kind of just fell asleep."

"Next time, you call me," Sammy said, their eyes flashing as they poked their acrylic nails against his chest. "It's my choice whether I leave a shift early, but I don't want you to bleed out on the carpet, or scrub the floors in the dark because you're worried about my feelings."

Sammy poked their nail into his chest a few more times, just to punctuate their point. But when they turned, Levi saw the glimpse of a smile on their face.

"Please tell me you're Owen," Sammy said, walking towards the other person in the apartment.

"That's me. Are you Levi's best friend?" Owen asked. He was dressed in something of Levi's, sweats that had been rolled up at the ankles, and a T-shirt that Sammy had bought him a few Christmases ago. It looked like a tourist shirt, all white with black letters and a bright red heart that proclaimed that the wearer loved the city of Ashton. Except this one proclaimed, "I heart Men."

"I'm Sammy," they said, giving Owen a once over. There was a smile and a quirk to their lips. "Has Levi talked about me?"

"A lot. Though he never mentioned your name," Owen replied, shifting in place. He looked far less comfortable now.

"That sounds like *our* Levi," Sammy replied.

Levi stifled a groan; they were massively misinterpreting the situation here. Which was fair, because this was the first time that Sammy had come over to find someone new and naked in the apartment.

"Yeah, I guess it does," Owen replied, his cheeks flushed again.

Come on, Sammy, don't drag this poor kid's feelings out like that, Levi thought, walking back to the kitchen to grab something to drink. Levi had been trying to keep Owen from falling too hard for him. At first, he had tried pushing him away, but Levi just didn't have it in him. He'd been lonely for far too long.

Owen had settled back into his chair, but he'd tidied up his research and packed the laptop away.

"So, when did you two meet?" Sammy asked.

"We met while I was out on a job," Levi replied. He hadn't prepped a backstory with Owen, because he and Sammy weren't supposed to meet. "We got to talking more after I got hurt again, and things just snowballed from there."

"Snowballed?" Owen squeaked, cheeks flushed all over again.

"Snowballed?" Sammy mouthed, an excited gleam in their eyes.

"Snowballed for me at least," Levi cut in, halting whatever thought they were having. He didn't know if he could take it tonight, and he didn't want to make Owen uncomfortable. "This is all new to me, so keep the teasing to a minimum."

Levi was being careful not to mention how Owen's dad was the one that had equipped him with all the clothes for his job, or that Owen had been part of the people that he was interacting with related to his work, or that Owen knew about the injuries to the extent that he did. Glancing at Owen, he tried to guess whether Owen was picking up on the small hints he'd left.

"Yeah, we're still trying to figure things out," Owen agreed, and Levi didn't know if he meant a possible relationship, or a way to break the Blessing. He knew how Sammy would take it. Levi felt his cheeks heat as he tried not to think about it.

The pointed look on Sammy's face was enough to flip them off. "Well, I'm glad to meet you," Sammy replied, ignoring Levi completely. "You must be someone special for Levi to have brought you home with him." They grinned as Owen curled up in the chair, ducking his head in embarrassment. "He's adorable, Levi. Don't fuck this up."

"I'm doing my best," Levi promised. He had been, until these two had ended up in the same room together. The mess that they could cause in his life was insurmountable.

There was a part of him that hoped that Owen could figure things out. A part of him that wanted to see Owen and Sammy get to swap stories and not have to hide their truths. Hope though, was a dangerous thing, because if that future was in fact possible, there were other beautiful futures that he wanted to find out about too. But there was no guarantee he could survive to see any of it. Besides, if ever he was free of the Blessing, there was no guarantee Townsend would let him walk away.

***

Owen felt like he was massively messing something up. When he'd stayed over to do research the first time, it had been because he had gotten so distracted by the chance that Levi was hurt and it would be too late to help, that he hadn't been able to do any of the research. He'd camped out on Levi's couch, taking up the space with notebooks and his laptop. When Levi didn't kick him out of the apartment, Owen simply stayed. When Levi got him the chair in the corner, Owen made the area his own. He went home to sleep and to make sure that his dad wasn't worried enough to call in the cavalry, but other than that, when he was free, Owen was at Levi's.

In his absence, homework and studying had piled up. He had an essay due on Monday that Owen hadn't started. The subject, and the class, felt far less important than the work he was doing now. He would write the paper in time; he still had a few days.

Messages from friends were filling up his phone. Janie was checking if he was going to show up to her next study session. Edwin wanted to swap class notes. Brooke wanted a ride somewhere. Alicia wanted a ride somewhere. Janie wanting a ride home from a bar—Owen replied to that one, double-checking that Janie was safe. She was, and even texted when she got home. Nothing from Vicki. That was usually troubling, but he had other things to worry about right now.

Sammy, the best friend, had not been in the equation at all. Owen had been too concerned about his nakedness to pay much attention to Sammy when they'd first met in Levi's room. But now, he was dressed in Levi's clothes and meeting Levi's best friend in Levi's living room. His eyes casting longingly at the comfort of his chair and wondering if he could hide there, instead of standing here and being a part of this awkward meeting. He wanted to meet Sammy, but not like this.

They stood taller than him, though he didn't know if that was because of the tall boots hidden under the oversized sweatshirt and slouchy pants combo, or if they were indeed taller. Their hair was a bleached white-yellow and cut short against their head. There was no makeup on their face, and their eyes looked tired, like they had been wearing something that had been recently scrubbed off. Either way, it was incredibly late for someone to come over. So, either this was a welfare check—which Owen could believe from the week and a half that he'd known the man—or this was a booty call. If it was the latter, he should leave. But neither Sammy nor Levi acted like he was the squeaky third wheel. He was even able to settle back into the chair, while Levi and Sammy teased each other.

When Levi left for the restroom, Sammy scooted closer. "So you two met at his job?"

"Yeah," Owen replied. "He caught my eye. I mean, look at him, I felt like I had to beat off men and women with a stick to even talk to him. I actually had to redirect one of my friends away from him, but only because she seemed to make him uncomfortable. Then we started talking about a project and hanging out, and…I've kind of fallen for him."

Sammy leaned back against the couch from their cross-legged seat on the floor. "Kind of?" they teased, eyeing the borrowed clothing.

"As much as I wish, that had been a different kind of shower," Owen murmured. "I guess I was preoccupied with research all day and started to stink. He told me to go home or shower, and well."

"You took the choice to stay longer," Sammy replied, a quirk of a smile on their lips. "Good for you. Levi needs as many people in his corner as possible. I know almost nothing about his job, but I know it's a dangerous one. He pushes people away because of it. That you could get this close is a good sign."

Owen felt his heart flutter, even if what Sammy was saying wasn't true. Levi *was* trying to push him away. It wasn't even subtle. Owen watched daily as Levi rebuilt part of a crumbled wall, over and over. The only reason he was this close was because Owen knew the secret, and was trying to break it. A secret that Sammy didn't know about.

It had hurt the first time Owen had learned that Levi's best friend didn't know about the Blessing. Looking at Sammy's face, that knowledge hurt even more.

The walls that Levi built around himself became clearer the longer Owen and Sammy talked: it was a way to protect the people around him. More importantly, though, it was a way to push down the guilt of knowing what was going to kill Sammy's best friend. A guilt that Owen now carried too.

CHAPTER 12

For an entire week, Levi waited for the moment that everything was going to come crashing down. Owen and Sammy had traded numbers. They were hanging out at Levi's together, while Owen and Levi kept working. The research was moving at a snail's pace, with Levi or Owen hitting dead ends at every turn.

Through Sammy's presence, Levi learned Owen preferred Chinese takeout over pizza, and would eat anything sweet even if it was sour candy. When they got pizza, Owen preferred ham and pineapple over any other flavor combinations, which was another odd one for their collection. Levi was not a fan of pineapple on pizza, but he was more interested in there not being ham on his slice.

Owen also kept helping himself to Levi's shirts. Not the new expensive ones, the old worn in ones. First it was the "I heart men" shirt, and then it was an old band T-shirt, or long-sleeved shirt, or a hoodie. Owen still went home every night, and if he did wear something, he brought it back the next day, but it seemed to be a ritual now. Owen would get something on his clothes that might stain, so into the sink it went to soak or spot treat. Another borrowed shirt would then take its place. It insured that Owen always had an excuse to come back over and do it again.

While it was weird, Levi let it be. It seemed to make Owen happy, and there weren't many things that Levi felt comfortable doing that would make Owen happy, without letting him in closer.

Then it was the weekend again. Without the constant disruption of going to class, Owen and Levi had spent the day grasping at straws. Every search they made turned into a dead end, and it was a struggle to figure out the next steps. When Sammy stopped by that evening, Levi suggested it was time to take a breather.

Sammy and Owen were debating what movie to watch after dinner, when the pain hit. The smack to his forehead was followed by a dribble of blood and an ache in his rib. It hurt to breathe. His wrist ached on what was his good arm; he didn't think he had a good arm anymore. More, maybe? Or were was it just past injuries, flaring again when something new hit? Distantly, he could hear Owen's curse. Crap, Sammy was going to notice. But his head was throbbing too much to hold on to the thought. His vision was going dark. Shit.

What had Vicki gotten herself into now?

***

It was a Saturday night, and the second Saturday Owen had skipped going out. He didn't miss it, though.

What he hadn't expected was how much more comfortable he was around Levi and Sammy. They didn't nag him about his snacking, or the sweets that he liked to nibble on. No one cared that he might get sugar crystals from the sour candy on the furniture, as long as he tried to tidy up at the end of the day. Neither Sammy or Levi made snide comments about his weight, or that he might bring ants.

It was more than the snacking though. Levi would check in with Owen. He'd ask if Owen was okay with background noise, before moving to turn on the television, letting the news or old documentaries play through the public access channels from the old set. When the news was too much, Levi would switch to one that Owen didn't have access to anymore with the modern technology. The old set offered comforting sounds of static. The white noise covered the sounds of the world outside, or the noise from the neighboring apartments.

Earlier today, Owen had followed Levi to the nearby corner store to rent a movie and refill their snacks. It was the first time Owen had ventured out to one of the local establishments. He normally gathered supplies and brought them to Levi's, or sent money with Levi or Sammy when they wanted to pick up snacks, and he was in the middle of a project. But he wasn't buried in coursework, and Levi wanted his input.

Bars on the door and windows of the store greeted him, along with the goose pebbling of his arm; the static in the air from the anti-theft wards covering the walls of the place. At first glance, they seemed crude. The more that he looked, the more he realized that the feeling of being monitored by the wards was the same as the cameras on the side of town he grew up on. Their purpose was the same, even if the execution was different.

Years of foot traffic had worn down patterns in the speckled tan linoleum floors. The aisles were narrow, with barely enough room to pass another patron without bumping into them. Food overcrowded the shelves. Owen began to recognize items from Levi's kitchen. Boxed rice and noodle dishes, cans of vegetables and soups, bagged chips, crackers, pretzels, and cookies. Drink cases lined the back wall. There was a small section with gallons of milk, cartons of eggs, and packages of cheese. Freezer meals sat next to ice creams in flavors that Owen didn't recognize in neon bright colors. He'd never wanted to try bright green mint chip ice cream before, but now he had to find out what it was about.

"Don't overload yourself," Levi cautioned with a grin. "Remember, we have to walk back, and I only have one carrying arm right now."

"Spoiling all of my fun, I see," Owen teased, turning his attention back to the ice cream.

They'd returned home with several bags of chips and cookies, drinks, two cartons of ice cream, and a rented, well loved, copy of a horror movie. One that had been on Owen's list for a while, and one that Levi had seen more than a few times and was happy to share.

The break had been good for him; not looking at Vicki's face while she was doing something stupid was even better. For once, Owen was feeling good about his decision to let someone else do his job. To reclaim his weekends, when Levi stopped talking midsentence and started bleeding.

Cuts started forming on his forehead and his cheek. His eyes looked unfocused, and his arm drifted to hug his ribs.

Imaginary aches filled Owen as he watched the Blessing take over, bleeding the injuries through.

"Shit, oh fuck," Owen slid off the couch to look directly at Levi, trying to put the clues together. What had Vicki done? It was early enough in the night that they couldn't have been partying long. She should have been dancing or fucking with Edwin for at least a few more hours.

Sammy let out a yelp. "What the fuck? How?"

"Do any of these injuries make sense?" Owen asked, trying to calm himself, as he looked for the source. "Head, ribs...wrist. Oh, shit..." A scattering of cuts along Levi's other hand seemed to pull the pieces together. "Car accident, maybe? None of these look like a fight."

"What are you talking about?" Sammy asked, their voice high and thready. Hesitant to move at all, they dropped to their knees on the floor next to Owen to get a better look. Sammy's hands hovered, like they were afraid to touch. "What's happening?"

"I can't explain all of it, and Levi will kill me if I mention too much," Owen said, watching how dazed Levi was. Concussion? Did concussions get passed through too?

"Levi?" Owen asked, trying to remember what he was supposed to do in the case of a concussion. "Levi, can you hear me? How many fingers am I holding up?"

He tried to stop shaking while he held up a few fingers. The slow, almost nonexistent response was enough. Four was not the right answer.

"I think someone got into a car accident and Levi got the injuries instead," Owen explained, heart pounding in his chest. He'd said someone and not Vicki, right?

"Of course he did," Sammy replied, their words sounding like a bit-off curse.

"We need to lay him down and check for other wounds," Owen suggested, trying to be careful of the bad shoulder and his spine. "Can you get the first aid kit?"

Sammy crossed the room in only a few seconds, as Owen ran his fingers over Levi's scalp, checking for bleeding. Only when his hands came away clean did he start looking for anything he may have missed elsewhere.

"You're awfully calm about this," Sammy said. The kit rattled in their trembling grip.

"I'm not. I'm terrified and pissed," Owen replied, fighting to stay in control and not drop something, or worse. He was continuing to look for any other bleeding, bruising, or tenderness. "And this stupid lump will protest if we try to take him to the hospital."

Owen didn't know what one was supposed to do about bruised or broken ribs. He hated every idea he had. Either Owen could break Levi's trust and possibly get him killed by taking him to the hospital, or do an internet search, treat this himself, miss something and let Levi die on this couch from something preventable.

"But you knew?" Sammy asked.

"Yes, I knew, I've known since the cut on his arm," Owen replied, wishing that he didn't have to mark the stages of his relationship by the freshest scars on Levi's body. "The person who put Levi in this position is dangerous."

Memories of back when his father wasn't the head of security flashed through his mind. The late-night phone calls that lead to Owen alone in the middle of the night. Owen pretending to be asleep, when his dad got home in different clothes than he'd left in. The harsh smell of chemicals that clung to his father as he took everything he had with him to the shower.

Owen let out a shuddering breath as he continued. "Very dangerous. Would kill both of us and Levi if it got out that we knew."

Opening the enormous first aid kit, Owen flipped through to find alcohol pads to clean up the cuts that he'd found. The scrapes along his forehead and arms were the most obvious, though he was seeing blood through Levi's shirt again. Levi wasn't out of it, but he was mumbling and his eyes weren't exactly focused. He kept trying to stand up; Owen gently pushed him back onto the couch.

"I've got a few healing scrolls in my bag," Owen said, nodding to the backpack. "They won't fix everything, but maybe we can use them to clear the concussion and his ribs? I hope I can figure out how to use them."

"Healing scrolls?" Sammy asked, already moving to grab them. "I know how to use them a bit. I've only held them once or twice for real injuries. I've got a few clients that use them to hide evidence of their nights out."

Owen tucked that information away as he continued to clean and bandage. "I just wish I knew if there was anything else wrong," Owen admitted, his heart pounding over a knot of nausea in his stomach.

"That's where I can help," Sammy replied, rolling up their sleeves. The tattoos that Owen had seen glimpses of in the past were on prominent display right now, the forests and plants and trees. And there was something else. Something in the background that caught Owen's eye. It looked familiar, but also out of place in a tattoo.

"You want to know why this idiot has stayed alive so long?" Sammy asked, putting their hands on either side of his head.

"Sammy, don't," Levi was whimpering. "Sammy!"

"I've kept this man breathing before. This is nothing," Sammy promised over Levi's protests. The tattoo glowed, and now Owen recognized it. Sammy was a Healer. A true Healer. Levi had been protecting his friend from more than just the Townsends; he'd been making sure his friend didn't get found out.

Owen's eyes grew wide as he watched the magic start to knit Levi back together. With every passing moment, sweat built on Sammy's brow and their face grew paler. He'd heard healing strained the caster, but this was more than he'd expected.

"If someone asks, we used those spells, yeah?" Sammy prompted, their voice shaky. "Save those for when I'm not around to help."

"Yeah," Owen replied, taking the scrolls and holding them close. He didn't know how he'd gained even a little trust from these two. Both of them had gone through so much together that even getting to be allowed part of their lives felt amazing.

His phone cut through the moment with a stupid ringtone he'd picked out years ago. "Vicki," he said, reading the caller ID. "I've got to take this. Just focus on internal and life-threatening stuff. We can use those for the rest..." He waved a hand towards the spells before he answered. "Vicki?" he asked, trying to sound confused.

"Owen, oh thank god, I tried calling Dad and then your dad and no one answered," Vicki replied, sounding drunk. "Can you get me? My car is broken."

Owen had to fight the urge to say no shit. "Are you okay?"

"I'm fine. The Blessing took care of it for me, you know that," Vicki replied.

Right. She'd been driving drunk.

"Where are you?" Owen asked.

"Uh, I'll send you a pin," Vicki replied. "The street signs are a little wobbly."

"Is anyone else with you?" Owen asked.

"Brooke, but I moved her to the driver's seat," Vicki replied.

"Is Brooke okay?" Owen asked.

"Why do you care?" Vicki asked, and Owen knew that voice. Vicki was about to have another tantrum. *Shit.* He'd already started motioning for a second phone to call 911 and let them sort everything out. But in this state, Vicki might hurt herself just because she could. Because the wounds would just go to Levi instead.

"I'm just trying to figure out what happened, and what story I'm going to use when I pick you up," Owen replied. "How about Alicia and Edwin? Do I need seats for them?"

"They stayed back at the club," Vicki replied. "Janie's not here either, thank you very much. Didn't need that mothering hen telling me how to live my life."

"So you and Brooke, okay? I'm on my way," Owen replied. "Send me the address when I hang up, okay?"

"Yes, dad," Vicki grumbled. The line went dead.

Owen felt his knees go weak as he stared at her contact picture on the brightly-lit screen.

Sammy's hands were no longer touching Levi's head; they were inspecting the scrolls instead.

"How's he doing?" Owen asked.

"As good as he can," Sammy replied as they rolled their wrists. There were circles under their eyes. They looked like they had just done a 48-hour finals cram.

Levi was trying to get up. This time, Owen and Sammy let him.

"I told you not to do that," Levi grumbled, his arm braced across his ribs. His eyes landed on the scrolls. "They're just bruised. I'm fine. What was the phone call?"

Owen looked down at it; nothing yet. "Vicki. She crashed the car, and it sounds like she moved Brooke to the driver's seat to take the blame."

"Shit," Levi replied.

"I think I'm Vicki's get-out-of-jail-free card," Owen replied as his phone chimed with the location pin. She wasn't anywhere remotely close.

"She would never see jail, regardless of what she did," Levi replied. "Her dad would have covered it up."

"Doesn't mean that Brooke should take the blame," Owen cursed. "What do I do?"

"Call in the emergency, someone's hurt even if it's not Vicki," Levi replied, leaning back against the couch. There was pain on his face as he closed his eyes. He let in a sharp inhale, before speaking again. "Then call your dad, tell him that Vicki just called you to pick her up, and that it might be a mess. Leave nothing that could incriminate you. We don't want whatever mess that Vicki got herself in hurting you."

What about you? Owen wanted to ask. If Levi wouldn't get hurt by it, he didn't know how he could keep himself from punching Vicki when he saw her. This whole situation was messing with his mind.

"Don't die while I'm gone," Owen said, wishing that he could give Levi a hug, or even take his hand, without hurting him.

"Don't worry. If I do, Sammy will drag me out of hell for both of you to give me a lecture," Levi replied, reaching out. That hand, Owen squeezed, gently. It felt like a broken heart.

***

Vicki leaned against the side of the building, watching the lights of the emergency vehicles around her car. High rises blocked out most of the sky. Heating along the streets kept Vicki from freezing. Janie's condo and Owen's apartment were supposed to be around here, but Vicki didn't recognize any of the buildings. Not that she was headed towards either when the car slammed into the wall.

Brooke was being loaded into the back of an ambulance, something about a head injury or back, something like that at least. Vicki was injury free, even if she'd had to wipe away some of the blood that the Blessing had left behind. If she were to redesign the spell, that would be one thing that she would change. She was really sick of it messing up her fit.

The buzz of the alcohol was lifting, and it *sucked*. She'd been working hard to get that, and now it was ruined because of a stupid vehicle block that hadn't been on this road before. Looking at her phone, she grumbled. What was taking Owen this long? His apartment was right around the block. That's why she'd called him. That, and he was the only one that wouldn't imagine starting a lecture with her.

Tapping her foot against the pavement, she scrolled through her phone to try calling him again.

She could hear his phone ringing and looked up to see Owen hurrying up the block. He stopped to check, only to hang up on her. Rude.

"Sorry, I had to park around the block to avoid the emergency vehicles," Owen said when he jogged up to her.

"What took you so long?" Vicki demanded.

"I wasn't at home when you called," Owen replied, pulling his jacket closer. "Where's Brooke?"

"Ambulance took her away a few minutes ago," Vicki replied. "Cops think I'm a bystander. Can I go home now?"

"Yeah," Owen replied. Even with his arms tucked around himself, he was shivering in the cold. Wuss.

"You're a good friend," Vicki complemented, giving Owen a smile. Maybe she had pushed him away too quickly. She was the one that had purposely planned trips to the nightclub and didn't invite him. Every friend group needed someone like Owen. She'd forgotten how nice it had been to have someone that was always willing to drop everything to help. "No one else picked up the phone."

Owen hadn't been hanging out with them for the past week, ever since he'd talked with Alicia and rushed out of the room.

"It's a good thing the Blessing was there to protect me," Vicki continued.

"Yup," Owen replied, almost before the end of Vicki's sentence. Rude.

"Who knows what injuries I could have had?" Vicki continued. Owen's shoulders hunched over and his eyes grew tighter and darker. "They healed so fast," she continued, looking for any untoward reaction. "I might have had a concussion for a moment, my mind was so fuzzy, and the pain in my ribs."

Owen was clenching his jaw! *What?*

"Does me talking about the Blessing make you uncomfortable? I didn't crash my car on purpose," Vicki pointed out.

"Look, I've had a rough night," Owen said. "Hearing about my friends getting hurt, whether it was Blessed away, doesn't make it any better. You could have died behind the wheel, and we don't know what the Blessing would have done about that. So don't make light of it."

"You are such a worrywart," Vicki replied with a laugh. Didn't he understand that the point of the Blessing was that she could just live her life as she pleased? The only thing that it couldn't fix was her overbearing father, but that's what alcohol was for.

Owen didn't reply. Instead, he walked her to the car and opened the passenger door. Everything seemed normal until they were on the road, and the coat dropped open. Now Vicki could see the shirt that was underneath, and it was unlike anything that she had seen Owen wear before. It was white with "I heart Men" on it, but that wasn't the part that caught her eye. No, there was a fresh patch of blood on it.

"Are you bleeding?" Vicki asked, scrunching up her nose.

Owen glanced down. "Shit. No. A friend had a kitchen accident. I helped him get patched up, but I didn't realize that I had got some on me."

"A friend? What friend?" Vicki asked.

"Levi," Owen replied. "We were going to have a movie night when you called."

"Is that where you've been this week?" Vicki asked, her eyes widening. "Levi's place?"

Owen shrugged, not taking his eyes off the road. The street lights changed the shadows over his features. "I've been working on a puzzle. Tonight was the first time in a while that I was just going to hang out with someone."

"What puzzle?" Vicki asked, leaning closer. Owen's car wasn't as nice as her own. The transition between gears wasn't as smooth, lurching her back and forth as she leaned away from the seat. She leaned back, a flash of dizziness from the movement rolling through her gut. "Is it Blessing related?"

"Maybe, kind of, not really," Owen replied, stumbling over his words. "Vicki, please don't lean closer. I'm driving and even you shouldn't get into an accident twice in one night."

"Why are you babying me?" Vicki asked in a flare of anger.

"Because I don't want to see you get hurt. I know it doesn't last, but what if the Blessing gives out someday and that hurt sticks?" Owen asked, anger and grief splashing across his face.

Vicki leaned back in her seat. Owen had to suck all the fun out of her teasing by turning on the waterworks.

Owen unmuted the sound system; talk radio and sports stats filled the car. No, thank you. None of that for her. Vicki reached forwards and flipped through the stations, changing the radio as she pleased, and getting more and more annoyed with each passing moment. None of Owen's preset stations had anything that she liked to listen to, and he was making no move to fix it!

She shot him a glare before she froze. The car slowing down drew her eyes to the outside world again. This time, she knew exactly where she was.

Turning into the driveway, the headlights washed over a pair of individuals that were standing on the path. One a short man with the light of a cigarette near his mouth, the other almost a head taller, and looking out of place. Vicki's stomach sank as she recognized them. These weren't security, or some dumb servant that she could just walk past or order away. Mr. Mills was there with his cigarette, and standing beside him was her father.

Owen pulled closer. The headlights illuminated both of them; the shadows emphasized the anger on her father's face. Shit. She was in so much trouble.

Reaching through the car, she looked for anything that she could use to cover up what had happened. "Do you have any mints?" Vicki asked, opening the glove compartment, the little cubbies in the console, anything that she could reach.

"I don't think so, but you can look," Owen replied, sounding tired of all things. Not worried, not angry, not anything—just tired.

"You've got to help me!" Vicki said, panic filling her voice. Her breath was awful, and if her dad was out here, he knew everything already.

"Sorry," Owen replied, parking the car and taking the keys out. He addressed both their fathers as he stepped out. "Evening, Mr. Townsend, hey Dad."

"Owen, thank you for bringing my daughter home safe," Father replied.

"It was the least I could do," Owen said, with an uneasy smile that didn't seem to belong on his face.

Vicki wanted to curl away from the door. Maybe she could hide here until her father's anger subsided.

Mr. Mills seemed to have a different idea as he walked over and opened it for her. "It's time to come on out. Your father was worried about you," he said, holding the door open wide.

The moment Vicki stepped out, her stomach lurched. She leaned over to spray vomit across one side of the driveway and into the grass. Her head was pounding again, and she couldn't tell if this was her hangover was starting, or something else.

They guided her into the house after that; the lecture was scheduled for the morning. She was not looking forwards to it, but at least it could wait until the world stopped spinning.

***

Owen just wanted to leave. He'd done his good deed for the day: didn't blow up at Vicki at her reckless behavior, and pushed down every ounce of self-respect that he had while she'd messed with his radio. The smug satisfaction, as Vicki realized she was already screwed, only lasted for a second. Saying no to her plea for help to cover up her vodka soaked breath? It could have made up for the phone call. But it did nothing for both Brooke and Levi, who had to live with her choices tonight.

Trapped in a conversation room with his father and the Devil himself, Owen could think of a hundred other places he would like to be.

"Can you tell me what happened?" Mr. Townsend asked.

"I wasn't there," Owen started, glad that Vicki wasn't in the room with them. If the Devil knew he'd been hanging out with Levi instead, it could be terrible. Though, his dad knew that was where he was, and his dad didn't know about Levi's curse. "I was working on a project, so I declined going out and partying this weekend. It's not like I get to enjoy those nights when I go, since I got put into the role of designated driver last year."

"So you were elsewhere," Mr. Townsend agreed.

"I was elsewhere, and then I got the call from Vicki that she was in an accident and needed a ride," Owen replied, trying to toe the line between telling the truth, and keeping parts of the story held back. "She said something about moving Brooke, and it sounded like she'd been the one driving, but I could have misinterpreted that. What I know is that they loaded Brooke into an ambulance before I got there, and no one was paying attention to Vicki."

A grim look crossed over Dad's face, and Owen tried not to spend the energy to figure that out. He'd spiral, wondering what was behind that expression. Had it crossed his father's mind that Owen could have been the one on the stretcher tonight? Or was he disappointed Owen wasn't there to stop it? Nerves ate through his insides, but Owen forced them down. He could panic later.

"Did you see anything else?" Mr. Townsend asked.

"Like what?" Owen asked. "I didn't look at the car too much. I think it hit those blockades that keep cars from going where people are walking? The retractable ones? But there were too many emergency vehicles to get a closer look."

"Anything else about Vicki?" her father prompted.

Owen thought about it,. Not because he didn't know what her father was asking, but because he wanted to point the questions away from the Blessing. "Vicki…how do I say this kindly? She's been hard to be around lately, ever since she nearly got shot," Owen replied, lacing his fingers together. "It could be the fear of her getting hurt getting to her brain, because she's been acting risky lately, and pushing everyone that asks for caution away. I'm terrified of seeing her get hurt, but she is just laughing in our faces…"

Mr. Townsend frowned. "I need you to answer this honestly, boy," he said. Owen froze, not even chancing a breath. "Has she attempted to hurt herself?"

Owen nodded, pulling his jacket tighter around him. The pressure was almost a hug. He forced himself to cut it out and set his hands at his sides. He could not show fear in front of this man. It was going to get out; she'd been so obvious about it. God, he hoped he was making the right choice.

"I've been trying not to think about it," Owen replied. His hands were shaking, and he had to grasp them together to make it stop. He didn't want to hurt Levi, but lying to this man was dangerous. "I didn't want to see it, and I'm trying to forget it."

"Mills, step out of the room, please?" Mr. Townsend said.

Owen looked up.

His dad was still sitting there, looking conflicted.

"Go on, Dad," Owen said, trying to smile. He didn't think it translated well, but it was the thought that counted. Right? He wasn't about to get murdered or anything. As soon as that thought crossed his mind, Owen tried to shake it away. Nausea bubbled in his gut that he had to swallow down with his fear. He could not let his dad get caught up in this too.

"I'll-" Owen tried, his voice shaky. He took a breath and pulled that smile onto his face again. This time, the words didn't catch. "I'll catch up with you soon?"

"I will not harm your son," Mr. Townsend promised. It seemed to hold very little weight.

Still, Dad got up and listened. "I'll be just outside the door," he said before he walked out.

Owen held his breath until the doors clicked shut. Only then did he dare to look the Devil in the eye.

"What did Vicki do?" Mr. Townsend asked.

With his finger, Owen drew a line down his forearm. "She took a knife, cut her arm like that…there was so much blood. Then she was waving the bloody knife at us and telling us to stop babying her because she couldn't get hurt. It freaked us out."

"Us? Who else?" Mr. Townsend asked.

"I know Janie and Brooke were there. Alicia and Edwin were in the house, but they weren't in the kitchen," Owen explained. "It freaked me out, so after we took the knife away from her, and I knew she wasn't bleeding anymore, I left. I don't enjoy seeing people get hurt, and her choosing to cut her arm like that, I just couldn't…" Owen looked at Mr. Townsend, trying to meet his eyes enough to make the point. Even that small movement took effort. Terror created tremors in his hands at being in the room with someone so dangerous, while rage that had settled into his gut from the injustice of it all. Levi had signed up to protect Vicki from the outside world, but Vicki had chosen to do that all on her own, no outside world required. His mind was dashing through what he could say to sound like he didn't know what he was talking about at all.

"We all know this isn't something to talk about, sir," Owen said. "I know you've got magic, and this is probably a special protective ward on Vicki to keep her safe, but it worries me she could test its limits. I don't want to be standing there when the protective spell has lost all of its power."

"Why did none of you tell me she was harming herself?" Mr. Townsend asked, his face dark.

Owen looked down at his hands again. The lie was easy, wrapped up in enough truth that he hoped it sounded real. He could imagine it would be, if he hadn't known the truth. "I can't speak for the others. I was trying to pretend that it wasn't happening, that I'd dreamed it. I had half convinced myself before tonight. But with Brooke getting loaded into an ambulance, and not a scratch on Vicki?"

Owen's throat was dry as he tried to swallow down the lie. His next words felt closer to honesty as his mind went back to Levi, bruised and bleeding. "What if that's me next?"

Mr. Townsend leaned back in his chair, looking thoughtful, and Owen looked down again. As much as he hated how terrified he was, loathed his shaking hands and the tremor in his voice, it helped to cover up his anger. That feeling didn't belong to someone that was watching his friend get hurt over and over from their stupidity, it was from watching the others get hurt around her. It was from watching Levi get hurt time and time again, knowing that someday his life was going to be forfeit, because of Vicki's stupid choices.

"I see," Mr. Townsend replied. "What could I offer you to keep this a secret?"

"Offer? What?" Owen sputtered out. Alarm bells in his head started going off. If he said that it wouldn't take anything to prove his loyalty, would that make him a suspect? If he asked for something, would that make him buyable? "I don't understand, Mr. Townsend. I don't want to tell anyone about this. I didn't even want to tell you, but this is your daughter."

"This information could be worth a lot of money," Mr. Townsend replied.

"Telling this information to someone could cost my friend their life," Owen shot back. "No amount of money can bring someone back from the dead. No amount of money could get rid of the guilt if my voice was the cause."

Mr. Townsend had a smile on his face, but Owen didn't know what that meant. God, what if his words were going to sign the death warrant to someone that he cared about? He wished he'd never picked up the phone tonight.

"Where were you tonight when you got the phone call?" Mr. Townsend asked.

It felt like someone had dropped ice cubes down his back. "What?" Owen asked, his voice breaking.

"There's blood on your shirt," Mr. Townsend said. Owen crossed his arm over his stomach. "Yes, there. Whose blood is that?"

"A friend had a kitchen accident," Owen explained, repeating the same lie as before. "I didn't know they got blood on me until I was already driving to pick up Vicki."

"I could pull it up on your phone," Mr. Townsend suggested.

"Why is this so important?" Owen replied, while a cold fear flashed through him.

But fear had kept Levi stuck, alone in that apartment, not allowed to have any friends other than Sammy. Levi could have friends. *He* could have friends. "I'm allowed to hang out with people outside of Vicki's circle."

"Because I heard from your father that you were hanging out with a man named Levi," Mr. Townsend replied. "A man that I employ."

The blood drained from Owen's face, and all of the air left the room. All those spells that he had gathered. Would they be enough to get him whole again? Was there even a point?

Owen tried to pull the fear to the forefront one last time, but all he had left was anger. He cast his eyes down to prevent the glare that he wanted to throw.

"You didn't say she earlier," Mr. Townsend explained, watching him with knowing eyes. "When you were talking about your friend that you wanted to protect. You didn't say she. You said them. Your eyes flash with anger every time you mention Vicki's name, and you haven't been able to drop the contempt from your face ever since your father left the room."

Owen raised his eyes to Mr. Townsend. Whatever emotion he had there was what the Devil would get. "I wouldn't sell Vicki's safety to anyone." Owen said, fighting to stay collected. "And there's nothing you could offer that I want. If you were to ruin me and my family, I still wouldn't sell Vicki's secret, and if you were to offer me all the money in the world, I wouldn't trade it for Vicki's safety."

"What if someone were to offer a way to break him from my grasp?" Mr. Townsend asked.

Owen grit his teeth. "Anyone that could break the spell wouldn't need anything from me to do it. They could get to you, or Vicki, without me—" Owen stopped himself from declaring anything. "Are you done with your loyalty questions?" Owen said, standing up. His legs shook. The urge to flee fought with the need to prove his point. "I have someone that is suffering from a concussion and bruised ribs that need some of my spell scrolls, so that he can keep taking the injuries that your daughter keeps causing herself."

Mr. Townsend was going to have him followed the moment he got back in his car; there was no reason to lie. "Also, no, he did not tell me anything. I figured it out when I was standing next to him, while your daughter got injured."

With that, Owen walked away. As soon as he crossed the threshold, the tingle of magic left his skin. The office wards? Truth spells? Compulsions? Owen didn't know. The knowledge that magic had been active in that room ate at him. He should have left immediately. He'd said too much, given away too much, and put so many others in danger for it. He walked with his head held high, until he stepped into the hall where his dad was waiting. Under his father's gaze, he just sagged. He wanted to hug his dad and sob, confess that he was making mistake after mistake. Instead, he pushed all of that down.

"I'm heading back out," Owen said, tucking his hands into his pockets and feeling for his car keys. "If I can, I'm sleeping over at a friend's place, but I'll text you if I'm going home."

"Heading to Levi's?" Dad asked.

"Yeah," Owen replied, reaching up and rubbing his eyes to stop the tears. "He said he would wait for me, but he might already be asleep."

"Have fun, and be safe," Dad said, worry still on his face.

Both of them could hear Mr. Townsend call for Owen's father, and Owen didn't want to stay to find out how it went. He could handle only so much worry tonight.

He took the drive to try to settle his thoughts. With each slowly passing mile, Owen's mind concocted a new worst-case scenario, until he was stuck with a dozen overlapping ways to watch Levi bleed out. Eventually Owen caved and turned on the radio, flipping through the stations until he landed on some kind of talk radio. Every time his mind started to wander, he switched the channel. Owen was nearly out of stations when he parked the car again.

The apartment was dark when Sammy let him in.

"Oh good," they said, with a tired smile. "Levi's been refusing to fall asleep."

"He should be recovering," Owen replied, sliding his coat off and glaring at the bloodstain on his shirt that had given him so much grief tonight. When he slipped into Levi's room, he found him in bed, sitting in the low light of a single lamp.

"You're back," Levi said, sounding surprised.

"You're still awake," Owen pointed out, stripping out of his borrowed shirt and digging through the drawers to find another one. "Why aren't you sleeping?"

"Worried about you," Levi replied.

The fluttering butterflies in his stomach escaped in the form of a smile. "I was worried about you, too. That's why I came back. Get into any trouble while I was away?"

Levi shrugged, which prompted Sammy to explain all of the ways that Levi had been a terrible patient while Owen was gone. From trying to drink a beer, even though he shouldn't have alcohol after a concussion, to not counting out the pain meds he wanted to take, which prompted Sammy to take over.

It was the first time that Owen was hearing about a belligerent Levi. Sure, the man was stubborn on a good day, but the way that Sammy was describing the behavior was sending his mind flashing back to Alicia and Brooke after a night of drinking. Annoying, but manageable. Nothing like Vicki's drunken recklessness, as evidenced by tonight. But he didn't want to think about her right now.

"Considering everything, it's a miracle you're alive," Sammy grumbled, scooting Levi to the middle of the bed. "There's room for you on the other side," they pointed out. "We'll keep this one from escaping in the middle of the night."

"I'm not going to escape," Levi explained.

Owen and Sammy shared a look. Then he crossed over to the far side of the bed and pulled back the covers.

"I'm sure you won't," Owen teased, kicking off his shoes and climbing in.

Levi puffed out his cheeks in annoyance, and Owen let out a giggle. Sammy reached over and patted the air above Levi's head. It had Owen laughing even harder.

The stress and relief of the night burst forth, and Owen didn't stop giggling until tears were in his eyes. Levi reached for his hand and ran his thumb along the back of Owen's hand, calming the giggles in its slow grounding motion. The emotions roiling inside of Owen were still trapped in his throat as he croaked out a, "thank you."

"The magic I used earlier should have cleared the concussion itself," Sammy said, voice soft with sleep. "But if you hear me waking him in the middle of the night, I'm double-checking for my peace of mind."

Owen nodded as the light on Sammy's side of the bed clicked off and the room was plunged into darkness.

With Sammy there, it felt like one big sleepover, but Owen was still getting to curl up in the bed with his crush. Having sex with someone was one thing, but laying there with no expectations except some possible cuddling, bedhead, and morning breath…that was something different.

The bed was big enough to accommodate, but small enough that they had to scoot close. Owen curled as close as he could, feeling the heat of the other two bodies radiating in bed with him, listening to gentle breaths.

Closing his eyes, Owen hoped for pleasant dreams, if he dreamed at all.

CHAPTER 13

A hand shaking her shoulder was the first sign of morning. Then the rolling ache and pounding migraine hit with full force. The sheets against her skin were cool and crumpled under the covers. Her clothes felt too tight, like she'd slept in jeans, even though her pajamas were loose silk. Laying amongst her soft pillows, she was aware the nausea was gone, but she didn't know for how long. Morning light drifted in through the windows, which meant that servants had already come through and drawn back the curtains. Her eye mask had slipped off while she'd slept. Squeezing her eyes shut, she felt around for it so that she could fall back to sleep.

"Miss Vicki, your father would like to talk to you," a voice said, shaking her shoulder again with each word. "You have a few minutes to shower and drink this. It will help."

Grabbing her covers and rolling over, Vicki waved the servant off. It would be so simple to stay in bed and rest, the idea of it dancing in front of her eyes. The image of her angry father ripped away any thought of it.

Rolling out of bed, she grabbed the drink and chugged it. Magic tingled on her tongue; the slightly syrupy taste made her stomach roll before the spell kicked in. Her headache cleared within a few moments. Quick showers were not her favorite, but there wasn't time for anything else. Time was money, or something like that.

Still, she made sure to look presentable. Her skincare and makeup were done, her hair styled, and her clothing chosen with purpose. Dressing as she would to go to college, which was as close to business as her closet allowed. Looking like a slob would only anger her father more and cause another lecture on looking weak. Besides, she could draw out her morning if she took her time. It was well over an hour later when she was strolling into her father's home office.

"Vicki, so good of you to make it," Father stated, motioning to a seat.

Vicki bit back a response as she picked out a chair. "Good morning to you too, father."

"I have several accounts from last night," Father stated, turning to face her, "of you getting behind the wheel of the car, completely intoxicated, with another friend trying to be a voice of reason. That friend is now recovering from the accident that you caused. The accident that you poorly attempted to pin on her."

"Poorly?" Vicki asked.

"Poorly," Father replied. "Your crash happened directly under a live video that showed you stumbling out of the car, and then moving your injured friend to the driver's seat. Do you understand that if Brooke had gone to jail for your mistake, it could have caused a cascading effect? Her family would have found this video, and pointed their fingers back at you. You, who walked away from that crash without a scratch?"

"What was I supposed to do? You didn't answer your phone, and I didn't have a scratch on me. No one thought I had been there," Vicki said.

"All of your friends would have pointed their fingers," Father replied. "Especially since you slit your wrist in front of them to prove that the Blessing worked." Father's eyes flashed with anger. "You gave that knowledge away because you were upset that they were babying you?"

"You don't understand," Vicki explained, hurriedly. This wasn't fair. Her father was never supposed to find out about that! *Owen.* Fury bubbled under her skin as she tried to reclaim whatever lies he'd spewed the night before. "They were supposed to be on my side, my friends. Then Levi just showed up and Owen was all over him, and Brooke had a crush on him, and Alicia was back together with Edwin because of that stupid trip you paid for that I couldn't go on."

Father cut her off. "I didn't pay to send your friends away for that week. Whomever suggested that I paid for any trip lied."

Vicki glared at him as she continued her original point. "And all of them were acting like I was too fragile to do anything."

"So you proved you were invincible," Father said. "If your life wasn't in active danger right now, I would take it away for your insolence. The Blessing is supposed to protect you from others, not from yourself."

Vicki rolled her eyes. "You can't take it away."

"Try me again, put yourself in danger again, and I will have your Blessing removed and lock you in this house," Father replied, his eyes burning. "Then you will have to face the consequences of your injuries the way everyone else has to."

Vicki almost choked on air as she nodded.

"Do you understand?" Father asked.

"Yes, I understand," Vicki replied, looking down.

"Good, now I have to deal with the rest of the mess that you left me," Father replied. "I have informed the staff that you are to remain at the house until it's time for you to leave for school."

Biting back what she wanted to say, Vicki walked out with her head held high as she shut the door behind her. She didn't slam it; that would have been childish.

How dare he trap her inside again? For the second time since school had started, and she hadn't even taken midterms yet. Locking herself in her suite, Vicki dropped onto her bed. First, she wanted more sleep. Then, maybe she'd redecorate her room. Demand the space to be repainted. Her closet needed to be reorganized.

Her stomach grumbled in protest, and with it, she debated a hunger strike. If Vicki was going to be stuck inside this house, then everyone else was going to be miserable with her.

***

Owen awoke the next morning to his phone ringing, pulling him out of a deep sleep. It was more than he'd slept in weeks. The room was comfortably warm; he could easily fall back into it, if it wasn't for his phone. He reached for the nightstand on his right out of habit, but he only found warm bodies. He didn't remember having anyone sleep over, but it would come to him, probably.

Reaching to the left, he found the phone by touch alone and pulled it to his cheek.

"Mmm, hello?" Owen asked. His voice was soft, still caked in sleep.

"Owen?" The fear in Alicia's voice tore through drowsiness until his heart raced. "Did you hear?"

"Hear what?" Owen asked. Memories of last night slowly trickled in. The car accident. Watching injuries spawn on Levi's skin in horror, powerless to make it stop. Climbing into bed with Levi and Sammy, to keep Levi from wandering away in the middle of the night.

Cold terror tightened in his chest and he reached out to feel the bodies next to him. Warm. They were both warm. His panic eased, breath slowing into something closer to normal. Owen never wanted to see that again. He didn't think he could forget it for the rest of his life.

"Brooke's in the hospital," Alicia's voice was hitching as she spoke. "She and Vicki left the club last night and crashed Vicki's car. She's in really bad shape."

"Bad shape?" Owen asked, keeping his voice quiet to try not to wake the others. He could feel Levi moving in bed beside him and lowered his voice. "Who's been to the hospital?"

"Edwin, Janie, and I are there now," Alicia replied. "I stepped outside to make the call. Can you come down?"

"Yeah, give me a minute," Owen replied, looking down at the bed in longing. It wouldn't take much to curl back up with Levi and Sammy, to pretend that last night hadn't happened for a few more hours. "Which hospital?"

Alicia relayed everything he needed to find them; she was always good for that. "Thanks, we're freaking out over here," Alicia told him.

"Yeah, I'm across town, so give me a bit," Owen explained before saying goodbye. He was wide awake, or as awake as he could be without coffee and a cold shower.

Pulling on the pair of jeans he'd shucked onto the floor, Owen began to track down his errant socks. The shirt he'd borrowed last night in the dark would have to do; he checked there wasn't anything crass across his chest at least. The faded band tee was from a group Sammy had introduced him to this past week; he made a note to switch his car's stereo to play their latest album. It would make the drive feel like Sammy and Levi were there still with him. Running his fingers through his hair, he might still be in better shape than any of the others, even with the bedhead.

Wallet and keys found, shoes added to his now socked feet, and yet he stopped. How could he just leave without waking anyone up? Were either of them the type to wake up violently? Owen didn't want to leave without telling someone. Even leaving a note could be a cause for misinterpretation.

"Go check on your Brooke," Levi murmured. Owen just about jumped at the sound. Levi's eyes were still closed. In the dim light of the room, it looked like he was still sleeping. "I can see you hovering. We'll be here when you get back."

"Uh, yeah," Owen replied, giving Levi a smile. "Be back soon."

The sleep-filled response that he got back didn't sound like words, so Owen took them as "get going" and did just that.

He turned the lock before he left. It wasn't the same as the dead bolts and chain Levi did up every time he left, but the main lock was the only one he could set on his way out. As trusted as he was, they had not gifted him a key.

The drive to the hospital was a slow one. Owen only stopped on the way to grab a set of energy drinks. If he had to guess, they'd either had less sleep than he did, or none at all.

Janie was the first one to call his name when he stepped into the waiting room.

It had been a long time since he'd been to a hospital, but it looked the same as he remembered. There was a nurse's station between him and the rooms beyond, where glass walls and doors opened into single bedrooms. He could barely make out the shape of the first. A privacy curtain blocked the contents of the room further down the hall. Somewhere back there, Brooke was being afforded her own private room and space to recover.

Arms around her stomach, Janie moved towards him. Beside her, Alicia and Edwin sat in a set of vinyl chairs. Edwin's arm was across her back; he was drawing circles on her far shoulder. Alicia remained focused on a spot on the speckled gray floor. The air was filled with the sharp smell of chemicals, beeping monitors, and the buzz of magic. Even for those that could afford it, healing scrolls and Healers could only do so much. The rest was modern medicine and hope.

There were tired bags under Janie's already bloodshot eyes. Owen couldn't tell if her eyes were that red because she'd been awake all night, because she'd been crying, or both. Janie hadn't been out last night either. He and Janie were in the same boat, sharing the responsibility of not being there. But Owen didn't feel the same guilt.

The realization of it hit him out of nowhere. Monitoring Vicki wasn't his job anymore. It hadn't been for a while. He glanced over at the others. Did they know it wasn't his job anymore? The weight of the grocery bag felt heavy in his arms.

"I brought energy drinks," Owen offered, offering the plastic bag. "What happened last night?"

"We went out, like we always do," Alicia said. "Vicki had been partying hard, and Brooke had been trying to keep up, like she does. We ended up separating from them. They were drinking in the booth, and we were out on the dance floor. By the time that we got back upstairs, the booth was empty, and we had a slew of voicemails and text messages on our phones."

"That makes sense," Owen said, rubbing his eyes. "I was the last one Vicki called last night. She needed a ride home from the wreck."

"So you drove her home?" Alicia asked, taking one of the energy drinks.

"I couldn't leave her out there," Owen replied. "She had already convinced the officers that she was just passing by, and who knows what kind of damage she could do if left alone. Or what her dad would do if he knew that all of us turned her away."

The memory of his conversation with Mr. Townsend came back with a shiver. Janie and Edwin made a similar involuntary response, while Alicia looked off into the distance. It took time for her to shake herself out of it. No wonder people called him the Devil.

Janie, however, just nodded. "I would have done the same if I'd heard my phone ring," she replied. She had taken none of the drinks, instead choosing to rub her eyes.

"So, I never saw Brooke last night," Owen said. "They had taken away her in an ambulance before I got there. How is she?"

"Bad," Edwin replied. "From what we've heard, she wasn't wearing her seat belt, which caused her to go flying and hit the wall. Her mom's in there now, and she's saying that Brooke might have to relearn how to walk."

Owen let out a curse. That wasn't good. The second feeling was the one that instantly made him feel guilty. He was glad that Vicki hadn't gotten that injured. As messed up as her injuries had been, they were at least manageable with what little he and Sammy had.

"Even with spells?" Owen asked, echoing his last thoughts.

"Even with spells, and any Healers trained in spine injuries are booked up," Janie nodded. "It might be months before she can see one, and by then it's a coin toss if they can help."

"Damn," Owen replied.

"They're trying to pin the driving on Brooke," Edwin added, his frustration evident in the clench of his jaw and the flash in his eyes. Then he let out a breath and glanced back towards the rooms. "We heard her parents yelling at someone about it earlier."

Owen didn't know how Mr. Townsend was going to spin this one. Hearing someone else say that Brooke might get the blame was a punch in the gut.

"But with Vicki walking away..." Alicia said, her eyes flashing.

Janie's face was pale as she hugged herself tighter.

"With Vicki walking away, it's hard to point fingers at the actual driver," Owen continued for Alicia. "When I dropped her off at home, her dad was pissed that she could use her gifts to put herself and others in danger like that..."

He couldn't say more, but they seemed to understand, regardless. Even Edwin, who hadn't seen the knife incident happen, gave a nod. No one here seemed surprised that Vicki had walked away from a crash that Brooke was lucky to survive.

"Are visiting hours open? Can I say hi?" Owen asked.

"I'll walk with you, see if Brooke's up for it," Alicia offered. The look on her face said that she had more questions.

Owen resigned himself to getting interrogated along the way, but what he didn't expect was to be led to an empty hospital room. The space was cold and dark. Panic began to spark as he glanced around; the bed was empty, and there wasn't any patient information on the wall or foot of the bed. Had something worse happened to Brooke? The possibility terrified him before Alicia started to talk.

"Vicki is a menace," Alicia started. "The Blessing has given her a blatant disregard for danger to herself and others."

"Okay," Owen stated, trying to look at her with something that conveyed calm and understanding, like he always did. He agreed with Alicia's opening thesis statement, but he didn't know where she was going with it.

"I thought that the Blessing could be worth it," Alicia continued, spitting out the name. "But it's a blight on humankind. Vicki gets to walk away at the cost of someone else's life."

"What do you mean?" Owen asked, standing in the center of this empty hospital room, and feeling like he wasn't allowed to touch anything in here. He turned his attention back to Alicia and took another step back.

There was a weight on his friend's shoulders. Alicia's posture was tired, and it looked like it was from more than a long night. He'd seen her like that before, sliding through listlessness, grief, and rage. Those months after her brother's funeral had been the worst, and the anniversaries were bad even still. It was ten years last fall.

He'd been telling himself that there was no connection there; Dylan's death couldn't be related to Levi getting the Blessing. The timeline didn't add up. Besides, this was Alicia, his and Vicki's oldest friend. If she wanted revenge against Vicki, why start now? Vicki's behavior prior to the gunshot had been the same as it had been since they were teenagers. There was nothing to set Alicia, or any of his other friends, on the path of murdering one of their own.

"You saw her last night. Was that someone that cared about her friends?" Alicia asked, her eyes narrowed in anger.

"Vicki's version of friendship has always looked different from ours," Owen tried to placate, even as a weight sank in his gut. Was he wrong in his defense of his oldest friend? Even now, he still wanted to keep her from doing something drastic. "She cares, but she's always been selfish, and takes risks that most of us wouldn't dream of taking. Why do you think I always drove you everywhere? That's not the Blessing."

"How do you know? The Vicki I know was kind once," Alicia spat.

"She was cruel when I first met her," Owen shot back. "Are you saying that she wasn't a bully in first grade? Because unless she's had the Blessing her whole life, I remember that."

"How would you know she hasn't had the Blessing her whole life?" Alicia asked.

It took him a long moment to search through his memory, before landing on one that Alicia had told him. "Do you remember the time that Vicki tripped during recess and skinned her knee? The next day, the teacher made the class skip recess until we told who pushed her. The kid that got blamed got kicked out of school."

Alicia opened her mouth, before closing it and nodding.

Oh good; he was worried for a moment he'd gotten reality confused with another lie. "What was your point of pulling me in here?" Owen asked.

"Where were you when Vicki called?" Alicia asked.

"At Levi's," Owen replied.

"That's where you've been all week," Alicia pointed out.

"Yup," Owen replied. Rocking back and forth on his heels, he waited for Alicia to get to the point.

"Is that where you were this morning? Why you were across town?" Alicia asked.

"Yeah," Owen replied. He stopped moving and shoved his hands into his pockets. "And before you get your mind all turned around, I wasn't there for sex. Levi got hurt last night. Not hospital bad, but I had to use a few spell scrolls for him, and now he's healing the slow way. And before you try to chew me out for not going to the hospital to wait for Brooke, I was helping Levi first, then got the call for Vicki, took her home, and then I went back to make sure that Levi was okay."

"If it was that bad, why didn't Levi go to the hospital?" Alicia asked.

Owen rubbed his eyes. "That's Levi's business, but the simple version, Levi and hospitals don't mix."

Alicia didn't look content with that answer, but Owen wasn't in the mood to play with her on this.

"Did you call me here to talk about the Blessing, or my relationship with Levi?" Owen asked into Alicia's silence. He could hear the sounds of the surrounding hospital, and wished it was Levi that was getting taken care of here. Instead, the person who he'd grown to have such strong feelings for was home sleeping it off, while Owen was here at the hospital for someone else that Vicki had managed to mangle.

"Have you been avoiding Vicki this past week?" Alicia asked.

"Can I visit Brooke and get back to my day?" Owen asked. Exhaustion made a home in his bones as the reality of this situation started to sink in. He'd come because Alicia had called and said Brooke was on death's door. Instead, Alicia was pushing her own agenda, rather than letting him check in on the person he'd came here to see. This conversation was why Alicia had really called, and he didn't need to be woken out of a dead sleep for it. "Vicki's choices have impacted everyone lately. Maybe I'm fed up with my role in this group. Levi treats me like a real person."

Though the words were spilling out on no sleep and without any filter, Owen found he *wanted* to share them.

"I don't have to keep track of when Vicki wants to leave the club and be the chauffeur," Owen growled, feeling the anger of all the nights that he'd had to give up so that Vicki didn't get to the wheel of the car first and kill them all. The rage bubbled in his stomach and his jaw clenched as he talked. "I don't have to keep sober while all of you are out having fun. I don't have to sabotage my relationships by picking guys that aren't in it for the long haul, because I'm worried that they'll see and treat me like the rest of you." His voice had risen, and he caught himself looking down at his balled fists.

He wasn't looking at Alicia anymore, instead Owen was thinking about that little apartment that he'd found a place in. How Sammy had just accepted him as another person who Levi could lean on. How Sammy had invited him into the bed last night, instead of making up the couch. How the shirt that he'd pulled on this morning was Levi's. He could still imagine the smell of Levi's shampoo, a mixture of citrus and cedarwood that clung to Levi's hair while they were curled up together on the couch. He wished he had taken the time to shower this morning, just to have that scent with him. He tried to stay with those simple pleasures, but a heavy weight settled into his gut, and a tightness filled his throat. He would have so little time with them if he couldn't stop this from happening again and again.

Dropping his voice to a whisper, Owen continued, even though he very much wanted to cry. "Maybe Levi and I aren't in it for the long haul either, but we want to enjoy the time we have together before it ends."

He didn't look up at Alicia as he brushed past her into the hallway of the hospital. Stepping to the side, he scrubbed his eyes against the tears that threatened to escape. First, he needed to check on Brooke. Then it was time to get back to where the world seemed to make sense.

***

There had been a time that Levi woke up without feeling pain, but today he couldn't recall any of it. His ribs ached as he rolled over onto his good side. What he wouldn't give to not have a good and bad side, and just be comfortable in bed.

It had been a while since Owen had left, though Levi didn't have a clue how much time had passed since. Sammy was in the kitchen trying to put together breakfast with the assorted items tucked away in the fridge, pushed into the backs of the cabinets. Even with the food that Owen had brought in, they had gone through the easy staples. It was already time for another grocery trip.

Despite the numerous dead ends in their research, Levi hadn't found himself frustrated with the lack of progress. Sure, there was a part of him that wanted Vicki's life to no longer be in danger. But on the other hand, would Owen stay once the job was done? When the allure of the mystery was gone, would Owen leave too?

"You better be resting in there," Sammy called when Levi got up. "I can and will strap you to the bed."

"I'm going to the bathroom," Levi called back. "You don't need to get out the rope."

"I was thinking leather cuffs," Sammy replied, stepping in to meet Levi's eyes with a grin.

Levi rolled his eyes as he shuffled to the bathroom. He didn't have any balance issues, which was good. But he wished he couldn't feel how his ribs were straining, his brain was rattling with every step.

"Where did Owen run off to this morning?" Sammy asked.

"Hospital, to check in with the other one that was in the crash," Levi replied. "I think he's coming back today, but who knows when?"

Sammy nodded, going back to their quest to figure out how to prepare food for the two of them.

Once Levi was cleaned up, he settled onto the couch to rest. Sammy had said that the dim light of his bedroom would be better on his head, but he didn't own enough pillows to make that comfortable. He would think that after a few injuries like that, he'd invest. But honestly, it wasn't his priority when he wasn't actively in recovery.

"Owen said that you would kill me if I knew too much of what was going on," Sammy started, waiting until Levi was comfortable enough on his bloodstained couch to start this conversation. "But you took the injuries of someone else that was in a car accident, and now Owen's visiting the other person who got injured. What's going on?"

"I can't tell you," Levi replied, flinching as he turned to face them. "I want to tell you, but I can't."

"But Owen could?" Sammy asked.

"The same person who keeps me from talking has not blocked Owen. He could, maybe," Levi replied.

"You were never a bodyguard or a bouncer, were you?" Sammy asked.

Levi shook his head.

"All those injuries, they were from this, whatever it was?" Sammy checked.

Levi wasn't sure if this counted as telling Sammy or not, so he didn't make a move in response. Sammy swore, the sounds of dials being turned off on the stove, followed by the rush of water from the sink. Levi leaned to see what Sammy was doing, but they were back at the stove and turning the burners back on before he could figure it out.

"Okay, okay," Sammy replied, pacing around the kitchen. They stopped at the stove to stir whatever they were making, before coming back to view. "Is this related to that job you took that got us into housing?" Sammy asked. "When you needed to stop living with me?"

"Yeah," Levi replied. "You have to understand, that was the one rule. No one, not even you, could know. I could pay for the house, until the city bulldozed it for the new Townsend high rises. Then I got you into an apartment when that got to be too much, keep you fed, do the things that we could have done if we lived together, and been able to keep you safe."

Tears were filling their eyes as Sammy turned off the stove and walked over to him. "Why? Why do all of that to protect me?"

"You know why," Levi replied.

Sammy dropped into the seat next to him and laid their head on his good shoulder. It still hurt, but that was a strain that he was used to. "Remind me," Sammy replied.

"Because you are the one- Sorry, one of two people in the entire world that makes me want to stay in it," Levi replied. A month ago, it would have just been Sammy, but not anymore. He glanced towards the chair in the corner, and the mysteriously appearing tray table, and the trash can to collect the clutter. If Owen turned into a permanent fixture, Levi could see adding a mini-fridge and a shelf for Owen's snacks and drinks. Permanent wasn't something that he should even daydream about, but he could pretend for a few minutes.

Sammy glanced over to the chair and smiled, too. "He just fit, didn't he?"

Levi gave a one-sided shrug. "Came in like the Kool-Aid man, and I can't even get mad at him for it."

"Give him permission to tell me," Sammy said, pulling themselves back into the kitchen. "He cares about you too much to tell me on his own."

"I'll try," Levi replied, laying his head back against the couch. The headache was starting again, so he closed his eyes to keep it at bay. It didn't feel like anything from the Chain; those usually started at his wrist or locked his jaw. Mr. Townsend's painful reminders never sent anything as nice as a migraine.

How had so much changed so fast? It was only a few weeks ago he'd been cleaning up the blood from the bullet wound that had started it all. Even though he'd been dreading it for a while, Levi was grateful for last night. This way, if something happened, Sammy would get answers. They could go to the underworld to scream at him after the fact, but Sammy wouldn't be left wondering anymore.

***

The apartment Owen and his dad shared should have felt like the home the two of them had built together. Instead, it had turned sour. The place was paid for by his father working for the Devil, and Owen's money that he got for doing errands for the Devil's daughter.

That he used to get, Owen figured. He wouldn't be doing Vicki any favors anymore, which meant he was going to figure out a new way to bring in cash. Another problem he was putting off in favor of figuring out who was after Vicki, and how to break the Blessing.

In his room, he checked for anything lying around that could help Levi. Grinning, he found a couple of pills for pain management and pocketed the tin.

"Owen? You home?" Dad called from the other room.

"Yeah," Owen called back, putting away his stash before he stepped out to meet with his father. "How did it go after I left last night?"

"It was a mess," Dad replied. He still bore the same tired look that he'd been wearing the night before, but his clothes were clean. A step up from Owen, at least. "Nothing you need to worry about, though."

Owen gave his dad a smile as he looked through the fridge. "I stopped by the hospital earlier. Brooke is in rough shape, but she didn't want to talk to me about last night." He paused, flashing back to the moment he'd stopped by Brooke's room. Even with the general Healers and spell work, bandages and bruises covered her. Between her injuries and the nurse's orders, Brooke wasn't allowed to sit up in bed. "I'm not sure if she just doesn't want to talk about it, or if she's blaming me for skipping and not being their designated driver."

The moment that Brooke had dismissed him, Owen felt numb. Years of trust and hurt between them had made it bittersweet. Even now, Owen wasn't sure how his friendship with Brooke would look after this. If there would be one. Time would only tell.

"You're not their servant," Dad grumbled into his cup of coffee. "All of them can pay for someone to drive if they aren't safe to on their own. You've been enabling their bad behaviors for too long."

While Dad had mentioned something similar before, it had always felt like a half-hearted statement. Owen had been raised to be Vicki's friend. Being there for Vicki, even when she didn't want him around. Following around the security personnel and learning about the job that was being done. Owen had followed in his father's footsteps in all the ways that he was allowed. While he might not be physically imposing like his father, he thought he would be a part of the same line of work. Maybe the behind the scenes person.

Now? When Dad said that he wasn't Vicki's servant, it no longer felt like an empty statement or a throw away compliment. It felt like a new opportunity.

For the first time, Owen replied with his full chest. "I know. As bad as last night was, I can't give up all of my weekends to follow Vicki around forever."

"Exactly," Dad replied. His father stared into his coffee before looking up at him. "I'm proud of you. I know they have been your friends for a long time, and setting new boundaries with them is terrifying."

Owen gave his dad a smile. "It's really thanks to Levi."

His dad's face offered only a flash of worry and concern.

"Is there something that I should know about Levi?" Owen asked, leaning against the counter. Levi had said as much as he could, but perhaps his dad could tell him something Levi couldn't.

"You know he's Chained, right?" Dad asked.

Owen looked down. Right. That. "I know," he sighed. "Whatever you think about Levi, he's been as honest as he can be about his situation. There's stuff that I know I can't ask, and questions that he's not allowed to answer." Owen let his fingers wrap around the cool metal of the tin in his pocket. "Even with all of that, Levi treats me better than anyone else."

"I know I can't protect you from everything," Dad stated. "But I don't want you to get hurt. Be careful, okay?"

Owen gave his dad a smile. "I'll be careful. Levi knows he can't promise me the world, and I won't let him. But we can have each other for a little while."

"That's the spirit," Dad replied, finishing his coffee. "And, let me guess, you're heading back to Levi's again. If you're there anymore often, he's going to charge you rent."

Owen felt the color fill his cheeks as he grinned. "I'm not moved in yet."

"Yet, he says," Dad chuckled. There was a shooing motion, and Owen waved cheerfully as he headed back out for the day.

It had been a while since his dad had teased him about a guy. The last time Owen remembered those kinds of comforting comments had been back when he was still in high school. It felt like a warm hug that he didn't know he'd been missing. Had the events from the night before scared his father so much that they were bonding again? Or had the events from last night scared Owen enough that he'd allowed his father to know how close he was getting to Levi?

He was looking forward to trying to restart the plan from the night before, a nice calm day of relaxation with Levi and maybe

Sammy. While they couldn't watch a movie until Levi was feeling better, they could hang out for a while. Together, they could make the plan when he got there. Stepping outside the apartment, Owen inhaled and let it out. For the first time in his life, he felt like he could breathe.

CHAPTER 14

O wen hadn't been there long when the phone rang. Levi knew who was on the other side before he pulled it from his pocket. There was a feeling, like a tightening vise over his heart, that only came from when the Devil took a hold of the Chain. Shushing the room, Levi lifted the phone to his ear and answered.

"Mr. Townsend, how can I help you today?" Pain shot through his chest and arm; he gritted his teeth through the swear he wanted to cry out. With the hand that didn't have the phone in it, he waved away Owen and Sammy. They didn't need to be involved in whatever had upset the Devil today.

Of course, that was going to be difficult, with Owen already seated to his left, and Sammy half sitting on the arm of the couch to his right. He couldn't concentrate on their emotions, trying not to pass out, and hold a conversation all at once.

He didn't catch Mr. Townsend's voice. Had he spoken while Levi had been trying to keep from collapsing, or was the man waiting for this wave of pain to be complete before speaking? "What, sir?" Levi asked into through gritted teeth.

"What about keeping the Blessing a secret didn't make it through your skull?" Mr. Townsend asked. Hot, spine-searing pain flared at the end of the question, before it ebbed again.

"I told no one," Levi flinched. "I deflected when injuries spawned on my skin in front of the others. I didn't betray that."

"Then how does Owen know?" Mr. Townsend asked.

Owen. Oh, good. The Devil didn't know about Sammy yet.

"He knew about the Blessing before he saw my wounds," Levi replied, looking at Owen and hating himself for putting this one good person in danger. "Vicki cut her arm in front of him. I got

187

wounds from a car crash while in front of him, and Vicki called to get picked up."

"I should have locked you away," Mr. Townsend grumbled. "I could still lock you away."

"Owen's not the one that put a hit out on your daughter," Levi stated, as the pain lessened. He could sit up again; he didn't know when he'd curled in on himself. "He has no motive, and didn't know about the Blessing until after. If I get locked away, then you'll be left trying this again by adding someone else to a now splintering friend group. I'm getting closer to finding your answers."

Levi made eye contact with Owen as he said the last bit. He still didn't have any idea who had taken the money from the account, who paid the failed mugger, and if those two were the same person. But he had Owen now, and between the pair of them, Levi thought they were getting somewhere.

"You have until Friday," Mr. Townsend replied before the line went dead. The weight on Levi's chest lifted and he could breathe again.

The strain on his chest and pressure on his ribs had only grown since the start of the call. A sharp pain pulled on his side when he sucked in a breath, and he hoped it would fade soon. Either through his mind choosing to ignore it, or through healing over what little time he had left.

Friday. How was he supposed to find out if there was a traitor in the group by Friday, when he could barely walk from Vicki's car accident?

"What was that?" Sammy asked, eyeing the phone with a fury that stole all the fire from hell.

"Did you tell him you knew?" Levi asked, rubbing his bruised ribs.

"He figured it out when I dropped Vicki off last night," Owen replied, his eyes wide and worried. "Did I fuck up?"

"No, no," Levi replied, cutting in before Sammy could react. Sammy still didn't know the whole story here, and he didn't need their protective streak scaring Owen away. This wasn't Owen's fault; Levi was sure of that. He reached over and gave Owen's arm a squeeze that he hoped was comforting. "I'm just trying to figure out who knows what. He doesn't suspect that Sammy was here yet, so we need to keep it that way. If Mr. Townsend didn't discover that you knew about the Blessing until he spoke to you last night, that means he's not watching my apartment. He doesn't know Sammy was here too."

"What kind of fucked up mess did you sign yourself up for, Levi?" Sammy asked, their expression shifting from fury to worry and back again.

"Dad mentioned you were Chained, but I've never seen that in person," Owen murmured. "That looked awful."

"I've had worse," Levi replied. Looking between them, he realized that might not be the best response. Guilt and rage flashing across Sammy's face, while Owen's skin turned an awful shade of green. "In his mind, no one's life is worth more than hers, especially mine." Levi wished that he could look at both of their faces at once, even though they were on opposite sides of the couch.

"This is why I didn't want you to get involved. I didn't want you to see this. The phone calls, the sudden wounds, the endless uncertainty," Levi continued. "I get it might be too much."

"Shut up, you idiot," Sammy said, scrubbing their face with the back of their hand. "You're not scaring me off that easily."

"What Sammy said," Owen added. "Like I've told everyone that has ever asked, I'm here as long as there's space for me. You are the best thing that has ever happened to me. Meeting you, meeting Sammy. Both of you have given me so much more than you can imagine. So, no, you're not too much, this situation isn't too much. But dammit, there's one thing that the Devil didn't count on."

"What?" Sammy asked.

"I'm doubling down on fixing your Connection," Owen replied, stalking over to his chair to turn on his laptop. "Neither of them deserve you."

Levi shook his head, trying to hide his smile. Sammy's expression almost got him to break.

"Connection? What Connection?" Sammy asked, crossing the room to pester Owen instead. "My Connection with him?"

"No, not yours. A different one," Owen explained.

"Someone came in and fucked with Levi's other Connection?" Sammy asked, looking ready for a fight. Sammy would fight God if it meant protecting their small family. Even a Connection that Levi never knew about, and would probably never meet.

"Taking over a Connection explains how Levi and Vicki can connect at all," Owen argued, showing something to Sammy on the computer screen that Levi couldn't see. "An idea I had was that if we could find the original Connection, the one that was overwritten, maybe together they could remove the corruption."

Levi had refused to burst Owen's bubble on that topic. If the Blessing really had overwritten it, the real one would be impossible to find. Levi could bump into them on the street and never know it.

"How? Through the power of friendship and love?" Sammy asked, scooting Owen over so that both of them were sitting in the same chair. "I better not find Captain Planet memes here."

"We're not trying to save the planet, just Levi," Owen grumbled, as they forced him to wait while Sammy scrolled.

Levi grinned as he settled back into the couch cushions. The sounds of their bickering lulled him to sleep.

***

At first, Owen didn't appreciate Sammy challenging his theories. It reminded him too much of his friends pushing his ideas down. Slowly, as the two of them bickered, Owen found as much as he had to defend the Connection that he was sure that Levi had to another person, Sammy wasn't pushing him down. They were trying to understand the arguments that he was making. Comprehend the logical steps that Owen was taking to get there, and challenge those ideas because Levi's life was at stake if he was wrong. The two of them were working together, not against each other, a comradery that Owen had never known his life was lacking. Levi had fallen asleep, so both his and Sammy's voices had lowered while they worked.

"Look, I've done my research," Owen whispered, showing off the scholarly articles on how they formed, and the unique magic that ran through them. "Levi has to have one for the stupid Blessing spell to work."

"Blessing? That shit stain of a spell is called a Blessing?" Sammy growled.

"Focus, we can talk about how the spell that Mr. Joseph "the Devil" Townsend invented isn't actually a blessing later," Owen pointed out. "It's the only constant and instantaneous transference system that someone could hijack. Otherwise, there would have to be someone that was actively sending or recharging the protective ward on Vicki."

"I'm not saying that's not a good theory," Sammy replied. "But, for someone else to have a Connection with Levi?"

"Someone else?" Owen asked, blinking at that. "Does Levi have a known Connection?"

"Yeah, with me," Sammy replied. "It's how I know when that idiot gets hurt. There's an uneasy feeling in my gut when it happens."

"Healer, Levi injury bloodhound. What other secret talents do you have?" Owen asked, looking over at Sammy, still sitting on his lap.

"Wouldn't you like to know," Sammy smirked, as they clicked through the tabs. They stopped with a frown. "What's this?"

Owen had to lean forwards to see what Sammy was looking at. It was a list of names that he and Levi had been gathering who had recently gotten out of prison, or been released from a long hospital stay, with any connection to the Townsend family. There was another list of people that had died a decade ago because of violent or unexplained means that he was cross-referencing against.

"I'm looking for someone that might have motive to go after Vicki," Owen replied. "The whole thing that Levi's tasked with, figure out which friend in the group wants her dead? Well, maybe one of them is backing someone on this list. I have two theories, but both would have the same motive. I think Townsend tested the spell, tested how well it would work, and what ways it could save his daughter. I think that someone involved wants revenge."

"What's the second theory?" Sammy asked.

"There might have been someone who was on the other side of the Blessing before Levi," Owen whispered. Alicia's story about finding out didn't match with Levi's experiences. Which meant there had to be another spell before Levi came into the picture. "Either way, ten years is a long time to wait to act."

"Yeah," Sammy replied, their face hard to read as they skimmed. "A decade is a long time…so your guess is that someone that died around the time that Levi got the Blessing is the reason Vicki's in danger now? Someone whose Connection was hijacked for the spell?"

"It would be a better guess than a generic family member," Owen replied, scrubbing his eyes. "Still, I watched someone that was supposedly well trained get sniped between the eyes for taking a shot towards Vicki."

"Do you know that guy's name? Compare it to this list," Sammy suggested. "If someone has already died for this, either this is more important than we thought, or you're going down the wrong rabbit hole. It could have been just a mugging gone wrong."

Could Mr. Townsend have been wrong all along? The way the man had moved out of the shadows, the flash of danger that Owen had felt when looking through the cars, the dead guards, all to get shot between the eyes—none of it made sense. It felt like a decoy. But for what, Owen had no clue.

"What about your friends?" Sammy asked. "How do they fit into all of this?"

Owen shook his head. "Money. It appears the shooter, the one that started all of this, was paid through one of Vicki's accounts. The only people who can pull that money are Vicki and her friends, myself included. Mr. Townsend is sure that one of us emptied that account to pay the shooter."

He handed the laptop over to Sammy and slipped out of the chair, carefully dumping them into the seat so he could move around while he talked. Levi didn't stir an inch, snoring gently on the couch as Owen paced.

"I've known some of them my whole life," Owen continued. "Even the ones that we met later, I've known them for years. Alicia, I've known since we were little. Brooke, we met in high school. She and Vicki had a rivalry that made the rest of us question if they liked each other, or hated each other. Alicia and I met Edwin freshman year of college, but he and Vicki have known each other for forever. Vicki and Edwin dated for a while, and then Edwin just went back and forth between Alicia and Vicki. Friends with benefits or something. I never understood it, but they seemed to make it work? I guess. Janie's the last one that we incorporated in, but even that has been since early college days. I think I introduced her to the group sophomore year? If one of them has been trying to get at Vicki or her dad, they've been playing the long game."

"Or the slight was recent," Levi mumbled.

Owen winced.

"If I wanted to actually sleep, I would have gone to the bedroom," Levi promised, waving away his concerns. He hid a yawn behind his hand before looking between the pair of them. "Alicia's been Vicki's friend the longest, but she's also Chained," Levi said through a second yawn.

Owen froze mid-step. Chained? The same thing that Levi had just gone through, Alicia could go through at any time? His mind flashed to an obituary he'd saved. The name that he had left off the spreadsheet. It was a motive, but Alicia couldn't hurt the Townsend's. The Chain would block it. Wouldn't it?

Levi continued talking. "Edwin's family recently lost a lot of money, thanks to some investments that went bad under Mr. Townsend's influence." Levi made a grab for a beer on the side table; Sammy batted his hand away and offered a bottle of water instead. He cracked the seal as he spoke. "Brooke loves Vicki, but Vicki treats her like trash. That Brooke was the one that was in the car when Vicki crashed it last night tells me she probably isn't the one that was involved. She would have had protections in place to keep her from getting caught like that. Janie...I don't think Janie's involved in this. I don't think she's on the up and up, not completely, but I'm a suspicious person."

"What about me?" Owen asked. His mind was swirling with all the information that Levi already knew about the same people that he had known for years.

Levi grinned and patted the seat next to him on the couch.

Nervous, Owen sat down, feeling like he was about to get scrutinized through a magnifying glass for appraisal.

"Even if you were the one to set up the first shot," Levi said, taking Owen's hands in his, "which I don't think for an instant, you don't have motive. You liked your place in that friend group, and you've been struggling ever since it got threatened. You've latched onto this little misfit family instead somehow, and found a new place for yourself instead."

Owen squeezed the hand that Levi hadn't hurt the night before with a hopeful smile.

"I've never suspected you," Levi said. It was the closest that Owen was going to get to a proclamation of something more.

Warmth flooded from his toes to his cheeks. "Well, I've never suspected you either," Owen replied, a smile on his lips that he never wanted to leave.

"Look, this is all very cute," Sammy said from across the room. "But we need to figure out which of your other friends is hurting Vicki and, in return, hurting our boy."

The bubble of laughter that escaped him felt wrong, but Owen couldn't help it. Meanwhile, Levi and Sammy had started bickering about how Sammy had called Levi "our boy," and how weird that was at that moment. They weren't getting closer to any answers today, but Owen wondered what tomorrow might reveal when they were all at school together. Vicki would be there, still believing that her actions weren't wrong. He would have to make the choice, again, not to fix things for her, while hoping that he wasn't also making things worse. And he was going to see Alicia again, knowing that she was Chained and stuck as Vicki's friend. Did that explain the awkward standoff in the hospital? He didn't know for sure.

Their time for answers was running out.

***

Vicki wasn't sure she'd ever been more humiliated in her entire life. She was a fully grown adult, but her father was treating her like a child that had been grounded. The only time Vicki could go out was when she was required to leave, and the only place she was permitted to go was the university.

A few of her dad's guards were stationed around campus, keeping far enough away that they weren't supposed to be interfering with classes, all while stopping her from making a run for it. She was certain she hadn't spotted them all every time she considered it.

"Can you drive me somewhere after class?" she asked Owen. Out of everyone here, she could twist his arm the easiest.

"Sorry," Owen replied, not looking even a little sorry. "I didn't bring my car today."

"Didn't bring the car? Why?" Vicki asked, her eyes widening.

"I accidentally put my keys in the wrong coat pocket, so we ended up taking public transit," Owen explained.

We? Who was we? Vicki looked around until she spotted Levi, at the back of the room on the phone.

He was laughing, leaning against the wall as he talked. His eyes looked up at Owen and he nodded in answer to an unspoken question. As soon as he hung up, Levi shuffled over to them. A limp that hadn't been there last week was now part of his walk.

"Found your keys," Levi said to Owen. "We can pick them up after class."

"So they were in the wrong coat?" Owen checked.

"Well, kind of. They were in the right coat, just the coat didn't end up on the right person this morning," Levi replied. His eyes slid to Vicki's, and the smile vanished from them. It wasn't gone from his face though, just his eyes. "Good morning. How was the rest of your weekend?"

She flinched. The question was like a slap to the face. How dare they act all cuddly and cute? The only thing keeping her from acting was her father's warning. One move out of turn, and she was back to virtual learning. If she was going to take that chance, it wouldn't be for something as low as wiping the smiles off of Levi and Owen's faces.

Vicki snarled at them, her nose crinkling as she crossed her arms. "Why do you want to know?"

"Conversation," Levi replied with a shrug.

Now that he was this close, Vicki was could see the speckles of old bruises on his face. He was standing so most of his weight was on only one of his legs. What had happened to him over the weekend? Owen had said there had been a kitchen accident, but this didn't look like that at all.

"What about you? How was your weekend?" she asked, turning the question around.

"Started off rough, but it turned around," Levi replied, leaning on a desk. "I heard about Brooke and your car. That's got to be scary. Are you okay?"

Vicki narrowed her eyes, looking at Owen and then back to Levi. "What did he tell you?"

"Not much, just that Brooke was in the hospital and that your car was totaled," Levi replied. There didn't seem to be any weird looks between him and Owen either. "I know he had to give you a ride the other night because of that. I'm guessing Brooke took your car and left you stranded."

Vicki blinked. Did he mean that? Had Owen spun the story to keep the Blessing a secret from Levi? Maybe he was a real friend after all. "Yeah, Owen helped me get home that night," she confirmed. "Was he hanging out with you all weekend?"

"Just about?" Levi replied. "We ended up having a couple of chill nights. Plus, we have a project that we're working on together that took a lot of time."

"What kind of project?" Vicki asked.

"We're trying to look into his stalker, see if there's a way to keep her off his back better," Owen explained. "We can talk about what we've learned."

Vicki squinted. The stalker thing was a fake-ass story to cover that Levi was part of her dad's protection squad. But Owen knew that. So, that had to be code for them doing work for her dad. If they were working, Levi might be done with his project soon. The sooner that weirdo let her life get back to normal, the better. She could live with giving up Owen for a bit, as long as there was an end in sight.

"I'm good, thanks," Vicki replied, reminding herself to be polite. "I'm going to see if someone else can give me a ride after class."

"Next time?" Owen replied, in a way that said that it might not be a real offer. Still, he offered.

If Vicki had expected the others to act the same as last week, or like Owen with his weird project, it turned out that she was wrong. Her frustration grew with every person she talked to. Alicia looked almost scared when she said that she could not give Vicki a ride. Janie outright said that she'd gotten a call from Vicki's father; it said that Vicki was to go right back to the house when classes were done for the day.

"He even told me to cancel our study session tomorrow," Janie explained. "Maybe we can study at your place, but it might be real studying."

Vicki glowered at her, though Janie didn't seem to think Janie was doing anything wrong at all. What were friends for, if not to help her sneak out and get back to the nightlife that she deserved?

Edwin, the coward, wasn't even here today. Something about a stomach bug, or eating something that had upset him the day before. Every day that Vicki wasn't in a relationship with Edwin was a day she grew more confident that Edwin didn't work, not even as friends with benefits.

It wasn't long before the school day was growing to an end, and Vicki was getting desperate. She even tried talking to other people at school, seeing if she could get a ride from one of them. That had almost worked, until she'd told them where she wanted to go. The student apologized and showed her that the nightclub was closed tonight. They were doing renovations for the next few days and wouldn't reopen until the weekend.

Which left Vicki with the only option of following her dad's security back to the house. She felt fourteen again as she stared out the car window at everything and nothing. The cool glass pressed against her forehead. The dark window tint hid her glare from the world. No freedom. No trust.

The sourness that had settled in her stomach had only grown with each turn onto another road.

"How was school today?" Father had the audacity to ask when she got home.

"What kind of question is that?" Vicki asked, dropping her bag onto the ground and stalking towards her father. "What's this about the club being closed?"

"We're adding the valet, just like you've been requesting," Father replied. "I should have added that before this point, and I apologize for getting that wrong."

Vicki blinked, and then scowled. "Why?"

"Because this weekend would not have happened if someone had seen you and Brooke head towards the car," Father replied. "It's a liability issue that is going to cost me greatly, but it would cost me a great deal more to ignore it any longer."

"Why does it require closing the club? It's just one parking lot!"

"Because I have to vet every single one of those valets in order to know which ones may put their hands on the keys of your car," Father replied. "Because I have to up the security of your parking lot to make sure that no one messes with your car. Vicki, this might not seem like a big deal to know, but this is twice that you've nearly died coming out of your club. If the Blessing hadn't been there, who knows what kind of hurt you would experience right now?"

Vicki scoffed. She was just going to have to find someplace else to party until then.

"You could just order Owen to be my designated driver again," Vicki pointed out.

Father's eyes narrowed before he shook his head. "I will let you think about why that was a foolish thing to ask of me. Then, I want you to think about what loyalty and friendship actually mean, because if you cared and trusted your friends to be the ones in charge of your safety, if you trusted the son of the head of security to be in charge of your safety for free, then you do not understand what loyalty means. If the lack of his presence is what you are blaming for last weekend's mess, although he is the only one to have answered your calls, then, no, I will not order Owen to pick up your slack. I raised you to be a leader, act like it."

Leader? What kind of bullshit was that? Raised you to be a leader—what did he think he was saying? Of course, Vicki was the leader of her friends. That's how it had always been. She told them where to go, and they went without question. Just because Levi was here now...

"This is Levi's fault," she said. "If Levi wasn't here, no one would have fallen out of line."

Father's gaze grew cold. "If another person in your group caused it to crumble away from you, then you need to reevaluate who your friends are. A single person joining you should not, and has not in the past, caused things to fall apart. This is on you. Not Levi, not Brooke, not Owen, not any of your other friends you have. You need to think about your choices and learn from your mistakes."

Vicki turned on her heels. This was utter bullshit. Magazine worthy rooms surrounded her as she marched back to her own. Servants stepped into side rooms as she passed, each hidden face only furthering the flame of her fury. It was Levi who had pulled her friends away from her. Owen had only stepped out of his place and turn their world upside down because of him.

Only when she was back in her room did Vicki let out a scream.

Punching her pillow, she cursed both Owen and Levi. They had been the first to splinter away. All of this had to be their fault, no matter what her father said.

***

Levi winced as he and Owen walked side by side to the subway station. It was the easiest way to get to and from school from his apartment, and it would be the easiest way to grab Owen's keys. Levi hadn't mentioned exactly where those keys were, other than who. At first, it had slipped his mind. But then, as they were walking, it just felt like an odd time to bring it up. It was a Monday evening after all, so there wouldn't be too many people out. But Sammy had swapped shifts with someone so that they could stay home with Levi over the weekend.

"Something wrong?" Owen asked, catching his wince.

"I think Vicki's punching something," Levi replied with a shrug. There was a repeated pressure on his knuckles. He guessed it was how a ring would catch and press into his fingers upon impact. "Nothing too bad though, just it feels like that."

"I swear that girl can tantrum like nobody's business," Owen replied. "I tried to let her down gently, so that she didn't pull another stunt today, but I guess that didn't work."

"She might have just talked to her dad," Levi pointed out. "I know I want to punch things when I'm done talking with him."

That got Owen to laugh, and they were back on track for the evening. There was a warmth in his gut that felt like a win.

The ride on the subway was one that Levi had grown used to. Crowded cars that thinned out the closer to his side of town they got. Subway stations went from clean and brightly lit, to grimy, dim, and graffitied.

Levi pulled Owen close when it was time for them to get off. That wide-eyed look of his was going to get them labeled as outsiders if he wasn't careful. They would be safe once they were out on the street, but the subway stations out here had a collection of squatters that made their money how they could.

He and Owen got off one stop before Levi's usual departure. It was about the same distance from either one, but it felt more efficient to be walking towards his apartment, rather than away from it.

"So, we're going to Sammy's work," Owen said, as they stepped out from the steaming underground and felt the sharp hit of winter air. The cushion of the earth kept the station out of the elements. During business hours, there was the added body heat of thousands of people passing through, along with the friction of the cars along the rails. The stations were never comfortably warm in the winter, but it beat being out in the elements. "What kind of place is it?"

"Nice, I guess?" Levi replied, steering Owen along the block. The people that were out and about were friendlier at this hour. Something that Levi had forgotten in the years of relative solitude. He ventured out for food, and to help Sammy, but both events happened at odd hours of the day. "This has been one of Sammy's favorite jobs, and other than a few bad customers, I think they'll stay working here as long as they can."

"That's good," Owen replied. "Though that didn't really answer the question."

The hot pink building was already coming into view. "Well, you can see for yourself."

Owen didn't seem to notice or make any comments about it, until Levi approached the front door.

"Wait, really?" Owen asked, looking at the iron bars on the windows and the neon signs behind those. The open sign was on, flashing through one letter at a time. "Sammy works here?"

"Yup," Levi replied, feeling a nervous pit form. "That okay?"

"Yeah," Owen replied. "Just…I guess I thought it was going to be a convenience store, a bar, or a tattoo parlor. Strip club works."

Levi kept Owen close to him as they stepped inside. He knew how to navigate without the floor creaking too much, and how to avoid the shin bangers that couldn't be seen in the low light. Should the chairs *not* blend into the background? Maybe. But there was only so much that could be done.

Sammy liked this place because the staff protected the dancers, and never gave them crap about being non-binary. The rest of the place had just enough work to it that it drew and kept a crowd, and that was it.

While the doors were currently open, there wasn't anything really risqué going on right now. Levi recognized this dancer, but didn't know their name, stage or otherwise.

"Looking for Hades, they here?" Levi asked. It was so like them to use a stage name that was supposed to invoke all the wrong feelings, but it seemed to work for them. They were better off than Levi most months. Sure, he gave most of his money to Sammy, but still, they didn't need it. The money was a way to give them more choice, or at least a cushion, for when things fell apart.

Slipping a hand into his pocket, Levi pulled out a couple of dollars and offered it to the dancer.

"I'll grab them," the dancer replied. There was no one else here in the room, so they stepped away from the pole.

"Thanks," Levi replied.

He led Owen over to a set of chairs so they could wait and talk. He had never been allowed back to where the changing rooms were, which was another reason that Sammy liked this place. It felt safe, because everyone played by the rules. Anyone that didn't got banned for life.

"So, this is where Sammy works," Owen said as he took it all in. "Is it weird for you?"

Levi shook his head. "Sammy and I both talked about this line of work before I got offered the other job, and while I rarely come over when they are working, I'll walk them home occasionally. Sometimes there's a customer that doesn't want to go away, and Sammy wants someone else with them just in case."

Owen opened his mouth, but the thought was never spoken. Levi turned in the direction that Owen was looking. Skintight leather booty shorts sat low on Sammy's hips, thin thong strings cutting across the top of their hipbones, and leather cups pushed up their breasts. The look put their stomach and extra weight there on full display, and Sammy was rocking it with confidence.

"You're missing your whip and cat mask," Levi teased. The thigh-high leather boots made them almost taller than him.

"I was still getting ready," Sammy replied, offering out a set of keys. "Missing my cat scratch gloves, too."

"Did you cut off the bottom of those shorts?" Levi asked, motioning for Sammy to do a spin. "I think I recognize those as the ones that you kept complaining were riding up."

"They can't do that anymore," Sammy replied, turning around and shaking their ass once before turning back. "The rest of the show will cost you."

"Don't give away anything for free," Levi replied.

"Damn. I'm gay, and that's still hot," Owen mumbled, his face red.

Sammy grinned. "Well, it's going to be a slow night, so I figured that I would try out that new routine if you two want to stay."

Levi looked at Owen, who nodded. If they were staying, Levi could start a tab at the bar, and actually pay the cover fee that he'd bypassed. He didn't normally stay to watch Sammy strip, but he'd been the one to help them set up a pole in their apartment for practice.

Besides, the hours that he and Owen were going to spend here wouldn't make a difference in the long term. Unless a miracle happened and something revealed the attacker without Levi dying in the process, Levi wasn't going to meet that Friday deadline. It would be better for Owen and Sammy to have good memories, before everything fell apart.

CHAPTER 15

I f Vicki had thought that Monday was bad, Tuesday was worse. She had thought that maybe she could convince her friends to help her get some place new, but Owen was mysteriously hungover and didn't want to talk to anyone. Levi was babying him, giving him electrolytes and taking notes for him in class, while Owen napped on his shoulder.

"What the hell happened to you two?" Janie asked.

"We accidentally drank our dinner last night," Levi replied, which was not fair. "We got caught up with everything, and now Owen's working through the worst of it."

"Not you?" Janie asked.

"Well, let's just say that I wasn't drinking as heavily as he was," Levi replied. "Someone had to make sure that we could get home, and I offered."

Wait. Vicki blinked, feeling like she had fallen into another universe. Owen partied like that when she wasn't around? No wonder Levi could pull him along like that. A pang of envy flashed through her, before it settled into a familiar dichotomy of want and betrayal. She had been the one to ask Owen to take her out drinking and dancing first. How dare he go without her?

"Damn," Janie teased. "Don't baby him too much. The point of a hangover is to tell yourself never again."

Owen waved her away, mumbling something that was lost in Levi's shirt. Something about neon lights? *What?*

Something was very wrong. Her father had forced her to spend a night inside, and Owen was the one that had a party? What kind of twisted world was this?

Edwin had actually showed up at least, but he refused to talk to her about breaking away from her father's hold. Not even an offer of a threesome with Alicia would sway him. "No means no, Vicki. You messed up this weekend. Learn to live with that."

"Or what?" Vicki asked.

"*Or what?* Use your brain, Vicki," Edwin replied, his voice clipped and his tone biting. "Your choices caused one of our friends to end up in the hospital. How can we know that one of us isn't next? That your next stunt isn't going to get one of us killed—"

Alicia grabbed Edwin's arm and pulled him back. Her touch was gentle, like herding back a cat that needed to be turned away.

"That's enough," Alicia told him. She turned back to Vicki. "We can't help you disobey your father. He would ruin both of us. When your dad is no longer grounding you, or whatever this is, then we can talk about going out again. Not yet, though."

Vicki stared at the backs of her two closest friends as they walked away. What was happening?

"Vicki," Janie said, and she was back to her Mom voice again. "Understand, if he catches us helping you, our lives here are done."

"He can't *do that*," Vicki whined.

"Whether he can or can't isn't up to us," Janie said. "Talk to him. Maybe you can get him to listen. Maybe we can go out on Friday?"

Vicki shook her head and turned away. She would figure something else out. If her friends couldn't help, maybe she could try again with the people on campus. There were places on campus where parties were happening, with drinks getting passed around—party drugs too, if she was lucky. Something that could take the edge off these stupid feelings and her lousy friends.

A man approached her, someone that looked familiar. Like a classmate whose name she didn't know. "I heard you were looking for a ride somewhere," the man offered.

"Yeah," Vicki replied, standing a few feet back and trying to place the person who was offering her a chance at freedom. Freedom that she so desperately craved. She could imagine the words of caution from Owen or her father, but neither of them were in charge of her. She was a grown woman, and it was her life. "Do I know you?"

"I'm a friend," the man replied, the smile on his face stretching across his lips. "My name's Dylan. Do you remember me?"

Dylan? It took a moment for the name to ring a bell. When it did, it was like claxons in her head.

"Dylan!" she exclaimed, taking in his whole physique. This was even better than following someone new. Dylan had been there for her when everyone else wasn't. Before he'd left at least. "I thought you had died! Look at you, not dead!"

In the back of her mind, there was a memory that Dylan hadn't survived his accident. It was good to see that those memories were wrong. It wasn't the first time that they didn't match the real world. Servants around her appearing or disappearing without a trace, and no one commenting on it. Her nanny switched out with another woman with the same name. Dylan was standing in front of her right now, so he couldn't be dead.

"You look good," she complimented, an idea forming in the back of her mind. If her current friends couldn't step up, maybe it was time for a new friend, a new old friend. She could step up and be the leader of this new friends' group of one, without all the others dragging her down. "It's been a long time. How have you been?"

"As good as I could expect," Dylan replied. "I've been in recovery for the last few years, had to turn to the arts to fully heal."

He twirled his fingers in a sweeping motion, a mockery of someone casting a spell. She'd seen enough to know it didn't look like that though.

"So, are you still interested in that ride?" Dylan asked, holding out an arm.

Vicki smiled as she took it. A friend of a friend could be exactly what she needed right now. Someone that could show her old friends what being a true friend was all about.

"So, have you heard about the Neon Vibe?" Vicki asked, directing her new friend to a nightclub a few blocks from campus that she frequented when she wanted some place that wasn't owned by her father. It was her only option now that hers was being renovated.

"I have a better idea," Dylan offered. "Why don't we sneak into your father's place? No crowds, and all the booze behind the bar is free for the taking."

Vicki grinned. "I like you," she replied, holding onto him while they walked. If they moved together, she might sneak past her father's security on their way. Ducking her head, she moved with Dylan between her and the guards. She pulled off her coat, not bothering with the cold. Dylan offered her a hat and she pulled it on, tucking her blond curls into the knit material. Dylan walked with a limp, similar to Levi, but it was only noticeable while she was holding onto him. Besides, Dylan was a thousand times better than Levi.

As they got to the parking lot, Dylan suggested she ditch her phone so that her dad couldn't trace her. Into the snow covered grass her phone went. She didn't need her dad tracking her down and ruining tonight's party. Besides, tomorrow her father could buy her a new one.

***

When Levi felt the thunk on the back of his head, he didn't immediately think about it. Rubbing near his crown, he tried to check out the bruise, only to pull away fingers slick with blood. Dammit.

He was completely exposed out here. He and Owen were still at school. Janie, Alicia, and Edwin were only a few seats away, and class was about to start. Where was Vicki?

Owen had been leaning against his shoulder, but he was slowly sitting up as Levi looked at the blood on his fingers.

"Is that what I think it is?" Owen murmured.

"Yeah," Levi whispered back, reaching into his pocket for a set of tissues. "Can you distract your friends?"

Owen nodded as he stood up. "Have any of your guys seen Vicki? Class is about to start."

"She was asking about going to a bar," Alicia said, sounding dismissive. "Why would you care?"

Levi could imagine how Owen was biting his lip as he tried to invent a new lie. With mostly clean fingers, he finally pulled on his knit beanie. He could still feel some of the warm dampness on the back of his head. Hopefully the dark fabric could cover it long enough to get somewhere safe. Did he have enough bandages in his bag for this?

"Levi? What's wrong?" Janie asked.

Of course, out of everyone, Janie would notice. She'd grown to teasing him today about taking over her usual role, as he babysat Owen through his hangover all morning. Thankfully, Owen had started feeling better by their afternoon class, but that might not last for long.

"I've got to go," Levi explained, grabbing his stuff and hoping the slip of his fingers was nervous sweat. Bloody textbooks would be hard to resell. He wrapped them tight around his black backpack strap and hoped that no one looked too hard. Why did head wounds always bleed so much? It was nerve-wracking.

Between the head wound and the latest concussion, Levi swayed and nearly crashed into a desk when he stood. Dammit. He needed to get out of this room so that people stopped staring, including all of his potential suspects. If Vicki caused him to die right now, he was going to be furious in the underworld while he waited for her to join him.

"Shit," Owen cursed under his breath. Strong hands grabbed Levi's good arm and guided it over Owen's shoulder. Levi leaned into the touch as Owen gave a command. "Janie, call Vicki. See if you can find her. If she doesn't answer, call my dad and say that she's missing. It's important."

Janie had her phone in hand and pressed to her ear before Owen had even finished. Her eyes were full of concern as she followed Levi and Owen out into the hallway, while the last of the students hurried into the classroom. Out here, there weren't as many obstacles; Levi moved to walk on his own and grabbed the back of his head to add pressure. He needed to find a bathroom, or some place to give the wound a check, but Janie kept following them.

Janie hadn't said a word when she pulled the phone away from her ear. Pressing a few keys, she tried again. "Dammit Vicki, you can't just throw a disappearing act whenever you want."

Owen pulled out his own; Levi saw the flash of Mr. Mills photo on the screen before it was pressed to Owen's cheek. "Dad? Vicki's missing. She might be in trouble..."

There was a growing pit in Levi's stomach as he navigated the hallways towards the restroom. The longer they went without response from Vicki, the more his breath caught in his throat. Or was that another side effect of what Vicki was going through? The bleeding and the dizziness weren't helping.

Levi stepped into the bathroom and froze. All he could smell was blood. There were sprays of it painted over every corner and every stall. Throwing his hand up, he stopped Owen from stepping inside. This place felt like a trap, or worse, a slaughter house.

"Have your dad call the security detail?" Levi called back towards Owen, staring into the dim. On the ceiling, only one lightbulb was shining, casting a thin yellow light.

The sound of phones ringing filled the room. First one, and then another, all echoing the same ringtone.

Levi slammed the door shut.

***

The only reason that Owen didn't drop his phone as the rings echoed off the bathroom walls was thanks to Levi, pushing him and Janie away from the door.

The scent of death drew Owen right back to that night in the parking lot. The sprays of blood on the cars that he could not turn his eyes away from. But the man that had shot at them was dead. He'd seen the bullet go through his eyes; he'd watched him fall. The first time he had seen anyone die, and it had been bleeding out in a Townsend nightclub parking lot.

Vomit bubbled up in his mouth; Owen choked it back down. If he puked here, it would be part of the investigation. It would take time away from Levi and Vicki. Tears filled the corners of his eyes from the strain.

"Those are the guards," Owen said, voice rough, still staring at the door to the restroom as if it had any answers. "Someone took out all the guards with no one noticing. Again."

Levi grabbed a piece of furniture, a round table covered in brochures of local clubs, and pulled it until it blocked the door. "Janie, call Vicki's dad right now."

"What?" Janie asked, her voice high and thready. "Call…call him?"

"Janie," Levi said through gritted teeth. "Please?"

Janie nodded, her hands trembling as she scrolled through her phone to find the number.

Owen jumped as his phone rang again. His father's number.

"What's going on?" Dad asked.

"I think we found the security guards," Owen said, his voice catching on the words. He tried to shake away the numbness that had settled into his fingertips. "We don't know if they're alive or not. We heard nothing when you called but ringtones. A new detail needs to get to the college right away, and we need to find Vicki."

Janie was relaying information to someone over the phone, and Owen squeezed his eyes shut. He forced himself to breathe before he opened them again. To his side, Levi was leaning against the wall, his face pale, and hand still pressed to the back of his head. It could have looked more relaxed, if Owen didn't know about the bleeding that was still happening. He hoped the wound was close to stopping by now, because they had little time to waste. They had to get Vicki to safety, or else that was going to be the least of Levi's issues.

Dammit! His father had hung up on him again. Something about needing to concentrate on getting security forces, and coordinating with campus security. Emergency services. Owen felt a steel grip on his heart as he thought about what could have happened, if his dad had been here. What could still happen to Levi.

Owen reached over to lift the knit cap and check the wound, but Levi stopped him with a grunt. Right. First aid. Put pressure on bleeding wounds, and don't lift fabric that was pressed against it, or else it might bleed harder. He turned to look around for a first aid kit or something, and found the empty hallway now held two new occupants: Alicia and Edwin.

"What's going on? You all rushed out of there like there was a fire," Edwin stated.

"Vicki's in danger," Owen replied, sliding his phone back into his pocket. Glancing through the faces of his friends, Owen couldn't help but remember that Mr. Townsend believed one of them was behind all of this. Who was he supposed to be looking for? The person who took Vicki? The person orchestrating the attack? Both? Panic ate at him, but he kept talking. "We think it's the same person from the nightclub, the night Vicki and Edwin were shot."

"That guy's dead," Edwin pointed out.

"I don't think so," Levi replied, nodding back towards the bathroom. "According to the reports, there were two attackers that night."

"How would you know? You weren't there," Edwin pointed out.

"I was briefed on it," Levi replied, pulling himself off the wall.

Edwin and Alicia went pale, but Owen couldn't tell if it was guilt, or worry about what Levi might have been reporting back to Townsend behind their backs. Townsend didn't care that Edwin and Alicia might have cheated on Vicki, or whatever nonsense was going through their minds. They were Vicki's best friend and ex. That didn't make them suspects.

"I know no one could explain why such a lousy shot and lousy mugger could take out so many of his men," Levi replied, cutting through Owen's thoughts. "I'm sure that has been puzzling a few people since. I think that we're looking for someone else. Someone that was pulling the strings."

"You've been working for Vicki's dad?" Edwin asked. "Vicki was right about that?"

"Vicki knows that I work for her father," Levi agreed. The tension in the hallway was growing with each passing word.

"How did you know to look in there?" Edwin asked, his eyes narrowed in suspicion. "We were all waiting around for class, and then you two started acting strange."

Owen didn't know how to answer that; he looked to Levi to for help.

Instead, Levi swayed and leaned against the wall again.

"Another one?" Owen asked, biting his lip as he looked at his friends.

Levi shook his head. "No, just all the same ones acting up again."

Janie had put her phone away to walk towards Levi. Unlike Edwin, there was no suspicion in her gaze, not if the looks of concern meant anything.

Then blood blossomed from Levi's knee. The light wash jeans turned dark in an instant. Levi shoved his arm against his mouth as a bit-off scream filled the hallway. Dropping to the floor, Owen grabbed his jacket to put pressure on the wound. Hot rage flashed through him, heating his skin and making the room too warm. A numbness sat beneath his skin as the helplessness of the situation hit him.

Where was campus security? Shouldn't someone have noticed and called for help? Or was the emptiness of the corridor an answer of it's own?

"If any of you are involved," Owen declared, but the voice that escaped him was not one that he could control. He tried to ignore Levi's small whispers of, "Don't." Each one crashed against him. Every word from Owen's mouth felt like a betrayal. But he couldn't just watch and wait for the next sadistic shot to end Levi's life.

"If any of you are involved with the person who took Vicki," Owen continued, tying the jacket tight against Levi's knee. Looking for any other injuries that his stupid idiot had hidden. "Tell them to stop. Please, tell them to wait, or find another way…"

There had to be another way. Vicki and her father had caused a lot of damage over the years. Lives ruined and lost because of their disregard. Owen understood the burning desire to get revenge, but not at Levi's expense. He'd lied to Townsend the other night. He would give anything to keep Levi safe, even Vicki's safety.

"There are better ways to get revenge," Owen begged. "Other ways to hurt them. Ones that don't invoke the Blessing."

The surrounding hall was silent other than Levi's whimpering, as Owen scrambled to pull out a set of the healing spells from his pocket. He'd been stashing as many as he could get his hands on, carrying them everywhere he and Levi went. They wouldn't be enough. He couldn't even cast them.. Powering on and off his wards was a light switch anyone could do, but spells? Magically resistant, his school tests had said.

But Levi wasn't magically resistant. That had been clear enough when Owen had learned about the tests that Levi had endured from Mr. Townsend. While he wasn't strong enough to be a Healer, Levi could use these spells.

"Come on," Owen said, putting the first one into Levi's hand. "We've got to stop the bleeding. Can you do that? We'll find Vicki and stop this, but you've got to stop bleeding."

Levi's grip on the spell was tight, and Owen watched as the seal on the scroll card cracked and the power of healing coursed out. Magic tingled underneath Owen's fingers as it knit together into a scab. Color came back into Levi's face, even as weary lines stretched at the corners of his eyes.

Then Owen turned, looking to see if anyone had finally arrived to do *something*. Campus security was getting close; they could just write Levi off as another victim of the attacker. There were no crowds of students yet, all of them still in class or in the common areas of the buildings. The rest? Well, he did not know what he was going to say to his friends when this was all said and done. From the lack of eye contact he got from them, the feeling was mutual.

CHAPTER 16

Vicki blinked against the bright lights of the dance floor. The back of her head was throbbing, a pain that should have gone away and yet still lingered. She tried to move her arms and found resistance instead. A rope had wrapped around her chest, tying her to a chair. Her wrists were bound behind her back. Another rope wrapped around each of her legs, tight enough that she couldn't move either of them. The binds chafed against her ankles. Her shoes were gone, but the rest of her clothes seemed to be there. The momentary relief of that realization vanished as she looked around.

"What?" Vicki asked. The room looked empty as far as she could tell, but she was too close to the lights. Flashing in her eyes, they filled her vision with spots too numerous to see. The low thud of the bass echoed in the space, covering up any sounds of footsteps or breathing, if there were any.

"Help!" Vicki screamed. Her voice ripped through her throat. Echoes of her cries bounced back to mock her.

"Awake already?" Dylan's voice asked, but she couldn't tell from where.

"Dylan? What are you doing? Let me out," Vicki demanded, yanking at her bindings that refused to give an inch.

"Why? You're right where I want you," Dylan replied, stepping into her line of sight.

He was backlit with the lights, and the spots still danced in her vision. Still, she could see the glint of a smile on his lips. The sound of the music dimmed, though the pounding in her ears remained.

"Why are you doing this? If my father hears about this—"

"I expect he already has," Dylan cut her off. "That accursed protective spell gave them warning. The fool."

"What are you talking about?" Vicki asked.

"I've seen you heal, Vicki," Dylan replied. "I want to know what it will take for you to bleed and not make it stick." He reached into his pocket and pulled out a voice recorder. With a click, the familiar sounds of a conversation between began to play.

"Vicki's arm didn't heal until she took the knife away," Owen's voice rang through the room, echoing through the walls and bouncing through her brain. *"Which meant that if she were, say, shot with an arrow and it stuck in her, or stabbed and the knife stayed in, the Blessing couldn't heal her until it was out."*

"Shit," Alicia's voice cut through the room like a knife. *"She might not be as invincible as I thought."*

The recording clicked off, the sound audible through the emptiness of the room. This man had a recording of that conversation, the one that Alicia had set up so that Vicki could hear. Was it all faked? Was there a script that Owen and Alicia had been reading the whole time? Or did Owen or Alicia have that recorder on them to give to Dylan later? Out of the two of them, Vicki would put money on Owen. He'd been the one that had changed the most, digging into the Blessing, staying home like her when all the others were gone at the ski lodge.

The lodge...

It felt like a bucket of ice water had been dumped over her. After that first attack, her friends had all gone skiing. Alicia and Owen had said that her father had paid for it, but Father had confirmed that he hadn't. What if her friends had been visiting her attacker?

"That look," Dylan said. "I was waiting for that. The knowledge that one of your friends betrayed you. Do you think any of them are going to rescue you now?"

Vicki yanked herself to the side, fighting at the bonds again. She didn't stop when she heard the click of the gun, when the muzzle was pressed to her knee. The Blessing could take care of that. She had to get out of the hands of this man; she had to get away and tell her father Owen had betrayed them.

The scream she let out when the muzzle went off with a flash, between the bullet hitting her and the Blessing taking over, was not one that she could control.

"So it's true, you've got another chump tied through that curse," Dylan said with a twisted smile. "But you only heal once the weapon leaves your flesh."

He lifted a blade from his belt, letting it shine in the flashing lights. "Something like this should demonstrate my point nicely."

Slowly, the blade began to pierce enough to draw blood, until it was running warm down both of her legs. The healed gunshot wound on one side, and the knife on the other. Vicki turned, trying to pull her leg from the blade, but Dylan's other hand reached out and forced her to be still. Pain radiated from the source as the blade slid into her knee. Sharp and precise, it continued to move until her skin met the hilt. Slicing through flesh like it was made for it. Her brain whited out with the pain. It was nothing like anything she'd ever experienced. This was lasting. The pain was staying and screaming and nothing else mattered.

Vicki stopped moving, stopped shaking, stopped throwing herself to try and tip the chair over. Sobs leaving her lips, she stared at the blade sticking out of her leg. The blood was turning her jeans red, pooling onto the ground under her bare foot. It wasn't healing.

It wasn't healing.

"Exactly like your friend predicted. It can't heal," Dylan said. The smile that crossed over his lips sent a fresh spike of fear through her heart. "Which means you can die, without killing that unlucky bastard on the other side."

The Blessing wasn't healing. He could hurt her. He could kill her. She didn't care about the unlucky bastard, whoever he was. The Chain she held didn't cause the other person to die when it broke. She didn't want *her* to die either. For the first time in her life, Vicki realized she might not make it out of this alive. The tremor under her skin had nowhere to go, and the seat under her grew wet.

The desperate scream that leaped from her lips was sent to heights she'd never reached before. "Help!"

Dylan disappeared behind the lights, but he wasn't quiet. He waited until her shouts died down to sobs, before he spoke. "There are so many options, you know." When he came back into view, he was showing something off like a game-show host. It was a long piece of wire, stained dark. "The garrote is one of my favorites. It took out your guards without a sound."

He tossed it onto the ground, letting the wire bounce and crash. Vicki flinched as the wire bit at her jeans, leaving a dark red line behind.

"But that one's too quick for you, Vicki," Dylan explained, looking at the weapon on the ground with disgust. "I suffered. Your friends endured. Your new whipping boy languished. Now it's your turn to feel the pain your Blessing has wrought."

The *Blessing*? What did the Blessing have to do with it? Owen had never helped her figure out how it worked. It just saved her. Why did he hate it? Why did it call it a curse? There were too few puzzle pieces for her to figure out the image they were supposed to make.

He stepped out of her sights again, and her breathing grew ragged. The Blessing had given her everything. It gave her the freedom to have friends. To play outside. To not be stuck in her father's protective bubble! It was freedom.

When he didn't come back, Vicki started twisting in place, trying to get her hand on the knife. The ropes that tied her to the chair could be sliced apart. Her leg would heal once the blade was gone. The rough fibers scratched and tore at her skin as she tried to pull a hand, her thumb, a finger, anything free. Tears stung her eyes, but she couldn't look away. Couldn't close them in case he reappeared in those precious seconds.

Vicki had never felt so stupid in her life. Why had she even spoken to him in the first place? Alicia's brother was dead, and this imposter was pretending to be him. It had to be. Dylan had been a kind person. So full of life. The person in front of her was nothing like him. Just some twisted person obsessed with her and her family. When she was free, she would have her father find out the magic that had been used to cut through her guard.

"None of that," the fake Dylan said as he flicked the handle of the knife in her leg. A new rush of pain shot through her as the knife moved.

He held up a vial. The dark glass was bright amber in the center under the lights. Liquid splashed inside as Dylan wiggled it in front of her. "This is your future."

Vicki shut her mouth, tightening her lips. If she was going to have a future, she needed to keep her mouth shut until help arrived.

"No," Dylan said, dropping into a frustrated growl as he pushed on the knife in her knee again.

The slice of agony made her mouth part in a hiss. But she shut her mouth in less than a second.

"You will drink this," Dylan said, holding the vial closer to her lips. "You can do it by choice, or I can force you." The knife in her knee twisted. "I hope you refuse."

Tears welled in Vicki's eyes as she tried to bite back her scream. The sting of her teeth against her tongue was so foreign that she startled away from the pain. Her whimpers let loose as the knife continued to move. Violent hot liquid splashed down her throat and into her airways. She coughed and sputtered as Dylan's fingers gripped her hair, shaking her hard enough to pull some of it out.

"Your father is a blight on society, and you are a leech," Dylan pronounced. "No one wants you. Your friends saw you for who you are and sold you to the reaper. You can try again in hell."

She let out a scream. A scream of help, a scream in pain, a scream to cover up that vile voice. Twisting and shaking, Vicki fought to get free, even as the world seemed to blur around the edges.

***

The hallways of the university were still blissfully empty of the crowds, but that did nothing to calm the dread building in Levi's stomach. Security still hadn't arrived to process the bathroom. Whether they were scouting for another lead on Vicki's whereabouts, or ignoring them, no one could say. The used spell scroll lay on the ground where Levi had left it, bloody from pressing against his knee. There was another one in his hand, still charged. The first one had knitted the skin, but had left the rest of the internal damage intact. Did he use the other one now? What if the spell was needed later? What if he *wasted* the spell? Healing a body that wasn't going to survive this anyway?

Levi pocketed the magic and pulled out his cell phone. The chances of him living through today were slim. He should tell Sammy. He knew it was going to piss off the surrounding people, and maybe even the Devil himself. But if he had some forewarning, he would not make Owen be the one that had to tell Sammy after his work here was done.

Levi shifted his weight, trying to find a comfortable way to lean against the wall. Sharp pain radiated from the limb every time he tried to put any weight on it. Bending it made dark spots dance in his eyes. He could feel the fatigue beginning in his so called good leg. His body was breaking down. It would be a wonder if he got to walk again. Looking at the scratched up screen, he dialed the number.

"What's wrong?" Sammy answered almost immediately.

"Why do you think something's wrong?" Levi asked, trying to put a smile in his voice. It came out like a grimace.

"Don't you play those games with me right now," Sammy replied, anger quick on their tongue. "What's happening?"

"Vicki's kidnapped," Levi replied, trying again to breathe through another wave of hurt. Make it sound like a normal conversation, and not a goodbye. "My guess is this is revenge."

"Dammit," Sammy replied.

"I figured I should let you know, save you the trip to the underworld and all that," Levi replied. The old familiar punch line fell flat as he tried not to choke on the words.

"Don't you even joke about that right now," Sammy ordered. "If Vicki's in danger, then all we have to do is get her out of it, yeah? Where am I meeting you?"

"We don't know where she is," Levi started, looking to see if anyone had found anything at all. Owen was scrolling through his phone and texting someone back and forth. Levi could only assume that it was his dad, or someone else involved in today's attempted rescue.

Alicia and Edwin were holding each other, their faces tucked close enough that they were hard to read.

"Wait, I've got something," Janie said. Tapping something on her phone, her eyes were almost sunken in with worry. "The lights are on at the nightclub."

"Nightclub?" Levi asked.

"Yeah, it's closed this week, but people are posting that the lights are all on, and there's music playing inside," Janie replied, showing everyone her screen. The feed of social media posts was filled with text and a few pictures of the building. "They think it's a private party."

"But it's probably a trap," Owen replied, looking at Levi with worry etched into his features.

"It's better than nothing," Levi replied.

"I've got the keys to Owen's car, and the pile of healing scrolls he left here," Sammy said through the phone's speaker. "Which nightclub am I meeting you at? Because I'm in for a bad night if I go to the wrong one."

That last comment kept Levi from giving the wrong address.

"Janie, can we have the keys to your car?" Owen asked. He glanced over to the blood that was still drying on Levi's jeans, an obvious check about whether Levi was too much of a mess to be in a car right now. He added, "I'll pay to get it detailed later."

Janie reached into her purse, rustling through the contents to find the key. "I'm coming with you," she insisted.

Owen opened his mouth to protest. Levi could tell by the crinkle in his brow and the defensiveness in his stance.

"I can't sit here and do nothing while you two investigate," Janie said, her eyes hard, fingers wrapped around the keys. "I can help. I found the posts, remember? And your attention is going to be split between tending to Levi and finding Vicki."

The fight bled out of Owen, as Sammy's voice pulled Levi back to their conversation.

"I'll see you there, don't die," Sammy commanded.

"Love you too," Levi hung up and slid the phone into his pocket. He had no control over life or death. That was all in the hands of someone else, and stopping them was still uncertain. The nightclub could be completely empty. It could be a decoy, while Vicki was being tortured in a warehouse somewhere. Still, he wasn't entirely ready to stop. Even if he had to crawl into his future, Levi wanted it. He had been saving for his funeral almost half of his life, but for the first time in years, he didn't want it to be spent.

Looping his arm over Owen's neck, he limped his way outside, trying not to slow anyone down. If they hurried, even if she wasn't there, perhaps it was some sick scavenger hunt and a clue would be waiting instead.

"We're going to save you," Owen promised, as Levi slid into the back seat. Janie was getting into the passenger side, while Owen had the keys. It wasn't ideal, with Owen getting over a hangover and Janie looking like her emotions were about to be a wreck the whole ride, but it was better than no one at all. Better to have the few people he trusted not to be the one behind the trigger.

"I'll do what I can to stay alive then," Levi replied. He buckled his seat belt and closed his eyes.

The tires squealed as they sped from the parking lot.

***

Owen didn't have time for traffic laws. The person who was holding Vicki hostage had already killed once today. His own abilities to stop them were nothing compared to the trained and armed men, currently lying dead in the university bathroom. All he had were his words, and that might not be enough. They might not find Vicki at all, but dammit, he had to try. This cycle of violence needed to stop. He was going to get to snuggle up with Levi and Sammy tonight. Today would just be a bad dream. There were no other acceptable options.

The nightclub was only a few blocks away, but the time that it took to get there had never felt longer. Even with his disregard for traffic laws, it was a lot of weaving, and waiting, and cursing before he pulled into a parking spot. The car wasn't in the space completely, and it had pulled in at an angle, but it was good enough.

"Now what?" Janie asked as she got out of the car. The parking lot had never been emptier when any of them had been here. Already there was a crowd of people outside, people with cameras like always when they thought Vicki would be here. The crowd was smaller than it was on weekends, but Owen recognized a few faces all the same.

"Ask around. See if anyone saw Vicki?" Owen asked, biting his lip. There was another car in the parking lot, a slick black sedan with tinted windows.

Pulling out his phone, he snapped a picture of it and sent it to his father. The more information he could collect, the better.

Instantly, his phone started ringing.

"What are you doing at the club?" his father demanded.

"Trying to rescue Vicki," Owen replied.

"No, absolutely not. This man has killed a half dozen of my men," Dad replied. "He will not look at you and let you leave alive. Leave this to the professionals."

"When will they get here?" Owen asked.

"As fast as they can," Dad replied.

Owen looked around, listening for the sirens or the revving of engines. "ETA?" he asked.

"Ten minutes," Dad replied.

Ten minutes. He might as well have said ten years. A jittery numbness washed over him.

"That's too long," Owen breathed. If he could breathe. The air around him felt like it was cutting him apart from the inside out.

"That's as fast as they get can there. You aren't trained, you aren't armed, and you're just as likely to get yourself shot by the teams inbound to rescue Vicki as the people that took her," Dad replied, his voice sharp and commanding. "Stay outside."

Owen looked at the back of the car, where a new spot of blood was forming on Levi's jeans. Was that the same one as before? Had the spell only partially healed the problem? Or was there a new injury that they didn't know about?

"We're running out of time," Owen stated.

Levi grabbed his arm. The grip was weak, and he spoke through gritted teeth. "Wait. Reinforcements are coming. We can wait."

"What if we can't?" Owen asked. He could hear his father still speaking, but his attention was solely on Levi.

"If we go in now, you might get killed, too. There's no guarantee that our speed will increase my chances," Levi pointed out. "You have no weapon, no training, and no protection. Don't run into your own death trying to stop mine."

Owen grimaced before he nodded. "We'll wait for backup, but if this gets worse… You can't stop me."

"Please, we're only a few minutes out," Dad replied, and the call ended.

"Wait for professionals, or Sammy, at least," Levi agreed, when Owen slid his phone back into his pocket.

But help was so far away. If what he'd heard was right, Sammy had just left Levi's apartment. They were as far out as the officers, or security forces.

"Vicki's in there," Janie said, coming back to them. Her face was pale, worry painting lines across her face. "She walked in with this guy." She had a social media post pulled up on her cell phone when she handed it over. The image was of Vicki, walking with a man whose arm was wrapped around her waist. Her head blocked part of the man's features, though it was clear that she wasn't in distress at this point.

Owen stared at the image, a nagging feeling at the back of his head. He couldn't place who the person looked like, though. Neither Levi nor Janie had any other information. But this was the first real clue that they had. If Janie was involved, there was no reason to show him this. Any last doubts that he had about her were removed from his mind. It left him with Alicia—Chained—and Edwin?

"Are you sure that they aren't in there partying, and this is some big misunderstanding?" Janie asked, looking like she was trying to grasp at straws.

Owen gave Janie a flat look. There was no way that the wounds that Levi was experiencing were from partying. Even if

Vicki had walked into the space of her own free will, things had changed once they were behind closed doors.

"Send that to me," Owen said, his eyes scanning around the building. If he had to wait out here, he was going to pass along as much intelligence as possible. Pictures of the outside of the building, the suspect, the license plate of the unknown car parked in the parking lot.

"Her dad is going to be pissed," Janie murmured. "After this, I don't know if she's ever going to be allowed out of the house."

Owen shook his head. It sounded like something Mr. Townsend would do. There weren't any lines that the Devil wouldn't cross for his daughter. Looking around at Levi, Janie, at his own bloodied clothes, to the other side of the road where the paparazzi had their cameras set up. Every person here could be worth sacrificing for Vicki's safety, Owen included.

Leaning against the car, Owen shivered. His jacket was still tied around Levi's leg to keep the bleeding away. The healing spell had stopped most of it, but taking away the material would only make things worse. Besides, it was already covered in crimson stains; he wasn't getting it back anytime soon. It left Owen with only a sweater against the early afternoon chill. He sat back in the driver's seat and cranked the engine again to warm up. Levi shivered with the new blast of air, and Owen cursed to himself. He messed with the dials to get the car warm again.

Owen's car got some air as it raced over the speed bump, pulling into the spot next to them. The brakes had it screeching to a stop. Steam was coming off the tires as the driver's door opened and Sammy stepped out. They were dressed in leather, not the same kind from the club either. It was more Matrix or vampire hunter in nature, and Owen had to wonder why they'd been dressed like that before they got the call.

"How's he doing?" Sammy asked. Their stride was several inches taller than usual in their lifted boots.

"I'm still alive," Levi said, turning to face them. He frowned at their outfit. "Were you about to go to work? I can't believe you got here faster than the police."

"I was driving faster, and there's a more direct route," Sammy replied, ignoring Levi's first question. They rolled their eyes as they got a good look at him. "You look like shit. How's he doing?"

"He's sitting right here," Levi grumbled, turning in the car to put his boots on the ground. He grabbed Sammy's arm and pulled himself to his feet. The motion was unbalanced. Owen couldn't do anything from the driver's seat, so he stood up to help. By the time he'd made it around the car, Levi and Sammy had figured it out.

"Do you have a jacket in your car that I can grab?" Sammy asked, offering a few things to Levi from the pocket of their coat. The healing scrolls that Owen had left in Levi's apartment, a mixture of ready to use and ones where the seals had already cracked.

"Uh, maybe, I'll check," Owen replied.

There had been something tight in his chest when he'd heard that "Love you too." He knew they were practically family, and those words shouldn't have hit him like that, but they did.

Maybe it was because of how short the clock felt today. Maybe it was because he felt like he might never hear them for himself. But Sammy would. They would get to hold that message close long after Levi was gone.

Shuffling back to his car, he popped open the trunk and dug through it to find an old hoodie. He also grabbed a scarf, which seemed like a better wrap for Levi.

Putting a brave face on, he worked with Sammy to rewrap Levi's knee, both worried about what was hiding under the cover of his jeans, and glad that they didn't have to look at it yet. Owen saw how Sammy pressed power into Levi's knee with every touch, how Levi tried to tell them to stop so they wouldn't get seen. There wasn't any fresh blood, from what he could tell. Still, as Sammy pushed power into the joint, the distress and unease on their face grew. Owen tensed, wondering what Sammy knew that he didn't.

Sirens stopped him from asking anything about it. Men and women in riot gear flooded out one van after another and moved into formation, teams at the front and at the back of the building. Another security crew—less armed than the first—went after the crowd with cameras across the street to move the herd away. A security fleet that belonged to Mr. Townsend pulled in with a screech of brakes; the familiar logo on the side of the van was the same one that sat on his father's work badge. The security squad took point at the side door into the club.

There was no loud burst of sound, no announcement of entry. The rescuers, the professional rescuers, were outside one moment and inside the next. Still, Owen didn't breathe a sigh of relief. Until Vicki was safe— Scratch that. Until the spell was removed from Levi, none of them could breathe easily.

In the moments after the local police and private security rushed into the building, another car pulled up. A frazzled and out of breath Alicia and Edwin stepped out of it.

Spotting the group by Janie's car, Alicia hurried over. "What's the news?" she asked.

Owen shrugged. "Not sure. We've heard nothing since they got here," he nodded towards the big trucks that previously held the security forces. A set of flashing red and blue lights announced the emergency vehicles as they came racing up the lane. Ambulances stationed in waiting, prepping stretchers and IVs.

"What took you so long to get here? You left right after us," Owen frowned.

"We got held up by campus security," Edwin replied. "We had to take the long way around to get off of campus. Vicki's here?"

"Whomever took Vicki tricked her into going into the building with her," Janie started, showing off the picture on the screen. "Someone posted one with a better angle."

Owen leaned over to take a look. It had to have been taken at the same time as the one that she had shown before, but this one had a better shot of the man's face. The image was familiar, like he had seen a picture of him before.

"Do you recognize him?" Owen asked.

"He looks like someone I should know," Edwin admitted, frowning. "I can't place him, though. Maybe we saw him at the nightclub?"

Owen's eyes widened as he looked at the picture again. "The new guard for the booth. Robbie. The one at the bottom of the stairs?"

"The guy that took the shot?" Janie asked, her eyes widening. "I thanked him for saving us from the attacker."

"Instead, he took out the guy who could point to him as an accomplice," Owen said, muttering a curse. "All the while, letting us think the attacker was dead."

The sounds of shots firing echoed from the building. Sammy and Owen turned to look at Levi.

Owen held his breath for the moment that one of those bullets hit the wrong target. "This is my fault," he hissed to Sammy alone. "I should have tried harder. If I had just had more time, maybe..." He couldn't even finish the thought. Fear gripped his heart as he glanced back and forth between Levi and the building. Flinching with every bang and crack that echoed out. Levi was still healing, patch-worked together from all of Vicki's poor decisions leading until now. Owen wasn't sure how much more Levi could take.

Sammy moved closer, shoulder pressed against Levi's shoulder. Owen reached out and took Levi's hand. Fingers sliding along Levi's palm, they pressed into the pulse point of his wrist. Part of him expected Levi to pull away. The anxiety of it vanished as Levi wrapped his fingers around Owen's grip and held on tight.

"We don't even know what the Blessing is," Sammy hissed, keeping their eye on the building as they picked at their fingers. Their acrylic nails clicked together with each movement. "How are we supposed to remove it?"

"It has to be a corruption of the Connection," Owen replied, despite all the arguments that Sammy had made before. "And if it's a Connection, then redirecting it or booting off the fake Connection should remove it, right?"

"If, *if!*, it's a Connection, then how come I can't kick that princess off of it?" Sammy asked. "There aren't that many studied magics around these things, other than breaking them, or pacts to add someone to them. I'll be damned before I break my Connection to Levi just to get that bitch off of it."

"Wish really, really, hard?" Owen guessed with a shake of his head. He wished he had an answer. Few people even believed these bonds existed; there wasn't a lot that he had discovered. All the spells that he'd found that were supposed to show which people were connected had all been proven to be fake. A week of tireless work, with no solutions to show for it.

He could hear Sammy's frustrated sigh, and hurried on. "I've been looking into this ever since I found out, but it's not been that long."

"Fuck," Sammy murmured. The side doors of the building burst open with a bang that made everyone jump. "Fuck!"

A set of people rushed forth, and out came Vicki, carried by an officer in riot gear. Blood trailed down both of her legs, and she was swaying dangerously in the officer's hold. How was that possible?

Levi pulled himself upright, twisting in the seat to look. He winced at Vicki's form. "That will not be fun," he grumbled.

"What's not?" Owen asked, glancing back towards Levi and then to Vicki. Then he saw the knife in Vicki's leg. "Oh, fuck."

"I don't know what's worse, not knowing when an injury is coming, or knowing one is on its way," Levi said, rubbing his eyes.

Janie was looking between Vicki and Levi and murmuring something under her breath. Owen only caught snippets. "All those injuries…"

Owen didn't press. He didn't want to get involved with Janie's questions.

Alicia and Edwin had already started towards Vicki as she was being loaded onto the stretcher. A heavy feeling settled into Owen's gut. An officer was trying to get Vicki's statement, while the EMT was loading her up to try and get her to a hospital. The amount of blood on her legs alone was making the EMTs look worried. Owen expected that most of the hospital personnel that were working on this were about to retire, or mysteriously vanish.

"I'll be back," Owen told his friends, before jogging away from Sammy and Levi.

Alicia and Edwin were already by her side when he got there, standing on the far side of the stretcher, while the EMTs continued to work.

Vicki narrowed her eyes at him when he got close. "I know it was you," she spat.

"Me what?" Owen asked. What did he do?

"You're the one that sold me out to that madman," Vicki cursed. "I heard it on the tapes."

Owen blinked, staring at her. What on earth was she talking about? Why did she think that? As far as he knew, she walked into the building with that man on her own. "What tapes? What are you talking about?"

"The Blessing conversation with Alicia, Dylan had it," Vicki spat.

"The conversation that Alicia asked for, and you somehow knew about?" Owen asked. The name was sending off alarm bells. Could his death have been a lie? People didn't die and then come back for revenge a decade later. "The conversion that I didn't know was being listened in on, about how I didn't think you should hurt yourself? That conversation?"

"There were only two people in the room, and Alicia couldn't have done it, so it had to be you," Vicki spat back. "I can't believe that I trusted you. You're dead to me. Get out of my sight. Father will deal with you and your betrayal."

That should have scared him. It should have. Even a false accusation to the Devil of this magnitude could mean a world of hurt for him and his father. But her threats were nothing compared to what the Devil could do to Levi. That scared him far more.

Instead, he looked at the knife still sticking out of her knee and asked the EMTs, "What's the recovery for that look like? For someone that doesn't have Healers."

"We won't know until they get a look," the EMT replied.

Owen nodded and braced for the worst. Would Levi struggle to walk for the rest of his life, while Vicki continued on as perfect as ever?

"What are you looking at, pervert?" Vicki exclaimed. "Get away from me."

"Thank you," Owen told the EMT, ignoring Vicki's ranting behind him. Instead, he looked at Alicia and Edwin. His conversation with Alicia had been recorded and given to someone else. There was only one way that could happen, if Alicia hadn't done it herself.

"We were in your bedroom when we had that talk," Owen said to Alicia, trying to watch for her reaction. If Alicia wasn't involved, if she was another victim in all of this, maybe she could give the culprit away. He glanced at Edwin, but all Owen saw was a man wrapping his arms around his girlfriend. Someone here was behind this. But picking the wrong person could mean a death sentence. Then the true culprit would go free and try again. "Vicki's claiming that the person who did this had a recording of it. You should check the room for bugs."

"Bugs? Oh gods, what if there were cameras in there?" Alicia said, her eyes going wide.

Her shock and horror looked real. Fuck. He needed proof. *Real proof.*

Owen stepped back from the ambulance doors so they wouldn't hit him as it got loaded up. Alicia and Edwin tried to step into the back of the vehicle, but the EMT refused.

"Family only, you can meet us at the hospital," medical staff told them, and shut the doors in their face.

Hospital. Owen could only imagine the medical tests and spells that Vicki would have done to help her heal. The knife wound that would transfer to Levi as soon as they removed the weapon. It wasn't fair; Vicki got all the treatment, and Levi was left with the injuries. Levi was the one that needed a doctor. But could Levi even go?

He was deep in thought about how to get Levi to care as he walked back to the car where Janie was pacing. She was glancing back and forth from the ambulance and the nightclub, where there were still sounds of gunfire. Levi was leaning against the back of the car, tensed and waiting for when the Blessing was going to take over and give the injury to its new owner.

Alicia and Edwin were walking over to their own car, not back to the others. Owen caught a flash of something metallic in Edwin's waist band. Gun? Or was he being paranoid?

Janie had stopped pacing as the gunfire settled down; she looked terrified in the silence. Was he wrong about Alicia and Edwin? Was Janie involved too? God, he was not cut out for this kind of guesswork and suspicion. These were his friends that he was looking at!

There were still three cars in the parking lot that didn't belong to the police, or emergency personnel: Owen's car, Janie's, and the one that Dylan had drove. The police were starting their way, and he did not want to get caught up in a blockade. He stepped around Janie's car and started towards his own, offering his hand out towards Sammy to get the keys.

Sammy reached into their pocket and tossed them at him. For once, Owen caught them with ease.

"We're going to the hospital to monitor Vicki and make sure there's not another attack," Owen said, offering Janie's keys back to her. Maybe using Levi's directive to protect Vicki might allow them to get past whatever bullshit was keeping Levi from going to get medical help. He had to try. When Levi didn't argue, Owen continued. "You don't have to go, but I don't think you should stick around here."

Janie looked at the ring of keys in her hand, before following over to Owen's car. "I'm not staying here by myself," she replied, clutching her keys in her fist. "Meet you at the hospital."

Levi and Sammy got into the back seat together. Owen grabbed the spell cards and handed them back to Sammy, before he cranked the engine. If they started into surgery on Vicki before they got to the hospital, Levi would start bleeding again. He did not want to find out how much healing it would take for Sammy to start down the path to their own self destruction.

As he drove, Owen glanced back at the pair in the rearview mirror. Even at a glance, he could see how pale Levi looked.

"Use another scroll or two," he suggested, looking at Sammy this time. "Our patient was refusing them earlier."

"I can handle that," Sammy replied, their voice tight.

The weight of dread that had settled on Owen's skin didn't lighten as he drove. Disquieted fear only grew with Levi's muffled grunts of pain; they punctuated every bump in the road or turn of the car.

CHAPTER 17

Vicki found herself in a hospital bed, waiting for her father to show up. The Blessing had healed away the damage to her knee as soon as the blade had been removed, but the aching twist in her gut and the fire in her veins were still there. Vague memories were just out of reach of doctors and nurses, working with her to purge the poison coursing through her. No expense had been spared between the spell scrolls and Healers, and the raw ache in her throat from vomit.

In their wake, a numbness had set in. She wasn't allowed to get up and leave. Her lips were cracked and dry, but both food and drink were completely out of her mind. Her stomach was tight and twisting with the ice chips used to lessen the ache. Exhaustion weighed on her shoulders, and every time she closed her eyes, the memories of being trapped jumped back as if it were happening all over again.

No one wants you. Dylan's voice rang through her head. *Your friends saw you for who you are and sold you to the reaper.*

When the flash bang had filled the room, Vicki had been left with spots in her eyes, ringing in her ears, and no knowledge of where she was going. All she knew was that someone was leading her out while she'd limped along. She hadn't even seen Dylan go down; it left her nerves fried and her body tensing for another attack.

Alicia and Edwin were the first ones to reach her side. With all of their faults, those two were the ones that she could always counted on. Then Owen had showed up with a pleading face and ugly desperation. Owen. The traitorous bastard who had sold her out. The one that had figured it out just in time to use it against her. She shouldn't have trusted him with the Blessing, shouldn't have shown it off to him. With all the nerdiness that he put off, she thought Owen could tell her more. Instead he'd learned how to use the spell to make her suffer.

The doors to her hospital room opened and Father strode in. There was an anger in his eyes that told her that he was focused on getting something done. She knew that look. If she didn't voice her opinions now, he would take those decisions from her with no input at all. Pulling herself upright, she ignored the exhaustion and the terror, and put on her most annoyed voice. "Thank god you're here. The nurses put an alarm on my bed so I can't get up without them coming in and checking on me." Vicki crossed her arms in front of her chest.

"You are still under their care," Father replied, walking over to the bed. Anger melted into concern as he looked down at her. "Now that the poison is out of your system, I want them to look at your knee and check if the Blessing took the whole wound, or if the small amount of healing performed in the ambulance before the blade was removed has messed with the spell."

"You're saying that the Blessing didn't take all of it?" Vicki asked, sitting up further. "The pain is gone. There's nothing there to look at."

"We'll see about that," Father replied. "I'm concerned about the ramifications. The amount of people that are now aware of your current healing abilities has increased substantially. I've had to pay a few Healers to say that they did the work themselves, and bribe the surgeons to look the other way. That, and a number of your friends now know the side effects."

"Side effects? What side effects?" Vicki asked. That knot in her stomach was twisting again. Was this about poison not being covered, or was he talking about something else?

Father didn't answer. Instead, he looked over the chart at the end of Vicki's bed. A dark scowl took over her features, growing worse the longer he read.

"Fine, don't tell me," Vicki grumbled, releasing her crossed arms to lean back into the pillows.

"Tell me what happened," Father instructed when he put the chart back.

"Dylan took me by surprise. He hit me over the head, which got healed instantly but caused me to black out," Vicki explained. "When I came to, I was bound to a chair. Then he…wait, that's it. Owen. Owen sold me out to that guy. I know it."

"That's a very serious accusation," Father stated, his voice a dangerous calm. "Are you sure? With no doubt that it was Owen and not a trick by your attacker?"

Vicki explained all of her reasoning. First there was the taped conversation between Alicia and Owen, which she had set up and had listened in on, so she knew it was real. Then all of her friends had gone to the lodge after the attack, even though Owen had claimed that he hadn't been there.

Father shook his head the moment she finished. "Is that the only evidence that you gathered? What about motive?"

"What are you talking about? It's all there," Vicki pointed out.

"If there is something that Owen wants, it is that the Blessing be destroyed, not you," Father replied, anger on his face again. "Once again, you are blind in your attempts to lead your group of friends. Your evidence has so many holes in it, you may as well be giving me a net."

"Don't you trust your daughter?" Vicki asked.

"Owen spoke to me before I walked into this room, explaining how you had accused him at the ambulance," Father continued. "In his own words, he explained that you had set up the conversation with Alicia, but he had no idea that it had been recorded. How he and Levi had been the ones that noticed that you were missing. Janie corroborated how Owen had been the first to track you down, when no one else knew you were gone. He had nearly rushed in to rescue you—we had to tell him to wait. Yet, you accuse him, rather than think that Owen himself was set up."

Vicki shook her head. Owen had gotten to him, too. None of that sounded like the Owen that she knew. He was a worrywart, always calling out danger in corners, when there was none. Sure, he had been the first one to point out the mugger hidden in the shadows, but of course he had. Owen knew the mugger was there already.

This had to be a setup to prove something to her father, get a promotion or something else.

"It was his words that helped Dylan know how to hurt me," Vicki pointed out.

"How so? The recording has not yet been recovered," Father asked.

"Owen was the one that pointed out that the Blessing doesn't heal if there is something around the wound," Vicki explained. "Dylan knew that if he stabbed a knife into my knee that it wouldn't heal because Owen told him."

"Told your kidnapper, or told Alicia?" Father pointed out, his eyes blazing again. "Use your brain, child." His fingers gripped the edge of the bed as he stared at her. There was disappointment on his face as he lectured on. "Use the evidence in front of you, and not your prejudices. If Owen sold you out, then find the proof. If you pick wrong, and send the one friend that has been protecting your life away, then you are left with the ones that sold you out in the first place."

Vicki rolled her eyes. She wasn't wrong about her choice. No one else fit.

"Alicia is loyalty bound. She couldn't have done it. Edwin cares about me, and so does Janie. That only leaves Owen, who has been distant since this whole thing started," Vicki replied, trying to point out the obvious.

Father let go of the bed and shook his head. "You're missing a piece," he said. "Owen does not want you harmed. I hold something over him that is more powerful than a loyalty bond. Either give me stronger evidence of the contrary, or find another to accuse." There was a knock at the door, and he called for the ones on the other side to come in.

It was the set of nurses that had been bullying her before.

"Do the tests," her father instructed them as he stepped out of the way. "I want to see if there is anything that the Healers missed."

As he moved out of the room, Father stopped and looked back at her. "We will speak of this again soon."

Vicki grabbed her pillow and threw it at her father as he left, letting out a cry of anger. The pillow barely made it past the foot of her hospital bed. Her father couldn't see what was right in front of him. Owen was the only possibility. No one else fit.

***

There was a waiting room at the hospital set up just for Owen and the others, while Vicki got the tests done on her knee. The Devil's daughter was permitted to have an entire floor of the complex to herself. Owen suspected it was just to keep her friends contained, while Vicki was medically vulnerable. After this, Owen supposed that there might be a new wing to the hospital named after one of the Townsend family members, matching the one at the children's hospital. The only one that wasn't here was Levi; he had been whisked away to another room to get his knees and head treated. For some reason, it was frowned upon for someone to limp into the hospital, all broken and bloody, and then not get care. Mr. Townsend had even offered to put Levi in a single room, but Owen knew that wasn't out of the kindness of his heart. He was only trying to cover up the side effects of the Blessing. Owen did not envy the nurse that was stuck finding all the half-healed wounds on Levi, and left with more questions than answers.

Mr. Townsend's face was blank as Owen stepped up to him. He needed to know if he was allowed to talk to Vicki, to get more of the sides of the story, or if he was allowed to go to Levi. Both had been forbidden until Mr. Townsend was done with his visit.

"Was I accused?" Owen asked.

"You were," Mr. Townsend said. He concealed away all of his emotions from Owen's view, just as the man always had.

"Anything I need to prove an alibi for?" Owen asked.

"The ski trip Alicia set up," Mr. Townsend replied. "The one that everyone, except you, went on after the attempted mugging. Why didn't you go?"

That felt like a lifetime ago; Owen had to take a moment to even find his answer. "My Dad had been assigned a new project, and I was curious about it. I thought it might have to do with what happened with the mugger. Dad didn't tell me anything about it, but I figured it out on my own later. Enough, at least," Owen explained, knowing that didn't give him a lot of protection. If Mr.

Townsend thought that the rest of Vicki's friends had been sent on the ski trip so that he could talk to the attacker alone, he didn't have an alibi. "That, and I have bad ankles. I've only gone skiing once, and it wasn't a good time."

Mr. Townsend nodded, but didn't look convinced.

"I told Alicia what I did about the spell because it seemed like Vicki wanted to test it," Owen added. "Wanted to test the boundaries of healing, and what would be protected and what wouldn't. I needed to warn them away from that." His eyes drifted to the door of the hospital room that he'd been barred from. There was a pair of guards stationed outside Vicki's room. Another pair further down the hall. None of it helped his unease.

Mr. Townsend followed his gaze and nodded. "Your loyalty is commendable, even if it's focused on the wrong place."

It was a bold statement from Mr. Townsend, considering how Owen had pointed out his own loyalty to keeping Vicki safe when they all first got here.

It had been Owen who demanded that Levi get the care he needed. *The Blessing only works while Levi is alive. If your goal is to keep your daughter safe and whole, then my desire to keep Levi in the same state should show we're on the same side.*

Owen shrugged, figuring that was a better response than fighting the point. "Did we find the attacker?"

Mr. Townsend shook his head. "I have magicians scouring the building. We found concealment scrolls at the nightclub and the school, so there's a possibility he hasn't left yet."

Owen hummed, looking around the waiting room. If Dylan was still out there, then this wasn't done yet.

It seemed the Mr. Townsend was done with entertaining Owen's curiosity, because he stepped away, leaving the room to just the young adults. Sammy had since maneuvered next to Janie; the two were talking quietly with each other. It was either join them, or talk to Alicia and Edwin. He picked the ones who hadn't accused him of murder, twice.

"What are you two working on?" Owen asked.

"Trying to track down who Dylan is," Janie replied. "We know he said something to make Vicki trust her."

"Vicki knew a Dylan," Owen said, watching to see if there was any recognition of the name in Janie's eyes. There wasn't. Then again, Janie had never met Dylan. He'd been gone for half a decade before she'd joined their group. "Alicia's older brother."

"But he's…" Janie started.

"Yeah," Owen nodded. Still, it was futile to accuse a dead man. "So, someone's pretending to be him?"

If someone had pretended to be Dylan to Vicki, did that mean they'd pretended for Alicia as well? Or was the connection between his oldest friend and the attacker one that pointed blame on the wrong person?

Owen wanted to rip his hair out.

"What did Mr. Townsend want?" Janie asked.

"I was just asked about the ski trip that you and the others went on after the mugging," Owen said as he sat down. It made him miss the chair at Levi's apartment, all cozy and comfortable. These were too stiff and too new, impossible to find a good way to relax in.

"It was odd, Alicia said that it was something that Mr. Townsend set up for all of us to get away, and that Vicki was going to be there too," Janie began to explain, "but when we got there, it was just me, Brooke, Alicia, and Edwin at the lodge," She finally looked up from her phone. "I figured it was just some kind of mix-up, and it was a free trip, so why wouldn't I stay?"

"I would have thought the same," Owen replied. "Alicia's the one that told me about the trip as well, but I couldn't make it for other reasons, so I stayed home."

Janie nodded. "It was while we were there that Alicia and Edwin started hooking up again, which also wasn't out of the ordinary. They would go on these dates, or stay back while Brooke and I went skiing or were enjoying the lodge."

"So, is there a chance that either of them could have met up with Dylan while on the trip and you wouldn't have seen it?" Sammy asked, glancing at Alicia and Edwin.

Janie's shoulder slumped. "Maybe. Though Brooke and I weren't together the whole time, so maybe she…" Janie shook her head. "It's just, none of this feels right. Pointing fingers at our friends? What if it turns out to all be this Dylan guy and none of us are involved?"

"Then we clear our names, all of us," Owen replied. "That's what I've been doing. Even though I know I'm not involved, I've been clearing my name too. Dylan had a recording of a conversation between Alicia and I that happened in her bedroom. That means that someone had gone into that room to leave a recording device. The only ones that could have done that would be me, Alicia, Edwin, or Dylan. So we go through to figure out who didn't, and cross their names off the list."

"How do you prove a negative?" Janie asked.

"Very, very, carefully," Owen grumbled. All he wanted was the evidence not to point directly at Alicia and Edwin. As much as their friendship had fallen apart recently, he didn't want to believe that either of them were capable of kidnapping and attempted murder.

Janie turned back to her research, and Owen pulled out his own phone to do the same. All the while, he kept one eye out for mysterious shadows, and Edwin and Alicia on the other side of the room. Leaning against Edwin with her head tucked into his shoulder, he couldn't see Alicia's expression at all.

**

Levi didn't like how the medication that he was on was messing with his senses. He kept having to look down to double check that his leg hadn't been amputated below the knee—both legs were still there. It wasn't that there was no pain from that leg, but he was struggling to control his limbs right off the bat. The feeling of not being in control, and not having those he trusted to watch his back in here, had filled his mind with nightmares. He kept turning over to talk to Sammy or Owen, and finding himself alone.

The other part of the nightmare was that out of the corners of his eyes, he kept seeing movement just out of reach. If Dylan knew he was tied to the spell, then taking Levi out meant Vicki would be left completely defenseless.

Finally, the doctors came and talked to him about his healing journey. He was going to need to use a wheelchair at first, and then crutches and a cane while he healed and built the strength back up.

"If you choose to use healing spells, then you can skip a few steps, but you will still need physical therapy," the doctor offered.

Levi nodded, working on getting himself dressed so that he could get out of here.

"Wheel me to my friends, Doc," Levi said, once he had pants on. He didn't think it was going to work, but he didn't have the filter that he normally did. The medication had loosened his tongue, and he was not staying in this shadow-filled room anymore.

The doctor was not the one behind the wheel. After Levi pushed and navigated out of the room, a nurse took over to take him to his friends. Luckily they were in a big shot hospital with an elevator, because he would be stuck if he had to go up a flight of stairs.

Owen and Sammy rushed over the moment they spotted him.

"Damn, you look like shit," Sammy commented. "Whose pants are those?"

"Not a clue," Levi replied. They weren't his, those had been cut off the moment he'd been evaluated. He got sympathy pants instead, which were thin enough that he didn't think they would do anything against the freezing night air. "That was a bougie ass room though, so I want to leave before they stick me with the bill."

"They're billing Mr. Townsend," Owen said with a grin as he pulled the wheelchair closer to their seats. "I might have pointed out that it was in his best interest that you got the best medical care possible."

Levi smiled at his friends. He knew that both Sammy and Owen just wanted the best for him, even if that wasn't really achievable. The Blessing still tied him to Vicki. Even if this kidnapper and attempted murderer was captured, it would only be a matter of time before someone else stepped in to give it another go. Today, though, he had been given another chance, for at least a few more precious hours. Maybe he'd be out of the wheelchair before the next one appeared.

"So, now what, do we go home?" Levi asked, putting his hands on the wheels to see if he could lean back enough to balance in the chair.

Owen reached out to keep him grounded. "Come on, you're not even out of the hospital yet," he teased.

"I mean, if I'm going to get hurt doing something stupid, this is the place to do it, right?" Levi asked.

"Are you high?" Owen asked.

Levi shrugged. "Maybe. They gave me all kinds of pain meds. I'm not really a fan of them though, they keep making my legs feel weird. Plus, you know, I keep thinking I see someone out of the corner of my eye, so I'm hoping that nothing is coming for me."

"Yeah," Owen replied. "I can imagine." He looked around the room too, and Levi felt a surge of gratitude that he was here.

Rolling back and forth in the wheelchair, it was only as he fidgeted that he realized no one else was here. It was empty except for Sammy and Owen.

"Where's everyone?" Levi asked.

"Dinner, I think," Owen replied. "Vicki's still in her room. Something about wanting some tests done before she can leave."

"So we're all still here?" Levi asked, looking around. He didn't know if having everyone here provided a sense of safety, or dread. "Oh, Alicia's coming back, I think."

Owen turned to look in the same direction. But Levi was struggling to pay attention; what the hell was in those drugs? The light and shadows around Alicia's face kept changing, almost making her unrecognizable. Still, Levi wasn't looking at her face, but her gait. There was a purpose to the movement that sent alarm bells ringing.

Owen hissed as he stood up. "Stay back," he ordered, as he walked up to meet her.

Levi looked to Sammy, before nodding that they should follow. Something felt wrong, but the drugs that he was on made him too addled right now to figure it out. He rolled the chair along the floor as he crept behind.

Alicia was headed towards the room that he guessed belonged to Vicki. There had been no reason for him to visit her, so Levi didn't know for sure. He kept thinking that there was something in her hand, but his eyes couldn't focus on whatever the object was. Was this still part of his drugs, or some kind of spell?

Owen quietly hurried to catch up. Levi was having to focus to keep up, not wanting to be left behind with whatever was about to happen. His arms ached as he pushed the wheelchair forwards, the muscles not ones that he'd used like this before.

"Let go, I'll push you," Sammy hissed as Levi nearly crashed into the wall.

It wasn't his fault that his arms were noodles and he was high as kite. The moment that Sammy took control, they were cruising.

Alicia was already in the doorway of the only open room, before Owen had caught up to her. Levi was surprised to find that there were no guards standing on either side of the door. Nothing to block their path.

"Alicia! Hi!" Vicki's voice came from the room.

Owen followed in a half step behind Alicia, but Sammy stopped the chair before they got to the room itself.

"Stay out here, something's up," Sammy whispered, setting his chair next to the wall and away from the doorway. Then Sammy stepped into Vicki's room themself, effectively blocking the doorway.

Levi knew what Sammy was doing, trying to make sure that Levi wasn't in the line of fire if something started happening, or if Vicki needed medical attention. But it left him alone with all of his worried thoughts.

The conversation drifting through the door sounded off. It reminded him of a phone call, where he could only hear one side, but there were plenty of other people in the room to be conversing in return. A heaviness settled in his stomach as Vicki's voice rose in alarm.

"What? Alicia, stop!" Vicki called.

A yell filled the space, then a crack of a gunshot rang through the hallway. Alarm bells and screaming filled his ears, but he wasn't in any pain. Something was wrong. The meds clouded his senses, but the horror punched through him and knocked his breath away.

In front of him, Sammy dashed further inside. It gave him room to wheel closer. There were shouts at the end of the hall behind him, but he paid them no mind.

A smoking gun on the floor, a few feet away from everyone else. Alicia screaming out and writhing in pain on the floor. Vicki standing over her, hand clenched tight and twisting the air.

Something was missing. Levi's eyes scanned the room, finding Sammy kneeling on the ground.

Levi's heart froze, blood rushing through his ears. On the ground, was Owen. A trail of blood leaked from an open wound in his chest.

***

Owen hadn't recognized Alicia at first. The woman that walked passed them looked nothing like his long-time friend. If Levi hadn't called her out, Owen wouldn't have noticed her at all. But when he looked closer, he could see the effects of magic, trying to conceal Alicia's identity as she passed. The same kinds of spells that he had seen some of his father's plainclothes security use at Townsend special events, like their holiday parties. It was the piece of evidence that Owen had been hoping not to find, and Alicia was heading right to Vicki's room.

Hissing at Levi and Sammy to stay right there, out of harm's way, Owen got up to follow. Of course, when he checked back, both Sammy and Levi were close behind. Levi rolling along in his wheelchair, too stoned to drive straight, and Sammy with the same worried face that mirrored his own.

Owen glanced around for Vicki's security personnel. There were nurses on the other end of the hall, and a guard all the way at the back stairwell. The door to Vicki's room was unadorned with any protective detail. Where was the security? They were supposed to be here! Did something or someone draw them away? Owen tried to keep up with Alicia, without blocking her way. There were doctors, nurses, and staff that could get hurt if Alicia was planning something.

Alicia stepped into Vicki's room a half step before Owen. It was spacious and far emptier than he would have expected. There were no balloons, flowers, or get better soon cards on the side table. No one was sitting on the couch. There was no nurse keeping a constant eye on this very expensive patient. It was just Vicki in the bed, and the monitoring equipment strapped to her.

Her face lit up when Alicia stepped inside. "Alicia, hi! You made it," Vicki called. She was still in her bed, though she was wearing new clothes and not the hospital gown. She had her makeup out in front of her, and it looked like she was using a heavy hand on the concealer around her bloodshot eyes. There was another tray of food off to the side, which looked better than any hospital food that he had ever seen before, despite it all being liquid.

"I'm so glad that you could visit," Vicki continued, as if Alicia had responded, even though Owen hadn't heard anything. "I was just texting Brooke to compare our meals. Also, do you think you guys could bring me balloons and flowers? This might be my only time in a hospital bed, and I want the whole experience."

While Vicki sounded like herself, there was a slight tremor in her hand, and her smile didn't reach her eyes. From where he was standing, Owen could see that Vicki was trying so hard not to let her kidnapping get to her. So, it didn't surprise him that Vicki continued talking, that she didn't notice that Alicia hadn't joined the conversation.

Owen almost didn't see the gun. The concealment charms that Mr. Townsend mentioned before rang through his mind. The click of the safety was what finally clued him in.

"What? Alicia, stop!" Vicki called.

Owen didn't have time to think. This close, it would be a miracle if Alicia missed.

Charging forwards, his feet kicked off the ground without a thought. Grabbing the hand that held the gun, Owen tried to throw it to the side, while the rest of his weight sent Alicia crashing to the ground.

He felt the gun go off just as much as he heard it. The pain blossoming through him felt like regret.

***

Levi forgot all about the surgeries to both his knees when he pulled himself from the wheelchair to get to Owen. His debilitating injuries didn't feel like anything at all.

Sammy was already there, tears streaming down their face as they put pressure on the wound. Doctors and nurses would be flooding the room in seconds, but Levi didn't look for them. There was still life in Owen's eyes. With it, Levi latched onto hope.

"You're going to be okay," Levi promised, pressing his hand over Sammy to help stop the bleeding. "We're going to make sure of it. Okay?"

Owen was nodding, whispering something, and Levi wished he could pay enough attention to hear it. Instead, his mind had latched onto the injustice of it all. Of all the people whose wounds he could steal, whose life he could save, it wasn't Owen's.

Owen, who Levi had found curled up in that old recliner, asleep from the endless hours of reading up on ways to save Levi's life. The one that had crashed into his apartment when he got hurt, with the anger of a thousand souls because Vicki had tested the Blessing. The one who'd torn down all of his walls with the delicacy of an industrial demolition. The one that Levi had held at arm's reach, hoping to keep his own funeral small. It wasn't supposed to be for this.

Fury flooded him, as arms pulled Levi away from Owen. People in blue scrubs and white coats swarmed the scene. It wasn't supposed to be Owen there on the ground.

The dark red blood on his hands was too literal to feel real.

A scream erupted from his lips. "It should be me!"

Roaring wind flooded his ears as his vision dimmed. The world flipped inside out and upside down. All of his limbs were gone, and then reattached with a clarity that he had never known, and at long last, pain.

Blossoming in Levi's chest, right where it belonged.

CHAPTER 18

The sound of bustling nurses and the steady *beep beep beep beep* of machines drew Owen back to the land of the living. He could feel where those devices were hooked up to him. A hand was covering his own. He was alive? There was a heaviness to his eyes; it took a few tries to get them open to look around. A shape of a person sitting was there. It was their hand over his own.

"I swear to god, I will hunt you down if you don't wake up," came the whispered voice, and Owen would have smiled if he knew how to control his features right now. Sammy.

He pulled his fingers closed, trying to squeeze their hand. The movement alone must have been enough, because Sammy turned their attention his way.

"Oh thank god," Sammy breathed as they squeezed back. Their eyes were filled with tears. "You and Levi are going to be the death of me, I swear it."

"What-" Owen asked.

"You jumped in front of a loaded gun," Sammy replied. "They had to dig the bullet out, which admittedly would have been easier if someone hadn't decided to take the wound, but leave the fucking bullet." Their voice got louder with each word; there was anger in it near the end.

Owen flinched, even though the anger was not directed at him. "What?" he asked.

"Levi figured out a new trick," Sammy replied. "He's alive, thankfully. But you're the first to have woken up."

"Levi?" Owen tried to sit up, but the gentle push of Sammy's hand was enough to keep him stuck in bed.

"He's going to be okay," Sammy replied. "The best Healer around is going to make sure that the pair of you idiots heal up quick as can be. In the meantime, rest. Your dad will be back soon. This is the first time he's stepped away since you came out of surgery."

Owen leaned back into the pillows, wondering where the new wave of drowsiness was coming from. "Who's with Levi?"

"You two scored a double room, so I've been sitting with both of you," Sammy replied.

Their voice kept drifting further and further away. He was going to have to ask Sammy how they pressed the button on his pain pump without his notice.

***

Vicki was having a terrible day. Ever since she had gotten home from the hospital, everything in her life was falling apart. Alicia, gone. Edwin, gone. Janie had stopped by to say that she needed some time to reevaluate her life, and now when Vicki tried to call or text her, the number didn't go through. Owen, in the hospital. Levi was there too for some reason. It was the weekend, the first Saturday since her kidnapping, but Vicki barely noticed the time passing anymore. Stuck in her home provided her with no means of escaping her mind, or her boredom.

But the worst of it all was the burn on her neck from the curling iron this morning. The bruise on her knee from knocking it into the side table. The paper cut from the documents that her father had made her go through the night before, withdrawing her from university. Her father was forcing her to take a gap year, effective immediately.

The Blessing was gone.

Vicki didn't know how to live without it. Not that she'd dared to live dangerously; she didn't *seek* to hurt herself. But the clumsiness of the day just seemed to build and build.

By lunch, Vicki stomped over to her father's office to demand that he fix it.

"The Blessing is still gone," Vicki stated, arms crossed as she barged into the space.

Mr. Mills and Father were in a meeting. Perfect. She could get answers that way.

Mr. Mills didn't turn to look at her. He continued talking, as if she hadn't interrupted.

"Edwin and Dylan are still on the run," he read from some kind of report on a tablet in his lap. "I doubt they are travelling together, though. There's evidence that Edwin didn't know about the plot. He bought the gun legally for Alicia for self-defense. We're closing in on him now. Edwin booked a flight in his own name to Argentina."

Father nodded. "Good, continue working with law enforcement. I expect Alicia will not flip on her brother, even though she was the one with the gun. Her lawyer will try to talk some sense into her."

Vicki flinched. The gun. She thought that all the loyalty bonds in the world would have prevented something like that. Right until she'd seen the gun pointed at her face. Even with the protections of the Blessing, Vicki had flinched, scrambling to get her fingers around the pendant to get her best friend back under control. It had been something that she'd worn as a last resort, but Vicki had never expected to actually use it. How Alicia had just crumpled when Vicki had gotten her fingers around it was a new feature in her nightmares.

"What do you know about Dylan's whereabouts?" Father asked. He didn't look at her either.

Vicki slid into a chair in the office, looking from her father to Mr. Mills, trying to find out what was happening. Her father had his own methods of punishing her; this had never been one of them.

"Disappeared," Mr. Mills replied. "Though, now that I am aware of the Blessing, we found motive. It appears that Dylan cut his own Connection to break the previous hold and faked his death."

Cut his Connection? Vicki's chest tightened like a vice at the idea. Cutting Connections was akin to torture. It was something in movies and story books that caused heroes to give in to the dark side, or become a broken shell of themselves. *Dylan had done that to himself?*

"We found traces of him bedridden in a hospital under his assumed name," Mr. Mills continued. "There are reports that even with all of the Healers they could, he would not be able to walk again."

"Did he mysteriously get better?" Father asked.

"Not at first," Mr. Mills replied. "But the concealment charms are all from Artifact. Evidence suggested that he traded information to their board of directors, for a chance to walk again and carry out his plot."

Artifact? The tech company? Half the technology in her college was Artifact branded, though Vicki had never been allowed to own anything of theirs.

Glancing at her father, she could see the tightness around his eyes at the name. There was something more about the company that she didn't know. Wouldn't know unless she started digging into it herself. A gap year could give her plenty of time.

When he finally looked at Vicki, she could feel the pressing weight of her father's stare.

"Alicia found out about the Blessing the day of your ski accident, didn't she?" Father asked.

Vicki looked down at her hands and nodded. It had been years, and she still felt the same nervousness as she had the day it had happened.

Until recently, it had been the scariest day of her life. They were all supposed to hit the slopes together, but Dylan had backed out at the last moment. Vicki hadn't wanted to wait, so she'd grabbed Alicia and headed out. Vicki was young enough then that she was supposed to be making sure that adults knew where she was going, and old enough to sneak off anyways. Vicki didn't remember whose idea it had been to go down that particular route; the amount of trees she'd hit on the way down had made her lose a few brain cells. By the time the world had stopped moving, the Blessing had already kicked in. Alicia had been staring at her the whole time.

Blood caked in her hair, and lungs still aching from the impact, Vicki had made her way up the mountain. She and Alicia were halfway up the hill when they found Dylan laying limp on the ground. She still remembered how ashen Alicia had looked when they were told Dylan wouldn't walk again.

"Yeah, Alicia found out that day," Vicki stated, not looking up. "But it was okay, she didn't..." She didn't betray that secret. The Chain Vicki bound her with ensured that, or at least it did then. Her words died in her mouth. The sounds of the gun going off in her hospital room echoed in her ears. "Did you ever find the recording?" she asked instead.

"We found a copy on Alicia's computer," Mr. Mills replied. "It contains Alicia's side of the phone call with you before Owen got there." At that point, Mr. Mills pulled the screen protector over the front of the tablet, effectively closing it. "Speaking of my son, I'm going to get back to him. Considering everything, I hope that the conditions that his partner put forward will suit you?"

Partner? The simple word shot through her like ice, freezing her veins. There could only be one person who fit that description. That friend stealing bastard.

Father nodded, standing up from his desk. He walked around to shake Mr. Mills' hand. "You and your son have been loyal to this family, and that loyalty will be rewarded. Keep me up to date if you get any more information about either Edwin or Dylan, but you don't have to come in to do so. Take care."

"Thank you, sir," Mr. Mills replied, shaking Father's hand once. Mr. Mills had a closed off expression as he walked out.

The office seemed so much bigger now that it was just the two of them. Father didn't look her way at first. Instead, he occupied himself with pouring something expensive to drink from the minibar, before he settled back in his chair behind the desk.

"You're lucky," Father stated, taking a sip of the amber liquid with little fanfare. "If the Mills family had walked away from us after everything that you pulled, then you would be in far more trouble."

"Walk away? Why?" Vicki demanded, sitting up. She ended up sliding to the end of the seat. "What do we need them for, anyway?"

"Other than Mr. Mills being my head of security and true loyalty doesn't come cheap?" Father asked.

"Alicia had loyalty. Look what that did," Vicki pointed out.

"Alicia didn't have true loyalty. Alicia was Chained," Father replied, an edge to his voice. "Those that are Chained can never develop true loyalty, because they lose that choice. The Mills family has never been Chained, and yet Owen still stepped in front of you to prevent that bullet from striking. Anyone that would do that, that would get between you and a gun, without any protection whatsoever, has loyalty."

"Owen doesn't even like me!" Vicki yelled.

"He didn't stop the bullet for you," Father replied, cutting off her point. "Think about it. Really, really think about it. He didn't get between a loaded gun for you. He knew that you had the Blessing. He didn't need to rescue you. So why risk his life?"

Vicki shrugged, flopping back in the chair. "Because he's a worrywart."

"Because he was protecting the person who would have taken the bullet," Father replied, tapping the glass against the table. It was an agitated gesture that Vicki had only seen directed at her a few times before. It was used when the other person failed to grasp her father's meaning. It made her feel small.

Vicki still didn't get it. She had been the intended target, even if the Blessing was going to take it away. Not that she had the protection of the Blessing anymore.

"The Blessing is still gone," Vicki reported, now that her father could pay attention.

"Correct," Father replied. "That spell was shattered beyond repair."

"When is it coming back?" Vicki asked.

"It's not," Father replied, draining the rest of his glass.

Vicki blinked, not sure if she'd understood that correctly. "What do you mean, it's not coming back?"

"What it means," Father replied. "The Blessing, in its current form, is gone." He stood up, brushing away a few tired wrinkles that had formed in his suit. "I may look into granting you another, in time. But you have not earned that yet. Your blatant disregard for your own safety has shown that the next Blessing would extinguish faster than the first. While it's poor timing with Dylan still being out there, in time you will find that your protections will mimic the protections that I possess for myself."

Father looked at the clock, humming. "I've another meeting. I should be back this evening. Until then, you can take up your studies at home." With that, Father strode from the room and left Vicki alone.

The chill in the room grew with every second Vicki sat there. The warm blanket of comfort that the Blessing had always been was gone, and there was nothing to replace it with. Her friends were gone. Her father was as cold and callous as he had always been.

Vicki screamed until her throat hurt too much to keep doing it. She *had* to stop when something hurt because she was vulnerable now. Just like the rest of them.

***

Even with the many specialists and Healers, medications and treatments which seemed to be working around the clock, Levi's hospital stay seemed to stretch on and on. Years of injuries had built up; apparently that made recovery even slower than the doctors had originally anticipated. It was almost a full two weeks that he was stuck, though not all of it was in bed. Physical therapists and additional testing ruled his life. Owen had been lucky; he'd been discharged the day after Alicia's attack. Instead, Levi was stuck recovering with his tiny stream of visitors. So when someone was standing in his door besides Sammy, Owen, and the medical staff, it was a surprise.

Of all the people he expected to walk into his hospital room, Mr. Townsend was not one of them. Dylan, maybe, but not him. Still, Levi had little choice other than to sit and wait until Mr. Townsend shooed the nurses out.

"You know, I rarely make in-person visits," Mr. Townsend stated, sitting in the chair with the same relaxed ease that he had the day they'd met. The man looked the same as he did a decade before. Not a hair out of place. There were no new grays or wrinkles, at least that Levi could tell. It was strange, looking at the man that held so much power over his life for only the second time. "Still, I felt like it was appropriate for today."

"What brings you by, sir?" Levi asked, sitting up the best that he could.

"Loose ends," Mr. Townsend started, his face calm and his eyes as cold the winter's chill.

Levi felt the blood drain from his face. "What loose ends, sir?"

Owen tensed next to Levi on the bed. He held out his hand, and Levi placed his own there before looking back at the Devil.

"In a perfect world we wouldn't be having this conversation," the Devil replied. His perfectly patient tone painted a picture of Levi's death without ever lifting a brush. Instead of the Chain, or a gun, the Devil offered out a contract. The folder oozed with more magic than Levi could have ever expected. "This is a nondisclosure agreement. Sign it, and your other contracts with me will be wiped clean."

Levi couldn't believe what he was holding. Freedom? Real freedom? There had to be a catch. The life that he'd built had depended on the financial support that he and Sammy had been getting. Trading that away, even if he had Owen now, put him in a place of vulnerability that wasn't easy to swallow. Then there was all the medical bills and the lack of employment history; how would he even hold a job with the body he had now?

"All the contracts? The money, the chain, everything?" Levi asked, meeting his worst enemy in the eye.

Mr. Townsend smiled. There was no joy in his eyes that Levi could see, but it was a smile all the same. "Everything," Mr. Townsend replied. "This hospital stay will be paid for, but after that all contact between us will cease."

Levi scanned it over. The contract wasn't written in tiny letters of legalize. It had been drafted in a way that he could easily understand, and in sections to make it easy to reference. There wasn't much to it.

He couldn't tell anyone new about the Blessing, and how it connected to him. Owen, Sammy, and Mr. Mills were all listed as people that he could talk freely with about the Blessing and how it impacted his day-to-day life. Other than that, no one else could know. The details of what would happen to Levi and the people that were told caused Levi to shudder. The written words implied financial and social ruin, but Levi could read between the lines. Mr. Townsend's whistleblowers always disappeared.

As soon as the contract was signed, the Chain that Levi wore would be removed and destroyed. Any fragments that remained of the Blessing would also be removed, never to be added to Levi's person again. He would never belong to the Devil again, but he'd be left without any way to survive.

"This isn't enough," Owen stated, cutting through the silence. He'd been reading over Levi's shoulder, giving Levi both the comfort of having someone there, and the fear of someone else being in Mr. Townsend's sights. "Levi spent ten years under your control. That's ten years of damage to his body that he could not get medical attention for."

Levi's eyes snapped to Owen, fear coursing through him as he worried about what the Devil would say. But Owen wasn't done talking.

"This is not Levi's only hospital trip in the future. There will be follow-ups, physical therapy, medications," Owen listed. "Cutting all of his contracts means that he no longer will receive his stipend to pay for his food and housing. This contract, as it stands, is death."

"What are your terms, Mr. Mills?" Mr. Townsend asked.

Levi wanted nothing more than to keep the Devil from looking at Owen, but Owen was right. There was no way that Levi could heal enough to get a job, before the rest of his money ran out. There was the emergency cash he gave Sammy, and Sammy's job to keep them afloat for a while, but that wouldn't be enough.

"Levi's stipend for ten more years, or that amount in a lump sum," Owen replied.

Levi waited in the silence until Mr. Townsend agreed. A courier would deliver a new contract that evening, to be signed before Levi left the hospital. His hospital room was nothing like Vicki's had been when she'd left. No bouquets or balloons filled the space. Sammy had offered to bring flowers, but Levi hadn't wanted to watch them wilt.

That evening, Levi let both Owen and Sammy read it through.

"What do you think?" Levi asked, leaning against his latest mobility aid: a set of crutches. He should be sitting, but he'd been sitting all day. He just wanted to stand for a few moments.

"He's covered his bases," Sammy replied. "But why? Why offer this out?"

"Me," Owen replied, tapping the contract where his and his father's name were listed. "Because you two are with me. That creates a conflict of interest. It's very important to Mr. Townsend that the people closest to him are not Chained, that they act of free will to protect him. If you're Chained, then it's like the whole family is."

Levi nodded. It stung that the only reason that he was getting this treatment was because of his partner's father. Still, it was a blessing. He could be living with all of this, or dead because of that bullet, if Owen hadn't walked into his life.

Now that the Blessing was gone, Levi had found the Connection that had been stolen from him. From the pair of them. He hadn't needed to look far. Only to the other hospital bed in their shared room. He and Owen were still trying to figure out what their relationship looked like, but Levi knew that he wanted to be by Owen's side as they figured it out.

He signed the contract that night. Levi had decided that long before Owen and Sammy had approved the choice. The future was worth anything that he might give up. Hearing them agree however was a fantastic bonus.

When Levi was discharged from the hospital (with many, many follow-up appointments), Owen didn't take him back home. The apartment that Levi had lived in was a walk-up with no elevator. It didn't work for someone that was only allowed to shuffle back and forth to the bathroom, or navigate with a wheelchair. He had expected the new place, but Owen hadn't shared any of the details with him. Which meant Levi found himself moving into an apartment he had never seen before, in a part of town that was new to him. Not in the expensive neighborhoods that Janie's building had been in, nor in the neighborhoods that Levi and Sammy had grown up in. It was a curious in-between, and close enough to the subway station that commuting to the rest of the city would still be workable.

It was big, with wide doorways, and only a few stories off the ground. The elevator was decent; it didn't lurch awkwardly or make any weird noises like the one at Sammy's building.

There were three bedrooms, a living room, kitchen, in-unit laundry, and two whole bathrooms. One of the bathrooms was bigger than the kitchen at Levi's apartment. That was the one off the largest bedroom, a private en suite.

The walls were still a stark white; nothing looked lived in yet. There was some furniture, but the space still echoed as he moved through it. Sammy's plants and art would change that soon enough.

"Is this the place?" Levi asked, his eyes wide with awe.

Owen smiled at him nervously. "It's the new apartment. Sammy helped me pick it out."

"Both of you picked this out?" Levi asked, wheeling around as he tried to take everything in. There was a couch and a set of chairs already in the living room, along with a television, and only one of the bedrooms had a bed in it. It looked like it could fit all three of them comfortably. On nights when the nightmares took over, and Levi or Sammy needed everyone to be close. Officially, the bed would be just for him and Owen to share. The second room was completely empty, Sammy's room, he guessed, and the third room looked like it was set up to be an office. A study space for Owen. "Wow."

"We wanted you to come back to a place that you could get around in, so we didn't have a lot of options to pick from," Owen explained, looking around the place. "We can figure out the logistics of everything when you're more comfortable getting around, and your legs have healed more."

Levi heard the implied, *When we figure out how much you can walk now that your knees are busted.* Still, it was great rolling around without having to bump into the walls and scrape his hands. He didn't have to think about getting up all of those flights of stairs with a walker or crutches anymore.

"Are you sure you want all of us to move in together?" Levi checked. They had talked about it in the hospital. When Townsend's deposit had cleared, Levi knew exactly what he wanted to do with a part of the money. A new apartment that fit all of them.

"I'm sure. Are you sure?" Owen asked. "Sammy only packed some of your stuff. The rest of it is back at your place."

Levi couldn't help but smile at his awkwardness. When he'd wished that he could pull the bullet from Owen, he hadn't expected anything out of it. The pain had burst in his chest, and Levi had thought that was it. He was going to cross to the other side, and Sammy was going to track him down and lecture him for the rest of eternity.

Instead, he and Owen sported matching scars. The Blessing was destroyed when he'd pushed it aside for the Connection that it had overrode.

"You forgot to grab your chair," Levi said, spinning the wheelchair around in a circle. "The one that you took over back at my apartment. It doesn't fit with the rest of the furniture, so... Are you sure?"

Owen's face split into a smile. "I'm sure. I promise. I know this is fast. I know that we have lots to figure out about what kind of relationship we can have together, but I want to figure that out. I can offer this place that you can get in and out of, while you're figuring out the healing and walking again thing. And don't worry, Sammy's moving in too. They're taking over the spare room and redecorating this whole place."

Levi grinned. He couldn't wait to see it. The number of plants that would fill the living room, along the big window. How the surfaces were going to be covered in color, from pillows and blankets that had been stitched together, out of scraps of costumes or hand crocheted. It would change this place from an open and light space, to one as full as it could be with comfort.

"It's always been me and Sammy, until you," Levi said, admiring the light coming in through the windows. Those visions of the future that he'd never allowed himself to entertain couldn't compare to this. Making meals together, arguing about the dishes in the sink, Owen having his spot in the corner while focused on a project, Sammy calling for a pickup because that car held together by duct tape and dreams gave out again.

A phrase that Owen had said a few days ago, back in the hospital and before signing the contract, came back to Levi through the fog with perfect clarity.

"Is this...are we family?" Levi asked.

Owen's cheeks pinkened as he took Levi's hand. "We can be. Sammy and I might disagree about a lot of things, but we agree on one thing. We're Connected. How we choose to manifest that Connection is up to us. Also, you saved my life in a way that no one else could have," Owen said. "At the very least, Dad sees both of you as parts of my family, whatever we make of that."

Sammy and Mr. Mills had gotten to know each other while he and Owen had been laid up in the hospital. A pair of anxious visitors that had been watching for good news.

Family had always been a bad word to Levi. He had always been pushed away or forgotten. The only time that it had started to mean something was when Sammy's had taken him in. But like everything else in his life, that hadn't lasted. Still, Sammy had been by his side this whole time. Maybe that was enough to let Owen find a place there, too.

"Family," Levi replied, the smile on his face hurting his cheeks. He leaned his head against Owen's shoulder. It pinched his healing wound, but he didn't care.

Sammy opened the front door with a gentle kick that made it bounce off the doorstop. "My hands are full!" they called. "Owen, can you steal Levi's wheelchair so you can help me move this plant?"

"I'm using it," Levi called back. "What happened to renting a dolly?"

"Do you know how expensive one of those is to rent?" Sammy shot back. "I don't have dolly money, you know."

Levi grinned as he wheeled himself over to the door to help Sammy out, or at least give his opinion. There was a lot of work in store for them to get their life back in order. But tomorrow was Saturday, and for the first time in ten years, he was looking forward to it.

ACKNOWLEDGEMENTS

Mirror of the Blessing taught me a valuable lesson: writing the book is easy, publishing the book is hard. Going through all of the steps of revising and picking apart the story over and over until it was polished took far more work than typing the first draft. Without the community around me, this book wouldn't have happened. I have so many people to thank for making this book possible.

To my parents who continuously encouraged my writing, even when it wasn't very good. You taught me that editing was an opportunity to improve, not a mark of failure.

To my twitch community that gave me focus and motivation on the nights and weeks when I had none.

To Wendy, who had to put up with me working on this book instead of all of our other projects together.

To my husband, Andy, who encouraged me every step of the way.

And lastly, for Jackie... the one who asked to be acknowledged.

ABOUT THE AUTHOR

MC Warner began writing before the turn of the century with the plan to publish before she turned eighteen. Over a decade later, with a career in software engineering and a multitude of dogs to help, she reached her goal. Her debut novel, Mirror of the Blessing, came to life through the power of peer pressure and streaming with her writing community on Twitch. MC lives with her husband in Missouri.

https://toukagencreates.com/

www.ingramcontent.com/pod-product-compliance
Lightning Source LLC
Chambersburg PA
CBHW071554110726
47908CB00007B/2095